SAKURA

Without limiting the exclusive rights of any author, contributor or the publisher of this publication, any unauthorized use of this publication to train generative artificial intelligence (AI) technologies is expressly prohibited. HarperCollins also exercise their rights under Article 4(3) of the Digital Single Market Directive 2019/790 and expressly reserve this publication from the text and data mining exception.

This is a work of fiction. Names, characters, places, and incidents are products of the author's imagination or are used fictitiously and are not to be construed as real. Any resemblance to actual events, locales, organizations, or persons, living or dead, is entirely coincidental.

SAKURA. Copyright © 2005 by Kanako Nishi. English translation copyright © 2026 by Allison Markin Powell. A Note from the Translator copyright © 2026 by Allison Markin Powell. All rights reserved. No part of this book may be used or reproduced in any manner whatsoever without written permission except in the case of brief quotations embodied in critical articles and reviews. For information, address HarperCollins Publishers, 195 Broadway, New York, NY 10007. In Europe, HarperCollins Publishers, Macken House, 39/40 Mayor Street Upper, Dublin 1, D01 C9W8, Ireland.

hc.com

HarperCollins books may be purchased for educational, business, or sales promotional use. For information, please email the Special Markets Department at SPsales@harpercollins.com.

Originally published as *Sakura* in Japan in 2005 by Shogakukan.

First HarperVia hardcover published in March 2026.

Designed by Yvonne Chan
Crayon drawings background texture on page iii © aga7ta/stock.adobe.com
Dog silhouettes on pages 1, 147, and 215 © Loveleen/stock.adobe.com
Dog silhouettes on pages 43 and 99 © Ascreator/stock.adobe.com
Dog silhouette on page 285 © fennywiryani/stock.adobe.com

Library of Congress Cataloging-in-Publication Data has been applied for.

ISBN 978-0-06-338994-6

Printed in the United States of America

25 26 27 28 29 LBC 5 4 3 2 1

Contents

Part 1 1

Part 2 43

Part 3 99

Part 4 147

Part 5 215

Part 6 285

Afterword 323

A Note from the Translator 325

PART 1

The Beginning

Flower Bud

In my hand is an advertising circular.

A gloomy yellow, like a discolored banana. A somewhat dubious blue that you might see on a folding bike. And a disgusting red and white, like meat mottled with dull fat.

It's just an ordinary circular—nothing special about it.

The paper gleams when I pick it up, but it doesn't feel smooth. Like an old car that's been polished to a high shine, or some ostentatious platter that's actually quite cheap. However you want to put it. Either way, it's just an ordinary circular.

20% discount on liquid food pouches
Our store will be open throughout the entire New Year's holiday!
Pay 5% less consumption tax!
Got everything you need for New Year's?

The reason I'm studying such a thing so carefully is on the back.

I have to look closely for the faint letters to become visible.

Subtle penciling—in hard lead, of all things—on paper that would barely tolerate a magic marker. The writing is of varying legibility, depending on the light, and there are places where there hadn't been enough pressure applied, leaving the script almost unreadable. Nevertheless, with much effort, I can make out:

"The camellias are beautiful. The red ones are everywhere but the white ones..."

And:

"I tried making my own plum wine. Here's how..."

Nothing of any substance.

But these two lines might as well contain important chemical formulas or earth-shattering prophecies—well, maybe that's an exaggeration. It looks like the person who wrote them was just trying to fill in the blank space, like the text on the front of the circular. The characters are written in tiny script, close together. There's something very nostalgic about the way they incline slightly toward the right. This is the handwriting that taught me to write.

It's a letter from my father, the first I've heard from him in two years.

I'd spent the day with my girlfriend. Even though we hadn't seen each other in a while, things got awkward between us for no good reason (I'd trash-talked a TV show that she was excited about), and when I got home late that night, still in a bad mood, the letter was in my mailbox.

My apartment building is called Bamboo Villas, but the place has absolutely none of the bracing greenness or dignified beauty of bamboo. If anything, it's distinguished by gray soot from who-knows-where and the reddish brown of rusting steel, reminiscent of a small but forlorn ironworks. I had figured the kanji for bamboo (竹) must have been taken as inspiration from the landlord's name, but when I went to introduce myself, it turned out his name was Okubo (大久保), which made the "Bamboo" moniker even more mystifying.

The mailbox is a communal one in the building's entryway,

so you just take the letters that are addressed to you. "There's no privacy," my girlfriend had complained, but I am fine with that; I have no qualms about people seeing my mail. Most of it is utility bills—gas, water, electric—along with pink envelopes from my mother (she writes "Mom" on the back and, embarrassingly, "flower bud" to seal the flap) and threatening letters from my university saying that I missed too many classes and might not graduate.

So, when I came across a brown envelope addressed to Kaoru Hasegawa in messy, seemingly male handwriting, at first I didn't realize that it was meant for me.

I glanced at the back of the envelope before going into my apartment, and the moment I saw the name, I got a case of uncontrollable hiccups. This tends to happen when I'm surprised.

The sender's name—Akio Hasegawa—was written there, along with the deliberate "flower bud" (really?). Above it was the final line of the letter: "I'll be home at the end of the year—Dad."

My hiccups stopped. This tends to happen when I'm *really* surprised.

I was supposed to spend the end of the year with my girlfriend. We didn't have anything in particular planned, but she'd made a point of saying she wanted us to ring in the new year together.

She'd recently started wearing her hair in a way that was pretty cute, and I didn't have anything else going on, so I had agreed. Still, as soon as I read my father's letter, pathetically, I was already thinking about what excuse to give her:

"I really like the way your hair looks—now I want to change mine too. But the only barber I trust is back home. He's the only guy I let cut my hair, ever since I was little."

Or, "You're gonna hate me for bringing this up now, but the truth is, I speak Kansai dialect. And after all this time, I have a sudden urge to go home and speak it again! Maido maido!"

But after giving it much thought, I came up with the following while I was taking out the key to my bicycle:

"I really miss our family dog."

Our dog's name is Sakura.

A Shiba Inu mix with black spots, medium in size (about as big as a vacuum cleaner), and with black leg markings that look like little boots. The black spots on the tip of the dog's nose look like freckles—even being kind, you wouldn't say that Sakura was a handsome dog. Anyway, she's a girl. Before people learn her name, everyone always assumes she's male because of her drab looks. But I think there's something rather humanly feminine about the way Sakura gently scratches the scruff of her neck with a hind leg, or the haughty way she sniffs the ground as she moves along—a certain ephemeral grace and strength that I admire.

She turned twelve this year, which in dog years means she's quite the senior citizen.

I had conceived of this as an excuse, though once Sakura entered my mind, I could think of nothing else. The slightly stiff hair on her back, the way she would gently press her paw into my hand, the muscles of her hind legs flexing when she broke into a run. As the memories came rushing in, I could barely stand it—I had to see Sakura.

I now had a mission.

"It's all about how our teeth fit together, you know? Even when we think we're chewing normally, we're actually askew. That's fine when we're young, like when we're strong and can lift anything, right? See, way back when, I used to travel all the time, and I'd carry heavy skis on my shoulder. But now, take someone our age—someone in their forties or fifties—and try chewing with the same set of teeth. We're worse for wear!"

At year's end, the Shinkansen's ridership is well beyond capacity, which means that I have to be pressed up against a complete stranger for the three-hour train ride from Tokyo to Osaka.

Immediately feeling sick, I stand in line for the toilet, where two older women are deep in conversation by the washing-up area. Whenever the train sways, they cling to one another's shoulders, but since both of them are already unsteady on their feet, it doesn't help much at all.

"So, when you say that you won't get any better unless you wear a backpack—it's not about your fifty-year-old shoulders, it's about how your teeth fit together."

"I still have my wisdom teeth."

"Your wisdom teeth? You don't need those—not at all! Instead of wisdom, at this age you need common sense!"

"I have plenty of common sense."

"What's most important are your molars. As long as they work together well, you can stand up straight and your shoulders won't be stiff. How many wisdom teeth do you still have?"

"All of them."

"That's no good—no good at all! We humans need all our wisdom teeth about as much as we need a tail. Doesn't having them still back there keep your molars from fitting together properly?"

"But isn't it painful to have them taken out?"

"Come now—you gave birth to three children, and you're worried about the pain?"

"Four children."

"Compared to that, this would be like cleaning the lint out of your belly button."

"The lint out of my belly button?"

"The lint out of your belly button."

I finally make it into the toilet, where I proceed to have a vomiting spell. Something about the subtle horizontal rocking of the train and the peculiar constraints of the lavatory reminds me of the smell that rises from a just-opened rice cooker (an appliance I haven't used in quite a while), which only serves to churn my stomach further as its contents—the cream bun and Doritos I had eaten that morning—disappear down the toilet. I have no trouble vomiting. If I start to feel ill when I'm out drinking or if I've overeaten, I stick my finger down my throat. My friends worry that I might have an eating disorder but it's not a big deal. I think of it as a sort of ritual for improving my current state. Spewing out the contents of my stomach enables me to reset myself. I wish I could scrub my esophagus and my guts and my stomach with a brush, but since that's not possible, I vomit. My girlfriend recently reported to me the welcome information that apparently there's something called a colon cleanse, and she was even willing to pay for herself if I would let her come along with me, but despite how adorable she thought that might be, now that she's pissed about my taking this year-end trip home, that option seems to have gone down the drain, so to speak. In the end, "I miss my dog," had not flown as an excuse. After a barrage of complaints, she finally looked at me with tear-filled eyes and cried out the rather thorny question:

"So, who's more important to you—me or the dog?"

I fell silent. Terrible as it may sound, if forced to choose between playing with Sakura on New Year's and spending the holiday with my girlfriend, well, that's easy—Sakura, hands down! But of course, I couldn't just say that. The fight went on a bit longer, and it was settled with me agreeing to buy her a new bag at the beginning of the year. I can never seem to save money.

"Even when we think we're chewing normally, we're actually askew."

When I emerge from the toilet, the older women are still having the same conversation. The one who had said, "That's no good—no good at all!" is fervently recommending dental treatment. As I elbow my way in between them to wash my hands at the sink, they glance in my direction but quickly go back to what they were talking about.

"What are you afraid of, dentures?"

"Well, yes."

"I have them, you know."

"They fit them for you, don't they?"

"Of course they do."

I search my pockets for a handkerchief to dry my hands, but all I feel is the rustling of paper.

"Soon you'll only be able to eat soft foods like bananas and tofu."

Which reminds me of what's in my pocket—that circular with the faded banana yellow on it.

"Ugh, that would be terrible. I hate bananas."

With no regard for our feelings, the Shinkansen zips through fields and between buildings. It almost seems as if the train is trying to shake off something aggravating. I stand the whole time—there are no seats all the way to Osaka.

Cataracts

My childhood home is in a newly developed residential area in the suburbs of Osaka. I say "newly developed," but even after ten or twenty years it's still one of those satellite towns on the outskirts, now aging and somewhat desolate. Since the place doesn't have much history to speak of, there's nothing to stimulate the senses; on the other hand, having come to know the same neighbors over ten years, the interactions these relationships provide are not entirely dry. They know the names of people's dogs and keep track of what grade each other's children are in, but as for the more-than-three-years-absent father in my family, they can't be sure whether there's been a divorce or if he's just on an extended business trip.

Having not seen my home in a long time, it appears just the slightest bit smaller than it used to be.

The house is adorned with flowers so wilted they look mummified, and yet the other decorations are so shockingly bright it throws everything off. Even the nameplate is odd—instead of a sedate piece of wood, there is a big, shiny marble-like thing with the family name on it, seemingly out of place with the landscaping. Maybe this is a strange way of putting it, but the house looks like it's wearing clothes that are the wrong size.

When you open the gate, there's a poor excuse for a few steps, and then you're already at the front door. Sakura's doghouse is right in front of the entrance, and if you go halfway around the side of the house, you'll end up in the backyard. Not feeling ready to go inside just yet, I decide to look for Sakura.

I walk along the path beside the house calling for her, but she's nowhere to be found. Usually all I have to do is yell Sakura's name and she comes running, wagging her tail as if to say, "You wanted to see me?"

I head around to the back, still calling for Sakura, and find my mother doing yard work. She's crouched down with her back to me. She's gained even more weight, carrying more flesh around her waist and, as if her hips can't handle it, her butt is practically touching the ground. There's also more flesh clinging to her bent ankles, making her feet look tiny. From her head to her toes, there isn't a single part of her that's narrow, though her expanded shape does resemble something. But what, exactly, I don't know.

I had missed the chance to call out to her. Feeling guilty for not having said anything, I remain silent, watching my mother's movements. The western sun casts her shadow in my direction. I nudge her shadow several times with my foot, but of course she doesn't notice—she's completely absorbed in whatever it is she's doing, her shoulders heaving.

Finally, after several minutes have passed and I am basically at a loss as to what to do, my mother turns around.

She has a strange floral bandana wrapped around her head, which I had noticed as I approached from behind. When she turns around, I see that her cheeks are flushed the same scarlet as the pattern. It's a little hard to tell, given that she's backlit by the setting sun, but she seemed to be smiling.

"Welcome home!"

"Thanks."

Apparently, that's all we have to say to each other. My mother looks like she's searching for more words as she takes off and then puts back on her earth-covered work gloves. Now my mother's fidgeting shadow seems to be nudging me in return.

"Uh, where's Sakura?"

"Sakura!" she shouts in response, loud enough to startle me. "She's been hanging out over there lately."

My mother seems slightly relieved as she points to where the three bicycles my siblings and I used to ride when we were little are parked.

I hadn't noticed at first because the bicycle cover was hanging down, but looking closer, I can make out Sakura's feet under Miki's red bicycle. Those adorable little paw pads I had been longing to see were facing my way, defenseless.

"Ain't it kinda cold?" I say, slipping into Kansai dialect. "Wouldn't she be warmer in her doghouse?"

"That bike cover's like a windbreaker, it's probably pretty warm. Y'know, Sakura's hearing's so bad now, you hafta gently touch her to get her to notice you."

Despite the cold, my mother is sweating. Profusely—as if she's just run a sprint in the height of summer. She wipes her face with her work gloves, leaving dark smudges.

As I walk toward Sakura, my mother calls from behind, "Gently!"

Even when I call her name again, Sakura doesn't wake up. She's asleep with her mouth hanging open, as if she were dead. I feel a little apprehensive but am reassured to see her chest rising and falling lightly, so I call her name once more. She still doesn't wake up.

I pat her belly roughly and, finally roused, Sakura's tail gives a reflexive wag. Then, once she catches my scent, her tail wags in happy recognition.

Both of Sakura's eyes have turned cloudy with cataracts—she can probably only make out vague shapes. And yet, she comes up and nuzzles her head against my knee.

"You recognize me, don'tcha?"

I know that dogs age faster than people, but to see Sakura suddenly so old makes me feel sorry for her. I give her a good rub on the head, belly, and legs. Sakura seems to enjoy being rubbed hard—her body squirms around as if to say, "That's the spot."

However, when I rub the base of her hind leg, Sakura's body trembles and she bares her teeth, but her face looks so ugly that I have to laugh.

"Sakura, who's my girl?"

She wags her tail again at the sound of my voice. Sakura has grown very thin.

Every so often, my mother pauses in her work, her breathing heavy. Amid the smell of new earth, the quince leaves make an exaggerated rustle as they fall.

"Dad's home!"

I wonder if my mother is still smiling as she says this.

Pedicure

Not much has changed inside the house apart from the TV, which is now one of the latest flat-screen models. A family photo hangs above it. Every year in early summer, when the yard looked its best, the family would all go out to take a commemorative photograph. We used a timer, but we could never get Sakura to be still and look at the camera. Occasionally we'd think we might succeed because she'd seem to be looking at the camera, but the moment the shutter would click, she'd look up at us and we'd all burst into laughter. Which meant that our family photos always featured a blurry Sakura looking off in one direction while the rest of us made all sorts of faces.

Miki is sitting on the sofa, painting her toenails. She's giving herself what they call a pedicure. My girlfriend wears really sparkly nail polish, but the nail on her pinky toe is all messed up, so any pedicure looks kind of pitiful on her.

"Welcome home."

Miki doesn't look up when she says this, which is typical for her. On her pale feet, bright red smears stand out from her little toe inward. The red is too red.

"Here I am."

I just stand there with my backpack still on my back, until

Miki finally looks up at me. Her eyes look the same as always. They exemplify the description "almond-shaped," and there's a gentle curve to her slightly aquiline nose, which might make it seem like that's what deserves special attention. But the most distinctive thing about Miki's face is her mouth. Like a bright red life buoy that's been thrown into the sea, lips so lustrous they seem ready to burst, their corners always turned up.

"It's okay. I forgive you."

It is just the sort of thing Miki would say. She regards me—and this hard scrutiny of her face by her older brother—with skepticism as she closes the cap on the nail polish.

"You gonna sit?"

The sofa's armrest still displays my graffiti from when I was little. Well, not quite graffiti—I just scribbled a large "あ" in magic marker, but I had written it backward, as if you were looking in a mirror. When I was young and my father was teaching me my letters, I always wrote the hiragana character for "A" backward. No matter how many times he showed me, I could never get it right.

"Kaoru, think to yourself, *This is the right way*, but then try writing it the other way," he'd said.

From then on, I've been able to write it correctly, but something always seemed fundamentally misguided about his teaching approach. I developed the odd habit of doing the opposite of what I thought was the right thing. For instance, I always hesitate when writing the character "短." Does the "矢" go on the left, or is it the "豆"? According to my father, I should go against my instincts. And by doing so, I always end up being completely wrong—the "矢" that I thought belonged on the left is correct, but I always put the "豆" there. This happens in my everyday life too. I might want a coffee, but I tell myself,

Wait, what you want is probably going to change any minute. So, by this logic, I end up buying green tea or something. Then, at the moment when the thing I have no interest in drinking falls through the vending machine slot, I think, *Not that!* I still end up drinking it out of frustration, but I don't enjoy it. So then I buy a coffee. Like I said, I can never seem to save money.

In spite of this tendency, the one time I managed to be true to my heart and make the right decision is when I chose Sakura. Yup, she was definitely the right choice.

The first time we saw Sakura was when she was two months old. This was at a house in the neighborhood. There were five puppies in the litter, and Sakura was the smallest, the skinniest, the most forlorn. When we arrived, the other four puppies all scrambled over to us, adorably wagging their tails and playfully rubbing up against our legs, but Sakura was the only one who remained in a corner of the yard, watching us from afar.

Miki wanted this pudgy, pure white puppy that was especially cute, but for some reason I was drawn to Sakura. Even when I approached her, she didn't move. And when I picked her up, she just looked at me anxiously and didn't even wag her tail. Her floppy ears twitched, as if she were hearing some kind of noise. When I brought my face in closer, she returned my gaze with an expression of wonder, but every now and then, she seemed to look off into the distance, nostalgic. *This dog sure looks lonely*, I thought to myself. Sakura's eyes were moist, with a strange shine to them.

Seeing that I hadn't left Sakura's side, the lady said, "That one's so weak and timid, all the other pups eat up her food."

But hearing this about her also charmed me.

SAKURA

Miki was pretty set on the white puppy—she kept insisting that we take that one home, but I was convinced that I wanted Sakura. I don't know what it was about her, but I knew she was the one for us.

"This is the one I want," I said. "We'll take her."

Miki pouted all the way home, trailing behind me the whole time. Occasionally she'd pick up a stick and scrape it alongside a house's wall or fence. That's what Miki does when she's sulking. She doesn't speak, choosing instead to express her feelings by making a lot of other noise. It might take the form of kicking around bottles and cans that have been separated and sorted and put out for collection, or opening and closing a poorly fitted door so that it creaks incessantly—by and large, the kind of noise that makes everyone cringe. So I could tell by the scraping that sounded like she was whittling something down that Miki was more than a little hurt. It was her idea to get a dog in the first place, and in the end, she had also been the one who convinced our mother that we understood the seriousness of being responsible for another creature.

So what Miki was really saying was, *I had the right to choose which dog we got, but you shamelessly came along and picked out that scrawny thing instead—and I'm pretty miffed about it!*

Normally I'd just ignore her, but I knew I was sort of in the wrong this time around, so I said, "Miki, here, hold her. Look how tiny and cute she is."

I held Sakura out toward her.

At first Miki just said, "I'm fine. That dog's a wimp," and turned the other way.

But the scraping along the fence got softer and softer, so I tried again, a little more persistently this time.

"Miki, just hold her."

Miki pretended to dither about it, and then reluctantly took Sakura in her arms.

In Miki's small hands, Sakura looked even more helpless; she seemed to be trembling. But then, as Miki brought her face in close to see what Sakura smelled like, for some reason Sakura weakly wagged her skinny little tail. It was such a small movement—like the last drop trickling from an almost-dry glass—that I almost forgot for a moment that a dog wagging its tail is a sign of happiness.

"Look, she wagged her tail for you, Miki—that must mean she likes you. She didn't wag her tail when I was holding her."

I said all this to humor her, but Miki really seemed to take it to heart, and her mood immediately shifted.

"We're both girls, you know."

Smugly, Miki pressed her head into Sakura's belly, and Sakura seems to find this ticklish—she wagged her skinny tail a bit more vigorously than before.

At that moment, something pink fluttered down.

"Ah!"

Still holding Sakura, Miki crouched down to see that it was a pale pink flower petal—so pale it looked almost translucent in the sunlight.

"So pretty. What kind of flower petal do you think this is?"

Miki studied the petal in my hand in awe, and then she cried out happily, "It's a cherry blossom! This puppy gave birth to it—that's how we know it's a girl. Right? Girls get to have babies someday, but this pup's so tiny she gave birth to a cherry blossom petal instead. We gotta name her Sakura! Because she gave birth to a *sakura*. Sakura—what a good name! Don't you like it?"

Miki rubbed her cheek up against Sakura, and the dog looked elated.

"Sakura," I said it out loud. *Not bad*, I thought to myself—the name seemed like a perfect fit for this puppy that had watched us so anxiously from the corner of the yard.

"Sakura, Sakura!"

Now Miki was downright cheerful as she walked along, holding Sakura. Being so small herself, Miki wasn't really holding Sakura so much as trying her best to gather the dog up in her arms. Her skirt was riding up, and her underwear was showing. I walked behind her, choosing not to say anything about the fact that, though a flower petal happened to have been stuck to our dog's tail, I knew that it wasn't a cherry blossom.

When I close my eyes and recall happy memories from when my sister was six and I was ten, this is the scene that comes to mind.

Me, walking behind my younger sister. Our eccentric family awaiting us at home, and Sakura's small, warm, trembling body in Miki's arms. The early summer sun, demurely announcing the season's arrival, casting our shadows along the slope that led the way home. This memory is so sharp, it's like it belongs to someone else.

Something warm and round enveloped us. Who knows what it was—but like coffee at the break of dawn, or a phone booth on a rainy day, it kept us snug and protected.

Back in those days, we lacked for nothing.

"Ugh, it's so hot in this house!"

My mother's voice is as loud as ever. It has enough force to dispel my thoughts.

My mother's weight gain has caused her body temperature

to run high, but it's the kind of heat that warms up everything around her. On a cold winter day like today, when she suddenly bursts into a room where all the windows are closed, she seems to bring the heat of the whole world with her. It's a gentle, beaming warmth, proven by the fact that Miki looks over at me and finally smiles.

"Been ages since y'all have seen each other, huh?"

Delighted, she ties on a familiar apron. It has green shoulder straps and a dog embroidered on the front. Round, appliquéd letters spell out "SAKURA" in English, though the "A" at the end is coming off. Miki made it in her junior high school home economics class.

I can clearly remember her asking me, "Is SAKURA spelled with an 'R' or an 'L'?"

I still get them confused, but at the time I had thought that "R" seemed right.

"Kaoru, is there anything you want to eat?"

My mind races with all sorts of things I might like to eat but I don't bother naming them, knowing it is already decided.

"Nothing in particular."

"I mean, of course you know what we're having—your father says when the family's all together, we eat nabé!" My mother chuckles, and then starts singing an unfamiliar song to herself as she goes into the kitchen.

Whether it's due to the sound of my mother humming happily to herself, or the inevitable menu for our reunion dinner celebrating my father's return after all these years, or Miki seemingly forgetting all about those appliqués as she gives herself a pedicure—I don't know why, but I feel a sudden pang of sadness, and I squeeze my eyes shut. I can still see the flickering image of the television, tickling behind my eyelids.

"You really look like him, don't you?"

"I mean, you could tell someone you were him, and they wouldn't know otherwise."

"Do people ever ask you for autographs?"

"Oh, once or twice."

"I bet—they wouldn't know the difference. The resemblance is too strong."

The year-end special of one of those afternoon variety shows is playing on TV. A handsome, somewhat older-looking man is surrounded by the show's personalities, wearing a perplexed smile on his face.

"Just look at his profile."

"Wow, he looks just like him!"

"Totally amazing!"

Miki is annoyed. "They say he looks just like someone, but who is it?"

I have no idea. I don't watch much TV, plus I can never remember people's faces.

"Dunno."

Miki had changed the channel before I could answer.

As I vacantly watch the images on the screen change, I hear the door open. Miki turns the volume up and is speeding through the channels when I notice that our father is standing there.

"Ah, it's cold out."

He speaks in a low voice, and he appears to have lost an awful lot of weight. I feel the urge to cry, and I can't bring myself to turn around.

"I mean, I've never seen anyone who looks more like him than you do."

"He really does, doesn't he?"

The television has ended up on the same channel as before.

"They say that everyone has three people in the world who look just like you, and you must be one of his."

Reunion Dinner

Our reunion dinner is nabé. It had been my father's idea, but I have to admit that nabé is a nice choice. The sound of the simmering broth helps fill the awkward silences, and keeping the bulky pot on the table means that we can sit together without having to look each other in the eye.

My mother and Miki quickly take what are presumably their usual seats and busy themselves with adding the vegetables. My father and I, unable to decide where to sit, both eventually and sheepishly claim the spots that used to be ours. But I immediately regret this decision. I'm seated across from my father, which requires me to share the ladle and everything else with him. What's worse, as soon as I begin to worry that he'll ask me to pour for him, my fears come true.

"C'mon, Kaoru! Pour some beer for your dad!" my mother says.

Looking a bit startled, my father glances back and forth between me and my mother.

"No, no, it's fine. I'll do it myself," he says.

But because I can't bear to listen to his hoarse voice or to see him self-deprecatingly wave his hand in front of his face, I open a can of beer and slosh it into my father's glass. He hurries to raise it, but is too slow and the beer spills over onto the table, soaking his pants.

"Oh no! Beer stains are so hard to get out!"

My mother hurriedly brings over a dishcloth. As she scrubs his pants, my father utters pathetically, "M'sorry."

Then he keeps on saying it, bowing his head over and over. "M'sorry, m'sorry."

My mother keeps scrubbing my father's pants maniacally, and Miki, as Miki is wont to do, keeps adding vegetables to the nearly overflowing nabé. The food smells delicious, but none of us seems to be eating it.

I could at least try, I think to myself, but I've had this strange feeling in my throat for a while and I've lost my appetite. I have a sudden urge to smoke, so I reach into my pocket for my Marlboros, but give up when I remember that they're in my coat.

For some reason, despite not even having had a sip of beer, Miki lets out a belch and mutters, "Oh, crap!"

Our reunion dinner is nabé.

Once my father's "M'sorrys" had stopped, we ate the mushy and overcooked nabé. My mother kept eating prodigiously. She ate so fast and so much, I sat there holding my beer, surprised and agog as I watched her.

The words "vacuum truck" popped into my head—I know it's terrible, but it was all I could think of.

Miki appeared to be used to it; every so often she'd say to my mother, "You chewing?"

Other than that, Miki herself ate in silence. My father also seemed rather spooked by my mother's appetite. He stole glances at her as he held his chopsticks.

That whole nabé was gone in no time.

Somehow, my mother seems to still be hungry—amazingly, she starts preparing zosui, making soup by adding rice to the leftover broth. Rapt, I am recalling the peculiar vigor of the vomit I had experienced passing through my throat earlier when Miki says, "I'm gonna let Sakura into the house."

Bleary-eyed at being let into the house at this unexpected hour, Sakura looks sleepy as she comes under the table. Miki follows after her, lightly slapping her bottom.

"Ah, it's cold!"

Sakura looks happy for the slaps and wags her tail. She's so cute that Miki can't resist giving little slaps over the rest of her body. Sakura yawns, opening her mouth wide.

"Whoa, her breath is nasty!" Miki exclaims, as she crudely flops onto her belly to rub Sakura, who lets out a fart.

All of us are at a loss, yet we can't help bursting into laughter.

Even my father, mid-guffaw, says, "Sakura, you stink!"

Without thinking, I utter in agreement, "Right?" and immediately regret doing so.

My mother says, "Sakura's happy, isn't she? Happy that we're all together, right?" Then she adds with a laugh, "Is that why you farted?"

My father stares at the rest of us, and my mother starts serving the zosui.

Sakura fawns over each of us in turn, and then pronounces: "Gfft."

The whole time, my mother is murmuring to herself at the table:

"Say, Miki, tell those two about what you heard on TV, that drinking alcohol changes your cells."

"Kaoru, want some castella cake? You like the kind with the crunchy sugar on top, don'tcha? Had to look all over for it!"

"The neighbors got a dog too. What's it again? The one with short legs, uh . . . oh, right, a pouri!" (She probably means "corgi.")

Sakura is under the table, snoring. Her snores are regular and soft—it makes me think of the steam whistle of a repatriation boat that has traveled distant seas.

Like a big ship pulling into port, Sakura will always put us at ease.

"I'm going to take a bath."

Miki stands up, and the rest of us take that as our cue to leave the table as well.

More than an hour later, Miki emerges from the bath.

I've been watching a totally boring year-end show, and my mother is doing the dishes. My father is cleaning his ears while drinking the tea that my mother has shrewdly prepared for us. In a corner of the room lies the beat-up overnight bag that my father must have brought with him. *Instead of the dishes, my mother ought to be scrubbing that bag*, I think to myself.

Miki plops down in front of the fan heater, frantically drying her hair with a bath towel. The cloyingly sweet scent of her shampoo wafts over with the warm air.

"So, who's next?"

I look at the clock—nine thirty. At home, I always take a shower in the morning. I think about saying this, but figuring I'll get an earful from my mother about how I'll catch a cold and it's bad for my health and whatnot, I say instead, "You go, Ma. I get a chill if I don't take mine right before bed."

"No! I'll go last so I can do the cleaning!"

"I can do the cleaning for you."

"What chill are you talking about?!"

This exchange seems to irk my mother to the point of silence, so she turns her attention to my father.

"You go next, then!"

Surprised, my father pauses from digging in his ear. "Oh, no no no. Uh, you two go on ahead."

Seeing his utterly spineless demeanor, I resolve that I will definitely be the one to go last. In general, people should take a bath whenever they feel like it—there's no need to be this deliberate about what order we go in. But this is one of my mother's hard-and-fast rules, and she's not to be moved on it.

"Oh yeah? So be it, then. I won't take as long as Miki though." Shuffling her large form toward the bathroom, she adds, "But don't let me hear about it if any water spills out of the tub!"

My father glances at us with a wry smile, but neither of us laugh.

I guess it goes without saying that my mother is what you'd call obese.

She used to be thin, her hips so slender that you wouldn't know she'd had any children, but now she is stout all over—even when dressed in warm clothes it's obvious that she has many layers of additional flesh. You can't tell where her chin ends and her neck begins, and there are lines at her wrists that look as though she has rubber bands wrapped around them.

My father, on the other hand, is withering away, his cheeks hollow and emaciated. This may be exacerbated by his deep-set eyes and chiseled features, but his face appears shadowed and altered by anguish.

Miki is trying to use the warmth of the fan heater to dry her hair. She has her back to me and is stooped over to bring her head close to the vent. Her skin looks as pink as the flower petal that was stuck to Sakura's tail that day.

Out of the blue, Miki says, "Tomorrow's New Year's Eve."

Gyoza

I have always felt a sense of nervous excitement on the morning of New Year's Eve. It's no different now at twenty-two years old. The sun seems even bigger and more beautiful than usual, while also a bit apprehensive about the grand task that awaits: showing up for sunrise on the first day of the year.

Perhaps due to my own pleasant apprehension, I savor my breakfast, taking tender bites that I chew thoroughly.

My father and Miki and I each have two slices of toast on our plates, while my mother's plate has four. On the table there is a variety of bizarrely colored jams and expensive-looking margarine. From the sheer number of options there are to spread on our bread, you'd think we must rank quite high on the scale of Engel's coefficient (just how much do we spend on food?). Apparently, the money my father regularly wired and the earnings from my part-time job transform into these food products of dubious origin. My mother is enjoying her coffee, which gives off a strange aroma—I'm curious what it is but I doubt it's worth the trouble to ask about it. I'll just sneak a look at the package later.

"What's the proper time to eat toshikoshi soba?" Miki asks, her mouth full of toast. Her question doesn't seem to have been directed at anyone in particular, but my father appears confused.

"The 'proper' time . . .?"

"What?! No such thing as a proper time, is there? You can just eat 'em anytime on New Year's Eve! Right, Kaoru?"

My mother, unsurprisingly, is shouting. She inhales all her toast but leaves the strange, pretentious coffee. I had finished my toast before anyone else and washed it down with coffee.

"So, toshikoshi soba?"

"You eat it the moment the new year arrives, don'tcha?"

That's our New Year's Eve morning.

Inside with the heat turned on, the air feels dull and dense compared to the crystal-clear air outside. At some point my father's overnight bag had disappeared and now here he is, sitting at the table, blending right in with the scenery despite his three-year absence.

The day he left home, he had carried with him the same overnight bag, along with the morning paper. At the time, I was more upset about not being able to look at that day's TV listings than the fact that my father had left and probably wouldn't be coming back.

Miki appeared to have been scouring the house.

"Aw, crap," she'd said, and then left.

About ten minutes later, she came back into the house with Sakura and threw at least three copies of the morning paper on the table. They were all the exact same edition of the *Asahi News* and though I was now glad to have the TV listings, when I asked her, "What the hell?" she may have misunderstood and thought I was asking where they came from.

"The Asanos, the Kishis, and the Onishis had them in their mailboxes."

Sakura had looked uneasy, her eyes darting around us.

My mother had realized my father was gone sooner than Miki and I had. She wasted no time emptying his closet and then started burning his socks, underwear, and neckties in the yard. As luck would have it, it was autumn, right around the time when my mother had raked up the fallen leaves in the yard, so she could get away with doing something like that without arousing suspicion from our neighbors.

And when the Asanos and the Kishis and the Onishis announced that they hadn't gotten their papers that morning, my mother had hammed it up. "Us too! Should we complain to the delivery boy?"

My mother made for an excellent liar.

Miki is on the sofa, reading a magazine. Her legs are flung over the armrest, and I see that her pedicure is orange today. The polish is characteristically smudged over her pinky toe— she's never been very good at applying it and I don't why she's so adamant about doing it every single day.

There is a delicious aroma of garlic, and on the table I see that a heaping mound of filling for gyoza has been prepared. For New Year's at our house, instead of the traditional osechi feast, we eat a massive amount of gyoza. How much, you may ask? Well, enough for us to eat dumplings for two meals a day over the first three days of the new year (not counting breakfast—toast is a given since we all sleep in) and still have leftovers.

The reason our family has gyoza for New Year's is a bit embarrassing, but it goes back to my parents' courtship.

On their first date, the two of them went to Chinatown in Kobe. According to my mother, she was nervous, and there was no way she was going to eat dumplings in front of my father. She was worried about the garlic smell, and thought to herself, "Oh, how I wish I knew this man well enough to feel comfortable eating gyoza in front of him to my heart's content."

A year later, instead of eating her heart's content of gyoza in front of him, she found herself married to the man—a shotgun wedding, no less, which was unusual at the time. But my mother hadn't forgotten about her wish, so she suggested they create a tradition that, on the most important day of the year, together they should eat all the gyoza they wanted. It's an annoying story. And it's just like my father to go along with it.

There's a photograph in our house commemorating that first date, with my father trying his hardest to look cool and my mother primped to the nines. (While she may have reduced every last article of his clothing to ashes, the photo remained close to her heart.)

My father has an aquiline nose and chiseled, determined eyes and brows (which Miki inherited) and though his weak mouth and square jaw (which I inherited) might be considered flaws, they are compensated for by his overall air of sophistication. My mother's beauty was renowned, even at the place where she worked. She has the ideal oval-shaped face, arched brows with almond-shaped eyes, full sexy lips, and a round nose—all of which add up to a charming winsomeness.

I don't resemble either of my parents. Well, maybe I do, but my face is an amalgam of all their lesser features. You might think you notice a similarity to my father's chiseled eyes, but mine are a poor facsimile that cannot dispel a general air of plainness. My mother always compliments my "nuanced face," while my father emphasizes a trait that seems quite irrelevant: "Kaoru has great ears! They stick out perfectly, all the better to hear people with." Meanwhile, Miki's take on it is, "See his face once and you'll never remember it."

"Kaoru, help out."

Without my noticing, Miki has tossed aside her magazine and started preparing to wrap the gyoza. Wrapping all these dumplings is also a yearly tradition. Sometimes the whole family does it together, and sometimes just us kids do it.

"This is for the 'winners,' I guess," Miki says.

We end up stuffing some of the gyoza with tidbits from some year-end gifts like ham, cheese, or mentaiko, but Miki gets slaphappy, and we end up with too many "winner" dumplings. I have to keep my eye on her—there have been times when we run out of filling and she tries to stick in a cookie or something, to make what is obviously a "loser" dumpling. Since she was little, Miki's never had any sense of limits.

Even now, as we go about our task, there are M&Ms and Oreo cookies, and a peanut butter jar scattered beside us, which is making me nervous.

"Miki."

"Hm?"

"You're not gonna put these in there, are ya?"

Miki looks at the brightly colored jellybeans in my hand.

"So-so . . ." she says cryptically.

"Whaddya mean 'so-so'? Does it mean you're gonna put 'em in 'so-so' many? Or like, you'll put 'em in some but don't get 'so-so' mad?"

"Maybe it means both."

"Did'ja already?"

At a loss, I figure the least I can do is make some gyoza that will be edible, so I keep stuffing them in desperation. I work in silence, reluctant to ask Miki about our father's whereabouts but, as if she's reading my mind, Miki volunteers, "He's upstairs doing something."

"Uh-huh," I mutter back.

Then she says, "There's no point trying to make 'em so you know which gyoza are yours."

I don't know how to respond to this. I utter a vague "Oh," and then the potato starch that the wrappers are covered with makes me sneeze.

"*Hitschew!*"

My sneeze scatters the potato starch, and even some of the jellybeans fall to the floor. Miki kicks me with her orange toes, and then she sneezes herself.

"*Ktt'sch!*"

A cute little sneeze, not like her at all.

Having heard the ruckus (or having followed her nose), Sakura comes up to the sliding door to stare in at us.

The People's Forest

Bored with wrapping gyoza and faced with the futility of keeping watch over Miki, I decide to take Sakura for a walk.

At the sight of the chain leash, her tail wags like mad—despite her age, she's still happy to go on walks, which makes me happy too.

The air is crisp and still, and the setting sun unusually beautiful—I'm not all that cold, and Sakura seems to also be enjoying herself. Every so often, she turns back toward me as if dazzled, wags her tail two or three times, and then continues on her way. Even when we occasionally pass a dog that might seem aggressive, she pretends not to notice. Reliable and clever, that's Sakura.

I don't know what kind of walks my mother and Miki are taking Sakura on these days, but as soon as we leave the house, Sakura leads me around to various places, as if she's navigating. What once was a no-thoroughfare passage is now a new road; where there used to be a big house is now a sprawling vacant lot—I'm surprised by all the changes.

"A lot's different around here, huh, Sakura?"

Having gauged my reaction, Sakura takes her time sniffing at each of these spots and then, after peeing in salutation, she moves on. The sound of Sakura's paws flip-flapping on the pavement is a balm to my ears, and for the first time since coming back I think to myself, *Ah, it's good to be home*.

For the next half hour or so, Sakura proceeds to drag me to wherever she pleases. We circle past the same places, we pass through tufts of grass that are not so passable for a human in tow. Sakura basically goes wherever she likes, but eventually she resumes the same old route as always.

The People's Forest.

These are the words beautifully carved in marble at the entrance to the park. As I recall, the characters that are engraved had been written by the grandfather of one of my elementary school classmates, whose name I couldn't remember but who had always been a nasty little showoff. Our school song that hung on the wall in the gym had also been written by that same kid's grandfather—who I guess is a famous calligrapher or something—but I'm not one for those kinds of elaborate brushstrokes and fancy flourishes. I much prefer my father's penciled characters, even if they seem to lack confidence.

The People's Forest.

Sakura is staring at me as I stand there. Before, whenever I had stopped walking, Sakura would tug on her leash or stamp her paws to urge me along, but this time she's just waiting patiently for me to start moving again.

Upon entering the park, you see a building on your right—that's the civic center. Within this bare concrete structure, which had been in style when it was built, there had been a branch of city hall and a modest concert hall. We never had any reason to go to this building but, on hot summer days, we would come by to use the bathroom and cool off in the air-conditioned lobby.

SAKURA

Sakura sets off slowly, matching her gait to mine as I start walking again. She doesn't sniff the ground or look for a spot to pee—she just walks, keeping up with my pace. I approach the building slowly, one step at a time, as if there's something I'm trying to absorb.

At the entrance to the civic center hangs a placard that says, "Closed Today." It must have been years old because the "C" in "Closed" and the "d" in "Today" are almost faded. I try to peek inside through the glass but with the way the setting sun is shining, all I can see is my own reflection. When I use my hand to deflect the light, I can barely make out the lobby within, which looks the same as ever. The vending machine we used to buy soda from is still there, along with the sign indicating where the bathrooms are. The only thing that's different is, where there used to be a row of green public payphones, now there's just a single unit in a corner of the lobby. The phone's dull, whitish green seems out of place amid all the sterile gray.

There's a tug on the leash. I turn around and Sakura is scratching the base of her neck with her hind leg. But not as zestfully as she usually scratches—she moves her paw lightly two or three times. After scratching, she stretches her spine a little and looks at my feet. The long hairs growing above her eyes shine white in the slanting sunlight.

Hasegawa-kun.

I hear a voice. The quiet, halting voice of a young girl.

Hasegawa-kun.

My gaze snaps back to the glass door and I see a reedy boy standing there. He's wearing a down parka the color of the sky after the rain has stopped and jeans that are a little too big for him. He is staring at me with a sort of nervous look on his face. It's my thirteen-year-old self.

I blink with surprise and, a moment later, the sight of him disappears. In his place, a stubble-faced young man and a ragged dog stand there idiotically. I squeeze my eyes shut, as if I can still see that thirteen-year-old boy in my mind.

Hasegawa-kun.

That day, the late afternoon sun had not been shining the way it is now. That's why I hadn't been able to see the boy standing behind me in the glass.

My heart races like a rabbit's when I hear my name called, but I don't want to let the kid see how nervous I am. I'll turn around sooner rather than later, but despite how many times I'm called, I want to make it seem like I only just realized it, so I count to ten before finally turning around. You know how ten seconds can feel like forever.

One, two, three . . .

It's then that I realize the pocket of my parka is fraying.

Four, five, six . . .

There's a piece of mint gum in my pocket, and I poke at it with my finger.

Seven, eight . . .

The wind howls, carrying with it the sweet fragrance of the girl's hair.

Nine . . .

My thirteen-year-old self was impatient and, with just one second left to go, I turn around. With all my strength, I squeeze the gum in my pocket, squishing it. The wind picks up again, and there she is, the girl with long hair looking at me with upturned eyes.

Hasegawa-kun?

Ten.

The twenty-two-year-old me does not turn around after I

count to ten. Nor do I bother opening my eyes. I just stand there, motionless, my eyes squeezed shut. Despite the reflection of the late afternoon sun, there's no glare, and Sakura's leash remains completely slack.

I wonder what that boy's face had looked like on that day. What had he been thinking? And what about the me who watches him silently—how does he feel? Memories swirl, flowing like grains of sand. They whirl around me, as if forming a mist that refuses to take shape.

The feel of the gum, limp and rubbery in my hand, and the sweet scent carried by the sudden breeze—they just seem so real, like they're right here in the present. They keep me standing there, glued to the spot.

Hasegawa-kun?

The wind whistling past my ears and someone's faraway laughter echo with surprising brashness. But I can't tell if their buzzing, like tinnitus, is audible here and now, or if it's something I heard back then. It's as if the sounds are mocking me, looming and retreating, only to suddenly resonate again. Like a tornado that strikes the American South, or a squall gusting on a beach. There's a barrage in my brain; I'm unable to keep up with these changes.

My mother with her back to me, Miki toddling along, my father's overnight bag, the flower petal stuck to Sakura's tail, the green telephone—all sorts of images flash through my mind and make me nauseous, like the swaying of the Shinkansen. No matter how tightly I squeeze my eyes closed, the images won't go away; they're still there, soft and indistinct, making me feel even more sick to my stomach.

Unfortunately, among these indistinct visions, a single image persists clearly in my mind. It alone has taken up residence there and, no matter how the wind blows, no matter whose voice I hear, it remains vivid and unchanged.

The image of a tree.

A tree as white as the bones of something that's dead, bent limply under the weight of gravity. That tree had taken everything away from us—my mother's slender fingers, Miki's eyes that shone deep as a lake, my father's protective arms around all of us, the warmth of spring, even Sakura's nattering.

And now, in a show of resilience, the image that seems to be ingrained in my soul is about to chase me down. Caught by surprise, I steel myself so that I don't literally fall over. I have the urge to flee, but my entire body is entwined in the tree's branches, leaving me frozen in place.

Kaoru.

I hear my name again. This time, it's a male voice. From under the shadow of the tree, it sounds exuberant. The grains of sand that had been swirling around me morph into a great beam of light, aiming right at me. It surrounds me and Sakura and the tree too, and once we're enveloped, everything becomes clear.

It's a hot summer day.

In the park, a leaf as big as my hand falls from a tree, which sways as if overcome by the heat. Someone has left behind an issue of *Shonen Jump* beside the vending machine, and it lies there, soaking wet, either from a previous rain, or maybe it too is sweating in the sun.

I'm very thirsty and am about to buy a soda from the vending machine. At the time, it still cost only one hundred yen, and I used to collect the pull tabs from the cans.

I insert my coin and, just as my hand reaches out to select a soda, someone pushes the button for canned coffee. I don't even have time to register surprise before the can of coffee falls into the slot with a thud, glistening in the sunlight. Back then I was uninitiated to how delicious coffee can be, and in that moment, parched with thirst, I whirl around in anger.

The person's face is backlit by the blinding sun. I can't see it, but I instantly know who it is by the sound of their laugh.

Kaoru.

Miki is playing with Sakura off in the distance; I can hear her laughter lilting like a song. Ah, that voice from before must have been Miki's. Now she's shouting something and chasing Sakura gleefully, while Sakura trots along, her gait like a bouncing ball as she runs away from Miki.

"What're ya' doin'?!" I say, but the person just stands there laughing.

Ha ha, my bad, I'll drink that.

He playfully flings another hundred-yen coin at me, using his thumb to flick the edge. It emits a clear ringing sound, which makes him laugh even more, and now I'm playing along too, knocking him in jest. He easily dodges my punch, ruffling my hair before he slowly glances over at Miki and Sakura. He's tall, handsome, and strong—and most of all, kind.

Should we go, Kaoru?

Our big brother.

PART 2

Hajime

My older brother Hajime took his first breath on a hot August day, with a fierce wail after thirteen-and-a-half hours in my mother's birth canal, and he died twenty years and four months later. That was four years ago.

My brother had a dramatic origin story.

To be clear, it didn't transpire on the night of that dinner in Kobe's Chinatown, but about eight months after my mother and father's first date, as a teeny tiny egg lodged itself within my mother's womb. Three months after that, my mother became aware of my brother's existence—not because she realized she had missed her period, but because she was seized by a ferocious appetite and violent nausea. Hearing the unexpected news at the clinic, my mother muttered, "What a dope."

Counting backward, she realized he must have been in her belly since her birthday, and the reason she knew this was because that was when she'd had sex for the first time, and it hurt so much that she hadn't let my father touch her in the three months since—in other words, from the time my brother had been conceived until the moment she realized it.

Meaning that my brother was the result of the first—and only—time my parents had had sex.

I've neglected to mention the embarrassing nature of my brother's name. Hajime, written with the character for "one" in Japanese, takes on several awkward connotations.

"I'm number one and it only took once," my brother often used to say about himself.

But Miki, after having wheedled the story out of my mother, would animatedly reply, "You're not number one, you're just first!"

Miki was eight years old at the time. Really, it's appalling on two levels—that a mother would tell her own child such a story, and that my sister would want to hear it.

Anyway, because of the rather miraculous way that my brother came into this world and the multiple significances of being the eldest child in the Hasegawa family, he was always doted upon.

My brother was popular from a young age. In kindergarten, he managed to pull off an incredible feat: When the teacher posed the question, "Who do you like?" to Hajime and his classmates in the Snow class, all but one of the girl students pointed at him (that girl was enamored with the swimming teacher). The following year, in the Lily class, it was common for there to be catfights among the girls over who got to sit next to my brother, with one girl even using a pair of scissors to slash at another girl, in an episode that contributed to what would become known as the "Hajime legend."

When I was young, I often reaped spillover benefits from girls—like being included in playing house or being shown their strawberry-patterned undies—just because I was Hajime's little brother.

I was born almost two years after my brother, in May, the season of fragrant spring breezes, hence the character for my name, Kaoru. Thinking about it, the way my parents came up with our names was pretty simplistic. Even Miki's name was inspired by the characters for "precious and beautiful child" and, being their only daughter, my parents couldn't resist pampering and spoiling her. Which explains why Miki is quite selfish and stubborn.

My brother had a rather unusual memory—not only did he claim he could remember when Miki and I were born, but he also claimed to recall the color of the sky, our mother's hands, and our father's face on the day he himself was born.

"You're full of crap!"

"I'm serious! I mean, I even remember stuff from when I was in Mom's belly."

"Like what?"

"Like, floating in the dark. I'd gulp down water and then pee it out. I could hear Mom's voice the whole time, so when I came out, I was like, *Oh, so that's who was talking*."

Even now it's hard to believe, but he described things that only my parents would have known, things that they later said were true—details like "Dad brought yellow flowers, not sunflowers, to the hospital room, and lots of bananas," and "On the day we came home from the hospital, there was a big truck parked at the house next door."

When I told Dad about Hajime's account, he said, "It's true—those yellow flowers weren't sunflowers, they were marigolds, Mom's favorite. And bananas are supposed to be nutritious after childbirth. There wasn't anyone else around either; Mom's the only other one who knows about that."

And when I told Mom, she said, "Now that you mention it, the neighbors did move in the day I came home from the hospital with Hajime! They came over to introduce themselves, and I was in my pajamas, you know? I was so embarrassed. But how could Hajime know about that?"

When I asked my brother about the day I was born, he said, "The whole house stunk so bad, it made me barf."

Feeling kind of insulted, I asked Granny, who was still alive back then.

"He's right! The day you were born, Kaoru, a sewer pipe had burst! The toilet overflowed, it was awful. Hajime kept saying, 'Stinky, stinky'—and then he threw up," she recalled wistfully. Naturally, this bummed me out.

"But I was psyched to have a little brother," Hajime told me sheepishly.

That made me happy, even if he only said it in consolation. My brother always had the power to brighten my spirits with his infectious optimism.

Gift of Flowers

Unlike my brother, I don't have many clear memories from when I was little, although there's something I do remember from right before Miki was born. My brother and I would often put our ears up to our previously skinny mother's huge belly to listen or press our hands to it to feel Miki moving around. Miki was so big in our mother's belly, and she kicked my mother so wildly, that all comparisons with my brother and I were already off the table.

"This kid's rambunctious, gotta be a boy," my father had said. Miki did turn out to be a huge baby, weighing ten pounds at birth. And while my mother had labored thirteen-and-a-half hours with my brother and six with me, she said of Miki, "The third time's a charm, Miki slid right out—plonk!"

I liked the way that sounded. Unlike "squish," *plonk* carries with it the slight hint of a letdown. Plonk. It's the perfect way to describe a baby being born. The baby is trying to come out, and the mother is laboring, and they're breathing in sync—that must be what the result sounds like.

Anyway, it was raining on the day that Miki came into this world with a plonk. Miki was born on February 29. A leap year.

I was three years and nine months old at the time. We hadn't moved into this house yet; our old house had a yard even tinier than this one's, about the size of a postage stamp, but it was always brightened by the flowers my mother planted.

Granny was home with us that day, and my brother and I were eating the omurice she had made for us, which was kind of gross (she had put reconstituted dried shiitake mushrooms in it), when my father called with the news.

"Hey, you've got a baby sister!"

My father was overjoyed. While I understood the significance of our baby sister's arrival, I was a little flummoxed, having hoped for a younger brother to play with and dote on the way Hajime did with me. And more importantly, I had a concern.

"How'm I gonna teach her how to pee?"

I'd learned from Hajime, who, unbeknownst to my mother, had shown me not only how to pee in the yard but also how to direct my stream farther. I'd been eager to pass along this knowledge to our next sibling, but a baby sister presented a dilemma. I found out from playing doctor with the girls who knew me from the "Hajime legend" that girls didn't have a pee-pee, and since I already knew that girls squatted when they peed, I was at a complete loss about how girls might pee standing up or how they'd direct their stream farther. I looked to my brother to see if he had any good ideas, but he was bombarding my father with questions over the phone, enthralled by the news of our little sister.

"What's she like? How about her eyes? And her legs?"

My brother talked to him for a while and after he'd settled down, I asked him again about peeing.

"You dummy! Girls don't aim and spray!"

Hearing this, I was both disappointed and kind of relieved.

Although four years later, Miki would get caught by a lady in the neighborhood while he was peeing on a utility pole, which caused a commotion among the locals. Miki would get angry whenever anyone brought it up, so we tried not to.

The first Hasegawa daughter would arrive home from the hospital in three days. In preparation, my father and Granny rushed about madly to buy clothes and toys for a baby girl. I'm pretty sure all my things were hand-me-downs from my brother and that I never had any new toys, but for Miki, my father even splurged on a brand-new wooden crib.

The airplanes and helicopters that had swirled above my brother's and my head were replaced by butterflies and flowers, and the pale blue rattle that had amused the two of us was exchanged for a pink one with a daintier timbre. Inside the house, things suddenly seemed somehow gentler and sweeter—so much so that, though my mother wasn't home yet, we even hesitated to desecrate the garden.

"No more pissing in the yard, huh, Kaoru."

"Guess not. Don't want our sister to think it stinks."

We became a little more grown-up in that moment, and made our first pact with each other that if we peed outside, we would only do it away from home. Such little men we were. And then we came up with an idea that felt like an even bigger leap forward.

"When our sister gets here, we should give her flowers."

"Yeah, let's do that!"

My brother and I decided that we would present a gift of flowers to the little sister we had yet to meet. It would be my first time giving flowers to a girl. This was the height of the "Hajime legend" era, when the classroom was often abuzz with girls declaring, "I like Hasegawa-kun!" Knowing this, I would have assumed my brother to be savvy about things like giving girls flowers, but in fact he too was a novice—it turns out his expertise was in *getting* presents like candy, marbles, and meatballs from the school lunch.

We were excited about our first brotherly foray and eagerly deliberating about which color flowers would work best when we suddenly had a revelation:

"Where do we actually get flowers *from*?"

At that age, neither of us had any concept of how "buying" flowers worked. We figured it'd be fine to pick whatever flowers were blooming in the garden, but there had been one time when our ball-playing had crushed some pansies in the yard and when my mother saw the bedraggled flowers, she wasn't too happy. My brother and I loved our mother and didn't want to upset her, so the two of us put our heads together and reached the conclusion that we'd try to get our hands on flowers that didn't belong to anyone. Judging from how unhappy my mother had been, it was reasonable to assume that taking someone else's flowers would evoke a similar reaction, so it would be better to find ones that weren't anybody's. Hajime and I really had grown up. Looking back on those three days we spent anticipating Miki's arrival, we were quite the little men.

However, we now faced yet another question: Where would we find these "nobody's flowers"? We were clueless, but one thing we knew for sure was that there weren't any around here. The yellow ones in bloom four houses down from us on the corner, those were Kato-san's, and if you turned the corner and went a little farther, those fuchsia ones were Miyake-san's. Surely, we thought, "nobody's flowers" could be had wherever there weren't concrete walls or paved roads.

We decided to go on a neighborhood expedition in search of these "nobody's flowers."

Our biggest obstacle was Granny. Whenever the two of us wanted to go somewhere, she always demanded, "Whoa, where'd y'all think you're going?"

Granny was mostly an optimist but we, her grandchildren, seemed to trigger her wildest and most pessimistic imaginings (that we were irresistible kidnap-bait, or a natural disaster would befall us, or a sudden and inexplicable epidemic would occur) and she prayed often for our well-being.

The places where Granny allowed us to go were "Giraffe Park" (so called because it had a slide in the shape of a giraffe), which was about a ten-minute walk from home; Fuji Park (the origin behind this name is unknown), located even closer to us on the grounds of a nearby danchi public housing complex; and the local penny candy shop, Satchan's (although no one by the name of Satchan worked there), for which we occasionally would each receive one hundred yen to spend as a special treat.

My brother and I conferred with each other and decided that we would venture to the destination furthest afield, Giraffe Park, to start on our flower quest. Granny wouldn't come looking for us until around five, so we'd be fine as long as she found us innocently playing there then.

I urged my brother to hurry up and put our plan into action—that is, to lie to Granny and get out of the house by two o'clock—but of course he was savvier than me. Knowing that if we left in too much of a hurry it would arouse Granny's suspicions, during snack time he ate with his typical leisureliness and casually mentioned, "We're going to Giraffe Park, Granny." We still had three hours.

It was a beautiful day with weather that felt like spring. We were wearing matching down jackets in different colors—my brother's was red and blue, mine was yellow and green—that had on the chest the appliquéd letters "GO!" in English, which neither of us understood at the time, but nevertheless we thought were cool.

"Hajime, do you like these stripes?"

"Yeah, I like 'em."

"I like 'em too."

Our spirits high, we hummed as we walked. Taking note of Kato-san's yellow blooms as we turned the corner, we immediately encountered our first obstacle: an ardent fan of my brother's. I've forgotten her name, but she was a year older than me, a girl with bobbed hair like a traditional Japanese doll and narrow, deep-set eyes. When she saw us, her face instantly lit up and she let out a shriek, delighted to have run into Hajime Hasegawa.

It occurred to me that she might prove to be a nuisance.

Just as I feared, she asked, "Hasegawa-kun, where ya going?"

"The park," my brother replied, trying to get away with a vague answer, but she was quite persistent.

"What park?"

And then, as if demonstrating her maturity, she proceeded to rattle off details about various parks, such as "X Park is dangerous because a weird old man who pulls down his pants hangs out there," and "A dead cat was buried in the sandbox at Y Park and it's been there forever."

But we hurried along. "Thanks, see ya," my brother waved as he tried to pass by her, when suddenly her mature composure of just a moment ago vanished and she shouted, "I'll come with you!"

That was the impressive power of Hajime Hasegawa. Despite his annoyance, he sagaciously said, "No, today it's just my brother and me."

The key word being "today"—to maintain the expectation that she'd be able to join him on another day. Like I said, Hasegawa power.

"Your brother?" The girl looked taken aback, and she regarded me intently. Then, predictably, and with an unkind gleam in those deep-set eyes, she said, "Hmm, you guys don't look much alike."

My brother responded, flatly and with utter exasperation, "Whether or not he looks like me, he's my brother!" He grabbed my hand as he abruptly turned away from her and we went on our way. Then, in case she had any ideas about following us, he added, "Can't hang with us if ya ain't got stripes!"

As if he knew that wasn't a very convincing argument, he took off running. My brother was fast, so I had to book it to keep up with him, but somehow the fact that I too had on a striped jacket made me feel like I could run faster.

When we'd finally lost her, we resumed walking, but since there was a risk of running into someone else we knew at Giraffe Park, we decided against going there. Instead, my brother proposed a new destination: Ding-Dong Park.

This came as a surprise to me.

As its name suggests, Ding-Dong Park had a bell that rang on the hour, all day long. The park was vast—it even had a pond—and though it was quite likely that we would find "nobody's flowers" growing there, it would easily take an hour for two kids like us to walk there. Whenever we'd gone there before, our father had always driven us.

"But don't we need a car to get there?"

Seeing that I was daunted by the prospect, my brother replied with absolute conviction: "I know the way."

"You do?"

"Sure. Kaoru, you've been to Yusuke-kun's house, right?"

"Yusuke—that fat kid?"

"Right. He lives near Sunny Supermarket."

"Yeah, I been there."

"We always go right by there in the car, don't we?"

"Huh, guess so, but d'ya know the rest of the way?"

"Pass Yusuke-kun's and keep going straight, right? Then there's the meat shop, the place with the weird pig drawings, you know? Turn at that corner, go straight for a while, huh? Then go under the bridge, right? Then go straight again, and turn som'ere."

When I think back on my brother's description of how to get to Ding-Dong Park, there's no mention at all of whether you turn right or left or for how long you go straight, to say nothing of that final "turn som'ere"—it was all so very vague—but at the time my brother was a hero in my eyes, and I had every reason to believe that if we did as he said, surely we'd end up at Ding-Dong Park.

"So Kaoru, wanna go?"

"Yeah, let's go!"

And so, bypassing Giraffe Park, we headed off to Ding-Dong Park.

The Old Man

I guess I'll start with the ending. My brother and I didn't manage to find flowers for our new baby sister that day. And we rode in a patrol car for the first time.

We were nowhere near Giraffe Park at five o'clock—as a matter of fact, we'd just made it to Ding-Dong Park when we heard the bell toll six.

According to the girl with the bob who was smitten with my brother, Granny—after mobilizing everyone in the neighborhood and going from park to park in search of us—reached the conclusion that we had been kidnapped.

Kato-san, who had the yellow flowers, suggested looking for us at Ding-Dong Park, but the idea was resoundingly rejected; most assumed the park was too far away for kids our age to get there on their own.

My father arrived home from work, where he had been bursting with pride at the birth of his first daughter, to find a patrol car parked in front of our house, surrounded by our kind neighbors, smiling with relief, along with Granny, who was berating us through her wails, and the two of us with heads hung low, on the verge of tears ourselves.

I wanted to explain everything, but my brother set a mature

example in the face of such anger. Remaining tight-lipped, the only words he uttered were "I'm sorry."

At the tender age of five, my brother had something else on his mind.

At Ding-Dong Park, we had encountered a rather memorable character.

By the time we had gotten there, our striped jackets were dirty and sweaty (even though it was winter), and my cheeks were streaked with dried tears from when I had fallen on the way and scraped my knee, drawing blood. My brother had been leading the way and had managed not to fall down, but after deciding to take a shortcut, he had gotten pricked by a strange, thorny bush, which looked like it had hurt. And though he didn't cry in front of me, he turned pale with fear when it appeared we might be lost. That's right, of course we were lost. Like half-feral cats, we made it there successfully (who knows how)—though when, miraculously, the park's large bell came into view, we didn't even have the chance to be excited about finding it. Instead, we were too busy worrying about how we would ever get back home.

The park had a big pond, bordered by a walking path that looped all the way around it. Beside the pond was a small drinking fountain, and when we got there, exhausted from our trek, we lapped up water from it like dogs.

My brother and I washed our faces and hands in the fountain too, wiping ourselves off on our jackets. Feeling refreshed, we perked up a bit. Despite the looming challenge of finding our way home, we were proud of ourselves for having gotten this far under our own steam, the skinned knee and pale fear now forgotten, and we returned to our original objective of finding flowers to give to our sister.

"Hajime, what about these?"

"Look closer, see the sign on the tree? The ones with a name written on them mean they're somebody's."

"Aha."

Along the walking path there were plenty of unusual flowers in bloom, any of which would have made a lovely bouquet, but these orderly rows seemed like they definitely belonged to someone, so we ventured a bit further into the woods.

Though there was still daylight, the woods were dusky, and withered tree branches not yet decomposed made a brittle crunch under our footsteps. While there were a few benches here and there, the white paint on them was peeling and the seats were so overgrown with weeds, they seemed like rather unwelcoming places to sit. Occasionally an insect that looked like a grasshopper would whiz past us, and we would yell out in amazement at their leaping abilities.

Teensy tiny flowers and white clovers were sprinkled among the weeds, but we worried that our little sister might swallow such small flowers, and white clovers were what my brother and I always peed on, so we passed those by too.

We were so intent on our search that we lost track of time. Meanwhile, back at home, having failed to find us at Giraffe Park, Granny's pessimism had caused an uproar, though we had no way of knowing it at the time.

Once we tired of looking for flowers, we were clambering up the smooth tree trunks, playing and peeing in the woods, when my brother noticed an old man sitting stock-still, like a tree stump.

He was wearing a pitch-black coat and a red and white knitted wool hat. His pure white beard reached his chest, and he had a cane—the hand holding it looked like bark on a tree. The two of us stood there staring, not moving a muscle, as if we were rooted to the ground. The woods were dense, growing darker, but where the old man was sitting was the only spot glowing with the evening sun (by this point, the sun was starting to set), and it seemed like he was about to vaporize before our very eyes.

"Is he dead?"

"Shh!"

The old man looked just like the Grim Reaper that I'd seen on my mom's tarot cards, and he was completely motionless. The old man's right eye was green, the same beautiful color as the jade ring my mother loved to wear, and his left eye was gray, like the cinder-block fences in our neighborhood. Never having seen anyone with two different-colored eyes, I stood there transfixed. The old man's eyes were huge, opened wide as if in surprise, and I felt as though they might swallow me up like the plunge basin at the bottom of a waterfall.

As I was standing there, stupefied, the old man murmured, "Alley oop," and heaved himself to his feet, brushing away the earth and grass that was stuck to his clothing. Each pat of his hands dispersed more poofs of dust than I'd ever seen, so much so that I actually started coughing just from watching him.

"Ey there, sonny, 'ave ya caught a cold?" the old man said suddenly.

He was still staring straight ahead, so at first, I didn't realize that what he'd said was directed at me.

Now, the old man must have been unaware of the sheer amount of dust that had accumulated on his body. But I wasn't about to tell him that I was choking on it just by looking at him, nor did I want to worry my brother by lying about having a cold, so I kept quiet.

"Whatcha doing there, sonny?"

Those words brought my brother and I back to why we had come to Ding-Dong Park in the first place (to be honest, we'd been so busy playing that we had forgotten our original purpose).

Upon remembering, and with renewed pride in ourselves, we launched into a rapid-fire explanation to our newfound companion (well, my brother did most of the talking, but I threw in a few apt descriptors).

It wasn't clear that the old man was listening—the whole time, he was stroking an abrasion on the knuckle of his index finger, randomly throwing in an interrogative "Ho?" here and there that made me worry that my brother's story hadn't been properly conveyed. However, once we finished speaking, the old man arched his back as slowly as a cat, then took a deep whiff of the scent of the breeze, and said, "Well, sonnies, ya've done well."

He went on, "So ya say ya've got a lil' sister now?"

"Yeah."

"Ho!" he said again.

The old man rubbed his chin with his withered branch of a hand, narrowing his eyes approvingly. Then, he sort of drew in his breath before speaking.

"See now, sonny. Evverything in this here world belongs to somebody."

His words completely crushed us. We took them to mean that all the various adventures and perils we had encountered up to now had been for naught. All the flowers in this park were like Kato-san's yellow ones or Miyake-san's fuchsia ones—they too belonged to somebody and thus were not for our picking. I glanced at my brother, but he wasn't able to disguise his shock either, and he grabbed my hand and held it tightly.

The old man turned his right ear in our direction—it was dark, wide, and dirty. He seemed to be checking us out. He had yet to look at us even once, but his face softened a little into a gentle smile, as if he had registered our shock.

"But then again, evverything in this world also belongs to nobody," he said.

My brother and I were totally bewildered. *Everything in the world belongs to someone, yet everything in the world belongs to no one?* Those yellow flowers were Kato-san's, but then they weren't his? And the flowers blooming in our garden were my mother's, but they also weren't? My bloodied kneecap and my brother's reddened cheeks are both ours but then also not ours? Hajime just stood there, his eyes downcast—the pose he took whenever he was deep in thought. The old man, seeming not to have noticed that what he'd said had plunged the two of us into confusion, kept talking.

"I been alive for more than eighty years."

At that time, I had only just fully grasped the idea that I was about to turn four, and I couldn't count past ten. Which meant that even if the significance of the old man's eighty years was lost on me, the sight of his withered-branch hands and his long, pure white beard that looked like a spray of shooting stars falling from his chin registered that this must be an extraordinarily long time.

"I've had eighty years to bask in the sun like this."

The dust particles that he had stirred up before were still floating around him, which only added to the notion that the old man was letting us in on a secret.

"Aha—all of it is mine, and none of it is mine."

He shut his cinder-block eye to gaze up at the dazzling sun.

"This sunshine, this sky, the water . . ."

And of course, the flowers, the old man looked at us as if to say, but his gaze seemed to pass through us, as if he were watching who knows what—something bigger and slow moving, maybe. It was then that I realized the old man was blind.

"My eyes—for decades they'd taken in the sea and the sky, big mighty buildings and fair young women—one day they just stopped seeing."

The old man rubbed vigorously at these very eyes, the ones that couldn't see.

"Such is my lot."

We could hear a patrol car's siren off in the distance. The old man stopped rubbing his eyes and turned in the direction of the siren, then looked up at the sky again before slowly continuing his story.

"Yeah, ya know, I reckoned these eyes were mine but turns out they weren't. God can have 'em back. Now I can't see the mountains or the stars, but I remember what the foothills look like, their rounded curves, and even if I can't see the shape of the stars, I can feel their light. I may be blind, ya know, but evverything can still be mine and evverything can still be given back."

I cocked my head, focusing intently on what the old man meant and on what he was looking at—just like the way my father concentrated when he was playing chess by himself.

"Don'tcha know, sonny, that's how I can go on."

The siren had gotten closer. Right about then, my brother and I realized that the siren was coming for us, which surely meant we'd get a good scolding from either Granny or our father (or both). But we stayed rooted there, staring at the old man's wrinkles that looked like the Amazon River had etched itself all over his face, and his eyes that, though they no longer worked, had seen much more than we had.

The breeze that swept past us already carried the scent of evening and the insects in the trees began to settle back down on the ground. In time, the birds folded their wings, burbling and cooing in expectation of tomorrow, and the sun above unhurriedly prepared to shine its rays somewhere else.

Hajime pointed at the white clovers poking up beside him. "So these are everyone's," he said, slowly breathing in the air, "and no one's?"

The old man mirthfully crinkled his eyes—the right one now bathed in shadow and deep green, the left one having taken on the strange aura of the setting sun and almost pure white—and said, "That's right."

Hearing this, my brother arched his back just like the old man had and looked up at the sky. The sun had swathed the entire western sky in its colors and was just about to bid us farewell. He gazed at it contentedly, like the king of some realm watching the sun hasten to its next workplace, and murmured to himself, "I see."

Despite it being our first time riding in a patrol car—something we had always dreamed of doing—my brother and I were quiet the whole time.

The policeman who found us in the park had barraged us with questions. As the tall officer loomed over us, it became clear that what we'd done was pretty bad. We kept our eyes downcast.

The policeman then asked gently, "Has it just been the two of you, this entire time?"

This made us realize that the old man was no longer there. In the spot where he had been just a moment ago, there were only the swaying trees that had shed all their leaves and the flowers that now seemed to be covered with them. But we were certain that we still felt his presence, and that the old man's body was somewhere far away. It seemed to me that, wherever that was, it must be someplace very nice.

Even though the two of us were always too scared to go to the toilet by ourselves in the middle of the night, this notion didn't frighten us in the least.

It was quite an uncanny feeling. To be standing there, seemingly enveloped by someone we'd never seen before and yet, at the same time, confident that we had gotten to that place by our own efforts. Whatever it was before us was enormous, and though it both unnerved and reassured us, it was entirely ours, though at some point it would leave us to return to wherever it came from. Until then, we would do our best to appreciate the beauty and fragrance of the flowers, and show our love to our new sister. Our little minds had been blown for the first time. It was as if a door had been thrown wide open in front of us.

With a puzzled look, the policeman peered around at whatever it was the two of us were staring at, and then he said, "Why don't I take you home?"

Miki

We were banned from playing outside for three months after what became known as the "Ding-Dong Park Incident."

But to us that didn't seem like punishment at all.

Our little sister had arrived.

The first baby girl I'd ever seen up close, she was so soft and pliable that she seemed to change shape at the slightest touch, and she smelled sweet and reassuring, like milk warmed with honey. *The scent of being alive*, it seemed to me.

Her tiny hands were like konpeito sugar candy, and I was amazed to count ten perfect little shell-like nails on her fingers. Her downy golden hair seemed like it might float away on the breeze.

Every now and then she would gently yawn with contentment, and I would be mesmerized by the glimpse of her bright red tongue, which looked like a delicious tropical fruit.

Even though I had never seemed to be able to follow my mother's instructions to wash my hands when I got home, going into my sister's room became the exception—I would scrub my wrists and even under my nails. And anytime I spoke to my little sister, it was always in a soft voice, as if a robin were whispering a secret.

SAKURA

Sometimes to my delight, she would stare at me, and I'd ask her, "What is it?" The next moment she'd have shifted her attention to something else, eyeing it so fixedly I'd look over to see what it could be, but by then she'd have moved on to yet another spot. It was like chasing a cabbage butterfly. Her gaze was greedy, trying to drink in everything she saw, but soft and capricious enough to want for nothing.

The very first Hasegawa family meeting was called under the pretext of deciding what to name our little sister.

My mother sat in the middle, holding our sister. The corners of my mother's mouth were always gently turned up, her eyes moist with fondness for everything around her. Her swept-back hair gleamed, the blackest and shiniest in the world. Her button nose had the power to sniff out sadness among anyone around her and then instantly alleviate it. She was the happiest mother in the world, here with the handsome and kind man she spent the New Year with eating gyoza to her heart's content, to whom she now flashed a loving smile. Meanwhile, my brother and I, in our childlike way, felt comforted by the obvious affection between our parents, which prompted us to stretch and yawn, at peace ourselves.

My father was the one who decided on the name Miki: 美貴. The truth was there had been no need for a family meeting; his mind was already made up. The first time my father saw Miki, he thought she was the epitome of beauty (美) and the most precious (貴) thing in the world, and he was so astonished that the woman he cherished more than anything in the world—more than his childhood memories, or his bright future, or whatever glorious honor might await him—had given birth to this child, after already giving him those two wonderful rascals eagerly awaiting the arrival of their little sister. He was so amazed by the grace of such an ordinary miracle that he had wept aloud, and the name had come to him.

His wailing, too naïve for anyone to think it was that of a man, echoed throughout the entire maternity ward, loudly enough to dampen the eyes of the other mothers who heard it and to awaken the other babies yet to be seen.

If my mother was the happiest woman in the world, my father was the happiest man in the universe.

Things Without Form

I've heard it said that God made babies so sweet and angelic because, in their vulnerability and defenselessness, they cannot survive on their own. That the reason they're so cute and lovable is to inspire the people around them to instinctively take care of them. Whether or not this is true, Miki seemed to have been born with a preternatural ability to make those in her presence feel unnerved and, at the same time, to inspire a warmth that, when she looked right at you, would almost bring you to tears. Naturally, Miki grew up showered with love from everyone around her.

I'd lie awake, just thinking about Miki in the next room, the rise and fall of her breath that smelled of sunshine, her mouth the size of the first grapes of summer in some sunny and faraway land. Since Granny had grounded us, whenever I wasn't in school and except for the time I spent eating or going to the toilet, I could be found staring at Miki's face. On school mornings, that's where I'd be—chewing my toast up until the very last minute (often to my mother's exasperation), and then, as class ended and before the teacher could even finish saying goodbye, I'd be darting out of the classroom to race home.

My brother was at the age when he was starting to act like he was too cool for it all—having already been through this when I arrived, his attitude was more detached—and he'd say with the air of an old hand, "I was the same way with you, Kaoru." Yet whenever Miki would cry, he'd run into her room, and he was always similarly thrilled when she looked right at him.

Miki's golden hair soon turned dark as night like my mother's, and as soon as she learned how to lock her unfocused gaze onto something, she also learned how to heave her big bottom off the ground and walk on her own two feet.

I was the first one to witness this. Although my brother's affection for Miki gradually drifted toward other things, like the pretty teacher for his Moon class, his new catcher's mitt, or the rhinoceros beetles that would fall from trees when he kicked their trunks, he had happened to be by her side when Miki first uttered "Mama," as well as when she finally held her head up without wobbling. He'd taken a certain amount of pride in that. But on the day Miki stood up and walked, he had been out back, playing soldiers with the boys from the neighborhood. They liked to pretend they were paratroopers, which involved jumping off the wall that surrounded our house, and as they leapt into the air with a furoshiki cloth billowing behind them or an umbrella unfurled against the blue sky, they looked like bright and promising young boys.

Normally I would have been playing with my brother, but that day I was on my own and bored. My mother had been watching TV with Miki in her arms, and she was starting to doze off peacefully. Miki had shown no interest in the cute toys for girls my father and grandmother had bought for her, preferring boyish things and more interactive play like throwing my miniature cars at the door with surprising precision or stuffing my brother's

Kinkeshi figures into her mouth, both of which my parents found worrisome.

On that day, she had been slapping a slipper against her thigh or the floor, narrowing her eyes with delight at the thwacking sound, until she suddenly stopped. I'd been sitting at the table, scooping out the dregs of Milo from the bottom of my cup with my finger, when I noticed that Miki, always making noise, had abruptly gone quiet. I looked over at her.

Miki was staring out the window, mouth agape, like a child seeing an airplane in the sky for the first time. Though Miki had recently begun to look my mother and us directly in the eye, her gaze was still soft and unsteady, like she was watching that invisible cabbage butterfly.

Wondering what was going on, I called out to her, "Miki?"

And then she stood up.

I don't remember anything about the moment when I first stood up. But I know that it requires a great deal of effort for a baby to do so. For example, the first time babies stand up themselves, they might need the support of a wall to stand next to or the help of their mother.

But Miki stood right up as if it were easy-peasy. Although of course she did use her hands to push up off the floor, she looked less like a baby summoning her strength to support herself than an old lady reluctantly hoisting herself upright. She might as well have grunted.

With both legs holding her up straight, Miki stretched out her arms and, surprisingly, started off in a trot. Her gait made it clear that she was trying to catch something.

What awakened my mother from her leisurely nap was the sound of Miki crashing into the sofa and me shouting "Miki!"

Actually, that wasn't the only thing that woke her—hearing my shout, Granny had come rushing into the room, fearing the worst.

Despite crashing into the sofa, Miki's gaze was still fixed on something. Hearing this story when she was older, Miki claimed to remember it clearly. It's amazing to me that my sister as well as my brother possessed such gifted powers of memory, whereas I feel ashamed about how little I remember.

My siblings truly are extraordinary.

We ate sekihan that day to celebrate. In our house, we had red beans and rice for any and every happy occasion (even on the day that Sakura barked for the first time). If the peas at the edge of the garden sprouted or when I outgrew my brother's hand-me-downs—really, for any silly little event, to the point that, when sekihan would appear on the table, we even stopped asking, "What are we celebrating?" (Which, fortunately, saved us from an awkward dinner conversation on the day Miki got her first period, a little on the early side.)

My brother was pretty disappointed to have missed the historic moment when Miki took her first steps. Hearing the full details from me, he banged on the table in frustration.

After that first time, in a demonstration of her capricious nature, Miki didn't stand up at all for the next couple months, though once she did start walking again, her active play style became even more wild (like eating the dirt out of potted plants and catching cockroaches), further unnerving my parents and grandmother.

Granny died a year after Miki first stood up. In her general optimism toward everything except for us, she had failed to notice the cancer that had spread within her own body.

Three months after being admitted to the hospital, she died

quietly, and without becoming a burden to anyone. Her parting words were, "Everyone in the family's got to get along."

That was the first time someone died right before my eyes. The Granny I saw at her funeral was so pale and frail, she didn't even look like a human being. The body lying there was completely different from the Granny always running after us shouting, "Whoa there! Where do you think you're going?!" Now, her mouth was open just slightly, and the teeth that were visible inside were shiny and white, like wax.

Hajime was in Little League at the time, and he had broken his arm sliding into home base on an inside-the-park home run; the cast on his right arm made it difficult for him to light the incense offering with his left hand. After that he started practicing and eventually became quite ambidextrous, but it was certainly a challenging day for him, trying to eat all the food that was set out for the funeral with chopsticks in his left hand.

Wanting to get away from all the adults and their tearful conversations, my brother and I took Miki with us and went outside the funeral hall.

Miki seemed uncomfortable in her black velvet dress; she'd never had to wear anything like it before and kept trying to take it off, which I swiftly put a stop to. As we looked up at the grayish smoke coming out of the chimney I thought, *Is this what happens when a person dies?*

You become pale and frail, and then a thing without form, like smoke.

Staring at the smoke that must have been Granny as it went up into the sky, my brother said, "There goes Granny," and he cried a little. We were both reminded of the old man from Ding-Dong Park. *Everything in the world belongs to someone, yet everything in the world belongs to no one.* That included Granny, and even the omurice she used to make for us. As the wind blew, little by little Granny's indistinct, shape-shifting smoke now seemed like it was trying to reach its final destination.

The sky, so blue it may as well have been squeezed from a tube of artist's paint, seemed oblivious to the fact that Granny had died. Miki was staring, agape, at Hajime crying. She looked just like she did the first time she stood up.

I Dare You

Just as my brother inspired the "Hajime legend," my sister became a sort of celebrity at kindergarten too. Miki's fame, however, differed somewhat from Hajime's.

If my brother's popularity was mythic in origin, my sister made a name for herself as a brute.

If something upset her, she would throw things using the precise aim she had honed playing catch with us. Whether it was an uwabaki indoor school shoe or a plastic container from school lunch, Miki would fling whatever was ready at hand.

Or she would beat up whomever was close to her. And I don't mean typical girlfight stuff, like scratching, pinching, and pulling someone's hair—she would actually punch them with her fist. She'd take a full swing like a boxer. Sometimes she only lightly grazed her target's chin to intimidate them, but other times she used a technique befitting someone much older, trampling her opponent so they couldn't get away from her blows.

Her homeroom teacher brought her concerns to the other teachers, convinced that Miki was on the verge of neurosis. "Sometimes Miki-chan scares me," she said.

Whereas my brother's sweetness and affability made him a teacher's pet, my sister, on the other hand, was their least favorite kind of student.

Once, a teacher paddled her bottom so hard with a picture book for spitting out seeds from the watermelon that was served with school lunch that, like an old lady with hemorrhoids, Miki could barely sit in a chair. Another time, she was made to stand alone in the middle of the playground after reeling around out of sync with all of the other students as they practiced the dance for Parents' Day. It had been winter, cold enough for snow flurries, and not surprisingly, Miki caught such a severe cold, she was in bed for a week. But, like Hajime, Miki was too cool to say anything to our parents about any of this. Even the time she came home with what, thinking back on it now, was clearly a deep purple and worrisome-looking bruise.

"Goodness gracious, you poor thing!" my mother fretted.

But when my father, already plotting revenge, demanded to know who had done it to her, Miki said nothing. She just opened and closed the door of the fridge, keeping her mouth shut, only later revealing to my brother and me what really happened. And the story was relayed in such a rapid-fire, nonlinear fashion that when she abruptly blurted out the unfamiliar name of some kid, we still couldn't follow what she was saying. Nevertheless, Hajime patted Miki on the head (my brother and my father were the only two males in the whole wide world who were permitted to touch Miki on the head—if any other boy tried to, they got one of Miki's signature swift right hooks) and praised her. "You took it like a champ."

In reality, no one was less capable of taking it like a champ than Miki, but she seemed truly thrilled to receive Hajime's praise. Her handsome and kind brother was everything to her, with all other boys being, in her words, "poop" (as it was, I was "gomame," those little dried sardines).

Because of her beauty, Miki received a constant stream of

invitations from boys. They wanted to go on the swings with her (so they could gently push her soft back) or make mud pies with her (so they could look up her skirt while she squatted in the sandbox), and at recess these boys would line up outside the Star classroom, earnestly hoping she'd accept their requests. Miki might glance in their direction, but then, seemingly indifferent, she would then take over the organ in the classroom and bang away at it. Her classmates, familiar with her renegade ways, would have to wait patiently for their turn.

Miki's studiously nonchalant expression as she played the organ, ignoring the line of boys outside, wasn't about trying to keep any of them in thrall; rather, she hoped at some point that Hajime would hear her play. When she stoically and silently endured being paddled by the teacher, it wasn't out of chagrin but because she craved Hajime's praise. And her wistfulness when she was on the swing didn't come from melancholy, but because she was lost in thought over Hajime.

Miki's life revolved entirely around my brother; her emotions were completely dependent upon him. Her detached attitude, however, made the boys' hearts swell and only increased everyone's fascination with her.

And Hajime, being Hajime, could not help but adore his stubborn little sister who followed him everywhere, enveloping her with great affection that was uncharacteristic for his age. He brought her along wherever he went to play, even when it might have been unwise (be it baseball, sumo wrestling, or climbing trees), and always included her among his friends. He brought me along too, but I didn't have their guts, so I often copped out.

Back then, it was popular with my brother's friends to play "I Dare You." The game involved sticking a firecracker into dog poop (the fresher the better). Okay, so this may sound like par for the course for boys all over Japan, but their form of "I Dare You" took it up a notch. They would stick in the firecracker and then form a circle around the dog poop, waiting for it to explode. The ones who got scared and left the huddle were deemed wusses, whereas whoever lasted longest were deemed the heroes. In other words, it was a game of chicken, but with poop.

At the tender age of five, Miki achieved the feat of last man standing. In a throng of strapping elementary-school-age boys, she was obviously the one closest to the poop, but Miki made it until the end, along with my brother and Yamashita-kun (the catcher on his Little League team), and she got a face full of poop to show for it.

Hajime and Yamashita-kun would just hose themselves off, but Miki was of a different breed. Despite almost vomiting from the stench, she was so elated by my brother's gleeful approval—"Isn't she amazing? That's my little sister for you!"—that she announced she was going to take a bath, before making a brisk exit. Once home, she was pounced upon by my mother, who kept asking her what on earth had happened, but Miki said nothing as she washed herself off—and then, all clean, went right back to where my brother was and, undeterred, stuck a firecracker in another pile of poop.

Ferrari

When we were kids, there was a scary local guy we nicknamed "Ferrari." Near Park No. 1 was an open space with a big elm tree. The place was kind of creepy—long ago it had been the parking lot for the danchi public housing complex but, after the new garage was built, this space had become the dumping ground for abandoned bicycles and junk cars.

Ferrari was always loitering there, wandering among the abandoned cars, sometimes muttering unintelligibly and swinging around a steel pipe over his head.

There was something wrong with his hair—it was cut raggedly and bunches of it stuck out in places like fried karinto snacks. His eyes were swollen as if he'd been beaten up, and each one gazed in a different direction, as if he wanted to see where the sun rose and set at the same time. But his most distinctive feature was his nose, with its terrifyingly huge nostrils that didn't seem to belong on a human being. His nostrils were so big, they resembled black holes, trying to suck up all the available oxygen. And yet Ferrari's breathing was always labored, punctuated with grunts and gasps. Those noises, which sounded as if he were saying, "Not enough air, not enough air," served as a danger signal to us that Ferrari was nearby.

Ferrari got his nickname because, year in and year out, he

wore a T-shirt emblazoned with the Ferrari logo, and he was also startlingly fleet of foot. We kids would tease Ferrari and he'd snarl, "What the fuck . . . ?!" before sprinting after us like a carnivorous beast. The man was as fast as a lion chasing down a zebra. And if you looked closely, he was wearing wooden geta clogs, no less—a further testament to his prowess. If we ran right in front of him, he'd surely catch us kids, so when we saw him running, we'd race to climb the nearest tree.

Ferrari had another idiosyncrasy: He couldn't perceive anything that was situated above his head. He always kept his gaze down when he walked, and if he ever looked straight ahead or glanced upward, his head would wobble, and he'd quickly have to turn his face down again. Almost as if he thought that, by looking up at the sky, he'd be sucked up by the sun.

This meant that Ferrari couldn't climb trees, so we'd torment him from our perch in the branches with vrooming sounds, trying to imitate Formula One racecars whizzing past, but he still couldn't tell we were up there. Even so, he would swing his steel pipe around and yell as if the enemy was right in front of him.

"You fuckers!"

This terrifying character was soon incorporated into another version of "I Dare You."

Instead of a game of chicken with poop, it was chicken with Ferrari—that is, how close could we get to him? We vied to see who could wait until the very last minute when Ferrari sprinted for us before scrambling up a tree.

Panicked by his tremendous speed, most of us would take off the moment we'd see him turn and start running toward us. Even Hajime would bolt when Ferrari was about fifty feet away. Somehow the kid who held the record was a table-tennis player named Mochizuki-kun. He held out until Ferrari was fifteen feet away and when he finally shimmied up a tree, Ferrari had grabbed the hem of his parka. This frightening experience had afforded Mochizuki-kun hero status for a while.

Unsurprisingly, my brother did not include Miki in this game. She may have been the fastest of all the girls, but Ferrari's speed was no joke, nor was the fact that he carried a steel pipe. Dealing with him was completely different from getting covered in shit.

Yet Miki was super competitive, and if she realized that my brother and his friends were playing without her, she'd insist on being included. So he was extra careful to keep the Ferrari chicken game a secret from her.

One day I was home watching TV when Miki asked, "Where's Hajime?"

I'd heard him say that he was going out to play that very game, so I kept my mouth shut.

She watched TV with me, unenthusiastically, but it wasn't long before she grew impatient.

She stood up and said, "I'm going out to look for him!"

I rushed to placate her, saying that he was still at school and would be home soon, but Miki wasn't stubborn in an ordinary way. Once she set her mind to something, she held fast until the end, just like a soft-shelled turtle that, as the saying goes, won't let go even with a thunderstorm drawing near. Ignoring my efforts to keep her in the house, Miki pulled on her favorite rubber boots (she wore rubber boots even on sunny days).

Frankly, I was annoyed because I wanted to keep watching

the period drama that was on TV, but if I let Miki go, I wouldn't be able to face my brother, so I went after her.

Miki focused her search on the spots where Hajime usually played, like Giraffe Park and the schoolyard. Since I knew that my brother and his friends were over by Park No. 1, I casually chose a route that would steer her away from there.

Luckily, all the grown-ups had always warned us against going to Park No. 1, namely because of Ferrari. My brother had never brought Miki there, so she had absolutely no reason to think that's where he would be.

When Miki's extensive search was unfruitful, I suggested that we head back home. She seemed unhappy about it but, having looked everywhere that she could think of, she had no choice but to give up.

I started walking, and Miki traipsed along behind me. Every so often we'd hear kids shouting gleefully, and Miki would stop and stare off in whatever direction it was coming from, straining her ears to hear if it sounded like Hajime's voice and, when it wasn't, she'd walk on halfheartedly.

Just as I was thinking to myself with relief, *Here's Aoki-san's house, we're almost home*, we encountered a familiar obstacle, albeit one I hadn't seen in a while. It was the same girl who my brother and I had run into when we were on our way to pick flowers for Miki, the one with the bob. Of course, she had grown since then—the randoseru school bag on her shoulders didn't look so enormous, her breasts had begun to develop, there was more flesh on her hips, and her arms were soft and plump—but she still had that same doll-like hairstyle and narrow, deep-set eyes. Remarkably, her feelings for her beloved Hajime Hasegawa-kun had remained steadfast from kindergarten all the way through to sixth grade; she gave him presents for Valentine's Day, his birthday, and Christmas without fail, and often loitered near our house on the off chance of running into my brother.

Something about her that day gave me a bad feeling—I nodded vaguely at her and, taking Miki by the hand, kept walking. "Little Miss Obstacle" (even then, we still didn't know her name) scowled as soon as she saw Miki. This was because Miki was known to spit at girls who came near Hajime, or to throw dead frogs at them. Little Miss Obstacle herself had once been pelted smack in the middle of her forehead with a wad of wet tissue and, not knowing what had hit her, was so freaked out that she fell over.

At me, though, she grinned. "How ya doing, Kaoru-kun?"

Little Miss Obstacle had matured enough to know it would be wise to win over the younger brother of the boy she liked, in the hope that he would say good things about her to his older brother. She doted on me as if I were her own brother, seemingly testing out what it would be like to be married to Hajime. A number of girls who were friends with my brother would often talk to me like they were my big sister—"Hey Kaoru, got a girlfriend yet?" or "Look how skinny you are! You'd better eat more!"—which I figured was motivated by the same idea.

And here was Little Miss Obstacle, turning on the charm with her grin, conveniently forgetting how she'd once cattily remarked that I didn't look like my brother.

I too had matured, so I deflected with a breezy "Fine," and tried to hasten my way into the house.

Feigning nonchalance, Little Miss Obstacle's deep-set eyes gleamed with vigilance as she uttered the inevitable, "Where's Hajime-kun?"

Miki reacted to this query, and I worried that she was already looking around for something to throw. Playing it casual, I tried to get by with a curt "Dunno."

But Little Miss Obstacle seemed disinclined to allow this interaction with the siblings of Hajime Hasegawa to end so abruptly. Conjuring the composure of a much older girl, she begrudgingly smiled at Miki and tried to cozy up to her.

"Miki-chan, how old are you now?"

Miki snubbed Little Miss Obstacle and her wheedling smile, instead taking off her boots and stuffing them with sand and pebbles. I worried that she might throw these, but then Little Miss Obstacle, peeved about being snubbed, responded to this annoyance with a strange smugness.

"Hajime-kun sure has been playing dangerous games lately."

Miki stopped what she was doing and looked at Little Miss Obstacle, whose smirk seemed to say, "Oh, you don't know?" But what she actually said was: "Miki-chan and Kaoru-kun, you'd better look out for him, okay?"

Little Miss Obstacle was back at it again. I tried to pretend that what she was referring to was just the usual games, and I yanked Miki's hand to come along with me but, when it came to Hajime, Miki was nothing if not resolute.

"Whaddya mean?" she asked Little Miss Obstacle.

Rapt by the notion that there was something about her beloved Hajime Hasegawa that only she knew, Little Miss Obstacle kept her mouth shut, retaining the same innocent expression on her face while her body swayed around.

"*Whaddya mean?*" Miki repeated. Her right hand was already gripping her boots, which were packed full of stones, and I was semi-panicked, my emotions a jumble. I wanted Little Miss Obstacle to hurry up and tell Miki before she threw the boots, though I also didn't want her to tell Miki at all.

But that dilemma soon reached a resolution.

Cheekily, Little Miss Obstacle said, "You don't know? Lately in Park Number One . . ."

Without even waiting to hear the rest, Miki took off running, leaving a trail of pebbles and sand in her wake.

It happened so quickly, I was stupefied, and by the time I rushed after her, Miki was already out of sight. My mind raced with images of what would happen next—Miki covered in blood, Ferrari spattered in Miki's blood, the steel pipe lying on the ground. My dead grandmother's negative thinking had rubbed off on me and, in my panic, I was tripping over my own feet. To make matters worse, Little Miss Obstacle was right behind me, and I could hear her taking a double inhale for every exhale, as if she were in a marathon. This put a weird strain on me, making my own running even clumsier.

When we got to Park No. 1, it was pandemonium.

Just as Ferrari was setting off on his sprint, there was Miki standing in his way, and in order to stop this, my brother—who'd turned white as a sheet when he saw her—was about to drop out of the tree he'd climbed.

"Run for it!"

Little Miss Obstacle shouted this at Miki, not out of sisterly concern but raw emotion. However, Miki just stood there staring blankly at Ferrari, not knowing what she didn't know.

My only thought was that I had to protect Miki, so I broke into another run, while Hajime hastily leapt out of the tree, his body contorted, and then he too dashed over, dragging his right leg awkwardly behind him. But neither of us were a match for Ferrari's speed.

Up in the trees, my brother's classmates were yelling at the top of their lungs.

Sunlight glinted off Ferrari's steel pipe and I squeezed my eyes shut, not just against the glare but also in prayer.

Amid all this, Miki just stood there, staring curiously at Ferrari.

Ferrari vanished the same day that the abandoned bicycles and junk cars were removed from the area near Park No. 1. Various rumors swirled in his absence: that long ago he'd been a professor at a university, that he'd been committed to a mental hospital, that actually he was a millionaire and a servant had come to take him home.

But on that day, when Ferrari's swift geta-clad feet had galloped like the wind, he came face to face with a small girl standing before him. That girl had just stood there, curiously regarding him with his gigantic nostrils and his steel pipe.

Ferrari suddenly stopped in his tracks.

Miki was only ten feet away from him, a lot closer than Mochizuki-kun had been. My brother and I had finally caught up with her, and we surrounded her on either side. My eyes were riveted to the steel pipe Ferrari gripped in his right hand, while Hajime was attentively awaiting Ferrari's next move. My heart was beating wildly, the sound of it pounding in my chest interspersed with my brother's heartbeat.

Even though we were standing in his way, Ferrari still hadn't taken his eyes off Miki. Like a blind man who gains sight and sees the ocean for the first time, or the leader of a caravan journeying through the desert who sees an oasis shimmering in the distance, he looked as if he had discovered something terribly extraordinary and important.

And as she gazed back at him, Miki was the picture of composure—you'd never have thought this wild and reckless little girl had just bolted here a few moments ago, her boots filled with stones that she may have been about to pelt at someone—especially in contrast to her brothers, both terrified and on the verge of panic. It created a strange illusion, the feeling that we were in the presence of a grown woman (one much more mature than Little Miss Obstacle) and that, instead of us protecting her, she was offering us protection.

Ferrari's breathing was labored, as always. In a pause between gasps, Ferrari muttered, "I . . ." and we strained to hear what he had to say. Come to think of it, it was the first and last time that we ever really tried to listen to him.

"I . . ." he repeated.

Miki grasped my hand and my brother's. Her hand was as tiny as one of my mother's brooches, which reminded me of just how young she was.

Ferrari expanded his attention from little Miki to include my brother and me. He couldn't look at too many things at once, so he studied the three of us slowly, as if allowing his damaged eyes the chance to adjust. Then, he inhaled deeply and he said:

"I remember."

We had no idea what it was that Ferrari remembered.

Miki looked at us and asked, "What's this guy saying?"

Ferrari let out a sigh, like he had just taken off a backpack that had been on his shoulders for a very long time—and even though it scared him to take in so much, he looked high up in the sky.

"I remember."

That was the last time we ever saw Ferrari.

After Ferrari vanished, we kids were allowed to play in Park No. 1. But we never did. The abandoned bicycles and junk cars were removed, and the lot was cleaned up, but there was something unnerving about it, the space was cold and correct—and of course, without Ferrari, there was nothing to draw us there.

Despite Miki's impressive memory, which rivaled Hajime's, for some reason Miki does not remember that day. Whenever Ferrari's name came up, she'd just cock her head and say, "Who dat?" Which only deepened my brother's and my sense that Miki was truly a wonder child.

Moving Day

In the spring of that year, we moved.

Our first house was prefab and, like the other homes in the neighborhood, quite modest. After all, when Miki was a baby we could hear her breathing as she slept in her crib so, basically, there was no such thing as privacy.

Miki was the one who heard my parents doing "it."

Miki slept between my mother and father, but when they did "it," she would almost always come sleep in my brother's and my room. We had a bunk bed in our room; my brother got the top bunk, of course, and I was on the bottom. Hajime, caring as he was, had offered me the top bunk, but I liked listening to his steady breathing while he slept above me. It was always reassuring to look up and know that my brother was there. Sometimes I'd see one of his arms or feet sticking out from the bed, and it'd put me at ease, helping me to sleep soundly.

Miki would bring her pillow into our room and go straight up the ladder to sleep next to Hajime. Sometimes she'd dangle her leg over the railing, which would make me laugh. Then I'd hear:

"You up, Kaoru?"

Even if I might have been about to doze off, I'd perk up at

her question and we'd stay up talking much later than we should have.

Through the slats in the bed, Miki's voice reminded me of how the ocean waves sound when you put an empty seashell up to your ear. Her outstretched leg and Hajime's arm shone in the darkness, faintly pale like coral washed up on the beach.

That night, when Miki's "You up, Kaoru?" roused me, I opened my eyes to the unusual sight of her and my brother looking down at me.

Even in the dark, I could tell that their faces were turning red, but I also knew that it wasn't only because they were upside-down.

"Hear that, Kaoru?"

My brother spoke in a conspiratorial whisper. I didn't know what he was talking about, so I strained my ears to listen.

A sound, sweet and gentle, like a mother cat calling to her kittens.

It didn't take long to realize that it was my mother's voice, but it surprised me—I'd never heard her sound like that before.

Sometimes when she was knitting or something, she'd let out a contented sigh. It had a lively quality, like the cue for a small boat to cast off, and that would prompt us to glance at each other and grin, but there was nothing impish about the sound my mother was making now. Her voice was incredibly soft and kind of wistful, like hydrangea petals scattering. The three of us fell silent as we listened intently. We forgot about whispering or chuckling—we just stared up at the ceiling, as if waiting to see a shooting star. Of course, I couldn't see the ceiling but, on the slats above me, I could easily imagine a river flowing along with the beautiful grain of the wood, at some point branching off into the sky outside the window.

My heart was beating so fast, I couldn't just roll back into bed, and I figured the same went for my brother and Miki. But then, as we all listened spellbound to the rhythmic sounds my mother was making, we fell back asleep.

"What were you doing last night?"

Miki asked this the following morning at the breakfast table as she struggled with her toast spread thickly with peanut butter. Miki always disconcerted us with her bluntness.

Though I had yet to learn about that kind of thing myself at the time, I knew that when a man and a woman were naked together, dirty stuff would happen. As for my brother, he had just taken the obligatory sex-ed class where they split up the girls and boys in separate rooms, so he would have been too embarrassed to ask our parents about it.

In kindergarten, Miki had seen the boys flicking up girls' skirts or trying desperately to touch the teacher's boobs, so conceptually she understood that lewdness was a thing that existed in the world, but she didn't know how or what would prompt my mother to make those rapturous sounds the night before.

My father was the most flustered out of all of us. He wore a completely startled look on his face and then, like in a manga, he choked on his coffee and had a coughing fit.

The expression on my mother's face was incredulous; she looked at Miki and laughed out loud in surprise. Then, with a sigh, she sat down and looked around at all of us. I waited with bated breath for what my mother was going to say—the air felt buoyant, like when she would turn over her tarot cards, and the look on her face said, "Just watch and see."

She gave a short cough and looked at Miki, her gaze gentle.

"Miki, whose eyes do you have?"

Miki seemed a little thrown off to be asked a question instead, but her beloved Hajime gave her an encouraging look, so she gave it good consideration before answering.

"Yours, Mom."

"And whose nose?"

"Definitely Dad's."

"Whose mouth?"

"Yours."

"And ears?"

"My ears? Um, Hajime's."

My mother sighed the way she did when she was knitting, and patted Miki on the head.

"Miki, your head is the same shape as Kaoru's. And your fingers look exactly like mine when I was little. That whorl of hair on the top of your head looks like Dad's. You wear down your shoes the same way that Hajime does, and you both stick out one leg when you sleep."

As was always the case with Miki, the caress from my mother had enchanted her. Miki still looked like she had just woken up, but her big eyes turned glassy—this was my favorite expression of hers.

"Even though you were born at a different time, Miki, you resemble Dad, and me, and Hajime, and Kaoru, because your dad's and my love worked its magic powers."

"Magic powers?"

"That's right. The magic powers that your dad and I have had since birth. We combined our powers and put them to use."

"How?"

"By loving each other a whole lot."

"That's it?"

"Hmm, well—we love each other sooo much that sometimes we don't need our clothes. And even when we aren't wearing any clothes, we don't feel embarrassed."

"You're naked?"

"That's right."

"And then what?"

"When we're naked, your dad tells me he loves me sooo much, and he kisses me all over my body."

"All over your body?"

"That's right."

"Your tushy too?"

"Even there."

"And your boobies?"

"My boobies, my tushy, my legs, my hair—everywhere."

"Doesn't that tickle?"

"Your dad loves me sooo much, it doesn't tickle. In fact, it makes me feel really good."

"How good?"

"Like I'm floating up in the sky, flying."

"In the sky?"

"That's right. Floating up there. It feels amazingly good."

"Hmm."

"Then, your dad and I, we each work our magic powers."

"Magic powers?"

"Yup. Your dad has the ingredients for making your body, while I have the ingredients for making your heart. And this magic only works when two people love each so much."

"Huh."

"So then we combined them."

"How?"

"I have the ingredients in my belly. And Dad, he has them in his pee-pee. So he puts it in my belly."

"His pee-pee?!"

"That's right."

"Ew, gross!"

My mother erupted in laughter. My father, who had forgotten about choking on his coffee, looked at my mother with a sheepish but reassuring expression.

"It's not gross—I love your father's pee-pee."

"How does he put it in your belly?"

"You know the place where you came out of when you were born? Dad goes to the opening, and he knocks—*Can I come in?* he asks. And because I love him very much, I say, *Please do*, and I open the door."

"Hmm."

"And because your dad loves me, he used his magic powers to give me the ingredients to make you, Miki."

"Huh."

"And from that moment on, you became you, Miki."

"From that moment?"

"That's right. I loved your father, and your father loved me, and we combined our magic powers together, and from that moment on, you became you."

Miki may not quite have understood everything my mother said, but she had the sense that in order for her to have been born, a very important ceremony had been observed, and the idea of that seemed to satisfy her.

My mother let out another one of her knitting sighs, only this time it was sort of muffled, as if she were about to cry out in happiness.

"Thank you for being born, Miki."

Two years later, Miki would realize that my mother had been talking about sex, and she would learn about how it works in much more detail than either my brother or me—and the more she knew, the more she came to think that she had been born against tremendous odds, and it filled her with awe.

It rained on moving day.

A fine, misty drizzle—the kind that's hard to decide if you need an umbrella for—gently saturated our house.

The movers who showed up were so scrawny, even a lightweight like me worried if they were up to the task, but they were remarkably efficient, deftly loading cupboards and dressers and the washing machine onto the truck—so much so that Miki, who typically only had eyes for Hajime, exclaimed with admiration, "They're so cool!"

All our neighbors had shown up and, sure enough, none of them had brought umbrellas. My mother and father bustled around, thanking everyone, and there was barely time to contemplate the fact that all our memories were now crammed onto the flatbed of the truck.

Hajime was just as busy himself—the girls who had come to see him off had already formed a line—and even Miki had boys falling over each other to give her presents.

As for me, for some reason my classmates had brought me a string of a thousand origami cranes.

We exchanged the usual farewells: "Take care" and "Let's play together sometime."

A couple of them were even a little teary, which caused my ears to prickle in both happiness and embarrassment. But I didn't want to be seen crying in front of my family, so I just smiled and scratched around my ears to compensate.

When it was finally time to be on our way, something else happened. Just as I was about to put the cranes they had given me into my bag, one of the girls called out to me.

Her name was Yukawa-san. She had pink-framed eyeglasses, but she was self-conscious and only wore them during class. I had been impressed by how diligently she swept up when she was on classroom cleanup duty.

Yukawa-san's pale, thin fingers held a light blue envelope. It was speckled with raindrops, making the envelope look like it was covered in deep aqua-colored polka dots.

"Read this," Yukawa-san managed to say, her voice quavering, before taking cover behind the others. Because I was Hajime's younger brother, I knew that this must be a love letter. I felt the blood rush to my cheeks, so I scratched even harder behind my ears. But none of my classmates bothered to tease me or smirk about it, which made me realize what a great neighborhood this really was.

"Thank you," I said, not to anyone specifically, and at that moment, the guys in the truck tooted the horn to signal they were about to depart.

Our rain-sodden house receded in view, growing smaller and smaller but glistening brilliantly. The hydrangeas my mother had planted by the front door had yet to bloom, but the other flowers in the yard made up for it with their modest beauty.

I thought about how, since it was raining today, the cats in Ding-Dong Park wouldn't be able to bask lazily in the sun. And the fact that Little Miss Obstacle, who had been wailing louder than anyone, would one day fall in love with someone else, and that Yukawa-san would continue to wear her pale-pink glasses, but only during class. And that, up in heaven, Granny still worried about us.

My world was small, so small.

Miki sat on my brother's lap, staring out the window, while my mother kept on waving goodbye to everyone. In the passenger seat, my father looked at a map of our new neighborhood, while my brother rubbed Miki's head as he smiled and reminisced.

In my pocket was the polka-dotted letter, its warmth gradually spreading to my belly, chasing away any apprehension about our new life.

My world was so small.

And then, in the rain, it all vanished from view.

PART 3

New Town

There was a certain someone who would soon arrive to accompany our new life. Timid and skinny—who else could I be talking about but our Sakura? But it would still be a little while after we moved before Sakura came to live with us so, in the meantime, I guess I'll give you a bit of background.

Our new house was quite the big deal.

The foyer was so spacious that a leopard could have sprawled out there and we still would have room for everyone's shoes, and there was an open, spiral staircase that wound upward, even higher than the quince tree in the yard. The living room had windows on each side, so it got an amazing amount of sun—the particles of light seemed to delight in pouring into that vast space. The kitchen, which was adjoined to the living room, had a fancy counter where we kids would sit and pretend we were at a bar. There was a six-mat tatami room decorated with a memorial photo of our grandmother who had passed, and Granny, in her picture, seemed delighted by the scent of the fresh tatami. The bathroom tiles were a deep blue, like the color of the bottom of the ocean. The tub was so spacious that, even when Miki played with her favorite toy frog, making him swim around, he never seemed to touch the sides. Water would gush out of the showerhead fast and furious like a squall. There was a western-style toilet—no one was happier than Miki that the commode was a pale pink—and this room was also bathed in brilliant sunshine. The yard was big enough that we could swing a badminton racket without holding back, and we never had to go into the neighbor's yard to retrieve the shuttlecock. And my mother trembled with excitement at the different kinds of flowers she'd now be able to plant in the garden.

But what had us kids the most excited was the fact that we would each get our own room. Miki's room had wallpaper with walnut trees on it, mine had a huge walk-in closet, and the smallest room—but the only one that had a balcony—was Hajime's. We were thrilled about having space for ourselves and even Miki, who couldn't fall asleep by herself and still slept with Hajime, would contentedly rub her new room's walnut-tree wallpaper.

"I can smell the walnuts!" she would say, looking at us with joy, and my mother and father would break into smiles. We were surprised to see that a new king-size bed had already been brought into their room. It was as soft and plush as the belly of a whale, and they seemed so happy about it that, even though I didn't fully understand why, I remember thinking that we might have another little brother or sister on the way.

Those scrawny-looking movers worked tirelessly and with the same efficiency as before, briskly and nimbly carrying the furniture into the new house, and we were filled with even more admiration.

Our new house was halfway up a hill. The lots were neatly arranged, like a staircase, and since back then it truly was a new town, there were still only a few houses scattered here and there. Of the three neighbors whose newspapers Miki later stole, only the Onishis were living there at the time, so when my mother insisted that we go around to introduce ourselves to the neighbors, it didn't take long.

The house just above ours on the hill had yet to be built, so that lot served as our playground. That's where Miki rode a bicycle for the first time; it was also where we caught what we thought had been a grasshopper rustling in the tall grass, but it turned out to be a snake(!); and it was where we made a crown for Miki out of white clover (which we no longer peed on).

There were a couple of parks nearby, but with their shiny red slides and swings with chains that didn't creak at all, they seemed so brand-spanking new that they were kind of uninviting to us, and it took a while for us to get used to going there. There was something a little daunting about their prim appearance, as if everything in the neighborhood was saying, "Hey, uh, please don't get me dirty!" Which is why, for a while after we first moved to the new town, we always played in that vacant lot.

We transferred to the elementary school that was a five-minute walk down the hill from our house.

Since we had moved in April, which was the start of the school year, I figured I might not stand out so much, but it turned out to be a pretty small school. There were only three classes in my year, and each class had about thirty students. And while, three years later, there would be seven classes of forty students each, back then it was like the school was running during the offseason.

As this was my first experience as the new kid, when it came time to introduce myself to the class, I steeled myself for the comment that Kaoru sounded like a girl's name, but none of the kids said that. Perhaps a little disarmed, I launched into it myself:

"I'm Kaoru Hasegawa. You might think Kaoru is a girl's name, but I'm definitely a boy."

Still, nobody said anything. The teacher looked around at the nonresponsive students and said, speaking slowly so that they would remember my name, "Okay, everyone, let's all be nice to Kaoru Hasegawa-kun."

So *that's* the kind of school it was.

When we walked the halls, our uwabaki indoor school shoes squeaked on the polished linoleum (at my old school the floor only made that sound when we waxed it) and the urinals in the boys' lavatory were so shiny that I hesitated even to pee normally in them (at my old school my friends and I would "cross the streams," which got piss all over the place).

Even the school, which looked like it was in prime condition, seemed to be saying, "Hey, uh, please don't get me dirty!" Maybe that was why none of my classmates wore T-shirts that were stretched out under the arms (as all of mine were) or socks that had holes in them (my mother had darned mine so many times they were totally misshapen).

On the day that my brother introduced himself, all the girls were excitedly gossiping about the cute new boy, but none of them clamored to speak to him the way they had at our old school—though they did show up at the door of his classroom to steal a look at him. They whispered and giggled to each other and, when Hajime sensed their gaze and glanced over, they all hurriedly turned away.

Hajime thrust his right hand out to the girl sitting next to him. "Hi."

The girl turned bright red and looked down, while the other girls around them murmured among themselves.

It was that kind of school.

I guess it was a peculiarity of the school being in a new town, that certain awkward and aloof sensibility.

My brother would invite his classmates to play, and they'd all come over to our house, but their main amusement was video games. The fact that we didn't have any video games was another reason why we always ended up playing in the vacant lot on the hill above our house. We also gradually got used to the new parks, and really applied ourselves to getting them dirty. We'd use all our might to swing on the empty swings, and we'd climb up the slide backward.

Thinking back now, many of the children at that school must have come from families that were well off enough to move to a new town—they even played like rich kids. You couldn't throw a rock without it landing in a vacant lot, but all those kids cared about was watching TV and playing video games. None of them ever played outside.

Our new house may have been big, but it wasn't as if we were rich.

My father worked for a transport company. He didn't drive a truck; he oversaw what freight was on which truck and which routes they were taking. He worked the night shift about three times a week and would come home in the early morning with bloodshot eyes. Dad worked his ass off. He never missed a day of work and was never late, no matter how much he'd had to drink the night or day before. My father took pride in his work above all else.

"Your dad knows what cargo from all over the world is on

which road right now and who it's going to!" he'd say. "If I make one little mistake, important shipments won't get to where they're supposed to."

We were in awe over the fact that our father controlled the fate of the world's cargo, but there wasn't anything cooler than the CB radio he showed us, which he used to keep in touch with his truck drivers.

"*Ch, chh* . . . Breaker, breaker. Number two-two-six, come in. Accident on route twenty-seven, traffic is backed up, take a right off Old Yamate Road and go by Hanada Road instead. Over!"

My father knew all the roadways across Japan and what's more, he seemed to know where all the back roads and shortcuts were too. It thrilled us that a single order from him could determine the routes taken by hundreds of trucks.

Thinking back, my father's job certainly wasn't high paying, but that didn't prevent him from being the happiest man in the universe. He worked hard for his family and now he had a house that was his castle.

A lot of our classmates came from wealthy families, which may have been why they seemed puzzled by our working-class roots.

"What kind of car do you have?"

They'd ask us about things like that or make fun of us for not having video games at home. My family's car was a used van, and the engine didn't always start, but when we were in our van, we could look down on all the little sports cars and there was enough room in the back for us to play cards. We may not have had video games, but I'd never seen anything like the imported chessboard my father cherished or my mother's sleek tarot cards at the other kids' houses.

Most of all, though, we were immensely proud of the fact

that our father had been able to buy this big of a house at such a young age.

Miki also proved to be out of her element in the new school. At the opening assembly, she promptly cut loose with a huge fart, and then, bored by the principal's address, she tried to make a break for it. Needless to say, this did not bode well for her homeroom teacher.

But Miki did seem to notice that she got a chillier reception in this classroom. Jealous of how pretty Miki was, the other girls may have ignored her but, unlike in kindergarten, they didn't hide her uwabaki shoes or pull her hair; so, since there was no active aggression, Miki couldn't retaliate by flicking up their skirts or spitting at their shadows.

Some of the boys tried to make conversation with her, but instead of chatting her up, they seemed to be making fun of her name. Because of the ubiquitous eyewear shop, Paris Miki, they would ask: "You don't wear glasses?" Or, because of Mickey Mouse: "Hey, where's your tail?" Miki didn't follow what they were talking about, and it seemed pointless to swing at them with her fist, so she would just stare back at them vacantly.

Miki in torpor was kind of amazing. Faced with the loss of an opponent she could best, she just sat there in the classroom, slack-jawed, pupils dilated, nose and mouth inhaling and exhaling but her body immobile, like a mailbox that'd been there for decades. I would check in on her, worried about her clocking someone, only to see her like that.

From then on, Miki's torpor became one of her signatures.

Perhaps due to her dissatisfaction with school, Miki grew increasingly dependent upon Hajime. Whenever he was about to go somewhere, she'd jump up and say, "I'll go with you!" And even though Miki loved tomatoes, she stopped eating them because Hajime hated them (and eventually, it seems, she really did stop liking them herself).

Hajime, being Hajime, did actually want to hang out with Miki, and he was determined to do something about the gloomy atmosphere of our new school. In contrast to the way that I approached most everything—with resignation, that is—my brother was the kind of person who saw everything as a challenge, a chance to forge a new path. He was always trying to get his classmates to play baseball or soccer instead of just going home, or he'd try to draw the girls into conversation, asking things like, "Hey, is that a new haircut?" He picked fights with the kids who talked about him behind his back, throwing himself physically into the effort of overcoming this minor yet critical situation. That was just his way. He used his body before thinking things all the way through. He'd move his legs and wave his hands in order to attract everyone's attention. My brother had gotten into dozens of fights before, but he'd never had to get physical as often as he did now. He'd come home totally wrung out, stuff his face with dinner, and then fall into bed to dream of a more enjoyable life ahead.

Miki was quite distraught about no longer being able to play "I Dare You" with Hajime. Her distress wasn't about the lady who berated her for peeing outside, or Little Miss Obstacle who blatantly threw herself at Hajime, or even that there weren't any boys for her to beat down—more than anything, she was saddened to realize that Hajime was steadily drifting further away from her. None of us could even imagine how sad.

Purple Camel

So when Sakura came to live with us, the timing really was perfect. One day, out of nowhere, Miki announced that she wanted a dog, and it took no time at all for my brother and me to become obsessed with the idea too. I'm not exactly sure what Miki had in mind when she made that declaration, but it might have been the first time in her life that we were totally on board with what she said. My mother and father catalogued the demands of having a living creature as a pet but, well, I already mentioned how Miki's like a soft-shelled turtle that won't let go even with a thunderstorm drawing near—she wouldn't change her mind even after being swallowed by a whale. Eventually both parents finally gave in, and that's how we got a dog.

Let me say it again—we got Sakura!

That first day, when Sakura came home with us, she didn't leave Miki's side.

"What a skinny Minnie she is!" my mother said. Sakura really was tiny.

"Her name is Sakura!" Miki replied.

"So you've already decided on her name?" My mother seemed surprised that Miki could have already given a name to such an itty-bitty little pup. "Say, Miki, why'd you choose Sakura?"

"It's a secret."

The pink petal that had come from Sakura was tucked away in Miki's right pocket. It would then be forgotten until a week later, when it was rediscovered as a dried up and crumpled wisp—but at that moment it was as fresh as a newly hatched fish and gleaming like a jewel.

My mother, knowing how stubborn Miki was, looked to me for an answer. The expression on her face was so happy, and the look in Sakura's eyes was so sweet, it made me feel as if I had a stash of pink petals in my own pocket.

"Right, it's a secret."

Sakura really was timid—she didn't bark at all that day or the day after. At first, we marveled at how quiet she was; she spent that whole first week not making so much as a peep, and one week then became two weeks.

We decided to take her to the vet. Looking back now, it seems totally absurd, but that night, around nine o'clock, the entire family piled into the car with Sakura and we drove to an animal clinic on the outskirts of town. We were worried about Sakura but, at the same time, it was thrilling to have something that we could all be ridiculously involved in together as a family. It felt like being on a treasure hunt.

Sakura was also excited to be in a car for the first time. She stretched out on Miki's lap, watching the scenery go by.

Miki murmured to her, "Look at that, Sakura. Don't you wanna bark at it? C'mon now, woof?"

But Sakura just looked up at her uneasily, without making any sound at all.

The veterinary clinic was about to close, so the only other person in the dimly lit waiting room was a plump older lady holding a mean-looking Persian cat, which was wearing a paper collar shaped like a satellite dish. The lady, dressed in vivid purple, wore sunglasses that made her look like a dragonfly. Her body rocked at times, and she was singing a song in a language I couldn't understand:

Ii-zaa-raa, za-aafa-u-ebaa,
shin-yu-bii-ora-u, yoo-raa-pummi,
aa-zaa-toppo-rawaa.

The song was kind of ominous, like an incantation or something—it reminded me of the kind of music you hear hayashi performers play at a festival—and, having to sit there listening to it, I began to feel quite drowsy. Every so often, Sakura would timidly twitch her ears, squirming restlessly in Miki's arms, while Miki sat there motionless, her eyes riveted to the lady and her cat, as if under their spell.

The cat with the satellite collar was purring contentedly as the lady pet it, but occasionally it would suddenly remember to send a menacing glare at Sakura, who was now utterly spooked and fearfully trembling on Miki's lap, her skinny tail tucked between her legs.

Yoo-raa-pummi,
aa-zaa-toppo-rawaa.

The air conditioner in the waiting room was ancient; its loud rumble sounded like our washing machine at home, which made me feel even more drowsy—I wasn't too ashamed to put my head on my mother's lap to doze for a bit. My mother stroked my ear, and her silky caress made my eyelids even heavier.

Yoo-raa-pummi,
aa-zaa-toppo-rawaa.

I had a dream.

I was travelling through a desert of soft, roe-like sand, riding a huge purple camel. The sun was directly above, the wind blowing north-by-northwest, but the grains of sand didn't stir at all. In my pocket was a hot dog bun filled with eggs that my mother had made for me, and I had mistakenly taken Miki's water bottle that had pink flowers on it, which I felt bad about. I could see a town glimmering in the distance, but that wasn't where I was going. I was intent on seeing the ocean, so I asked a girl with long hair who was leaning against a rock and singing a song, "Where is the ocean?" She smiled at me and I saw that she looked like Miki, which made me suddenly realize that I needed to go home. I turned back toward the town, but now there was nothing shimmering there and, bewildered, I started bawling. I cried and cried, my tears flooding all over, and the purple camel murmured, "Take heart, now." Terribly embarrassed, I was about to explain myself when I heard, "Hasegawa-san."

The vet nurse's drawl woke me.

I stood up, dazedly rubbing the sleep from my eyes and, now self-conscious, shaking off my mother's hand from my head. She just laughed. We had to pass in front of the older lady when we went into the examination room. The Persian cat with the satellite collar was still giving threatening looks to Sakura. I glanced their way and when I did, I heard the lady say, ever so quietly, "Take heart, now."

I turned back, startled, and the lady grinned at me, then went back to chanting that same song.

As we filed into the exam room, Miki holding Sakura and leading the way, the vet greeted the lot of us with a dubious look. He had a bald patch on the top of his head, and the hair on the sides was unusually long. His face shone brightly, and he had googly eyes and a huge mouth that looked like it would split open. He could have been one of those yokai creatures that grown-ups warn you about—"If you don't behave, he's gonna come and get you." As soon as Miki entered the exam room, she hid behind Hajime, with Sakura still in her arms. For my part, I was scared to look at the doctor, so I immediately pretended to stare at the posters on the wall: *Did you know that dogs can get stressed out too?* and *Trim your pet's nails once a month*.

But the one who was the most scared—more than me or Miki—was Sakura. The pungent smell of disinfectant in the room, the yokai wearing a white coat, the examination table that made unsettling noises, and the mournful howls of other patients audible in the back of the clinic. Sakura's entire body shivered and her nose—a dog's most important feature—had gone completely dry.

"What seems to be the matter?"

The vet had a surprisingly high-pitched voice, and as he asked this, he looked at Miki with a kindly expression (or surely he intended it to appear kind, though all we could see was someone who was about to devour us).

Miki seemed to have forgotten why we were there. She held Sakura tightly and tried to take a step backward, which my mother prevented her from doing. As a grown man, my father was a far better match for a yokai; he lifted Sakura from Miki's arms and bravely faced the exam table.

"What do have we here, such a sweet little pup!" (Translation: "Looks delicious, how should I eat her?")

Putting on his utmost charm for us completely terrified kids, the yokai then tried to hold Sakura.

"No!" Miki shouted, in spite of herself, and right at that moment, there came a sound: "Wuooff!"

Sakura's bark echoed throughout the entire clinic. She must have been so scared that, once that first memorable bark had been loosed, it was like a dam had burst.

"Wuuooff! Wuooofff!"

I was dumbstruck, while my mother shouted with glee.

Miki gathered Sakura up and did a little happy dance. "You did it! You barked!"

For such a tiny little dog, Sakura had an improbably deep and low voice, as if she were warning her fellow wolves of impending danger. Sometimes she would growl so fiercely, it would take us by surprise.

As for the yokai, he turned to my father and asked, "So, what's the problem with this pup?"

My father tried to offer an awkward explanation but the rest of us had already rushed back to the waiting area, catching the nurse unaware.

"Thank you!" we yelled, laughing out loud as we took turns hugging Sakura.

The lady in purple and the cat with the satellite collar were nowhere to be seen.

In/Out

After coming to live with us, Sakura always slept by the front door. At first, she slept in a cardboard box that used to hold shimeji mushrooms, and as she grew bigger it became a carrot box, then a napa cabbage box, and then a carton for Elleair tissues. When she no longer fit into an Asahi Oolong Tea carton, Sakura slept outside for the first time. My father and brother went to the home improvement store and bought a doghouse that was too big for her. It had a red triangular roof like Snoopy's, and Miki put up a sign on it that said, "Sakura's House." To the right of the opening she wrote "In" and on the left "Out."

The first day that Sakura passed through that door—whether as an entrance or an exit—also happened to be the first snow of the season. The entire yard was blanketed in white. Though Sakura was excited to see snow for the first time, she played in it very daintily—she was a girl, after all, so instead of frolicking around in it, she sniffed her own pawprints and gingerly tasted it.

"Poor thing! Her first night sleeping outdoors, and it snows!" the females in the family lamented.

"No, no—dogs sleep outside no matter how cold it is!" the males insisted, as Sakura trudged into her doghouse, the powdery snow falling lightly all around. She just went around in circles, smelling all over the place, still unused to her new home. Finally, she settled down in a corner, resting her head on her front paws with a satisfied groan.

"Gmph."

It was quite cold that night. The snow absorbed all sound from the surroundings, though every so often, the north wind howled through the still silence. The only warm part of my futon was where my body was lying and, not wanting to move, I lay there as my exhalations transformed into a white haze above me.

The first noises I heard were made by my father.

There was the slight creak of a door, followed by squeaking as he went down the stairs, the jangle of the chain being unlocked on the front door, and lastly, the slapping of his oversized slippers as he walked out to Sakura's doghouse. I strained my ears as best I could, paying close attention to what my father would do. But when I heard him say softly, "Sakura, come inside," I leapt out of bed with joy.

My father was standing by the front door with a bleary-looking Sakura.

"I figured it'd be okay to wait a bit longer," he said sheepishly.

Despite my delight, I made the comment, "But we don't have a box for her."

Before we knew it, the whole family had gathered by the front door, and everyone was taking turns petting Sakura, who looked befuddled as we laughed and smiled at her.

"Who's a good girl?"

From then on, it became one of our secret pleasures to sneak Sakura back into the house at night. When there was heavy rain or thunderstorms, or even sometimes when there was no weather to speak of, we'd bring her inside and spread a blanket in the foyer. Even before we opened the door, Sakura seemed delighted to be let into the house—apart from being fed and when she saw the leash for her walk, this was when her tail wagged the most, and she'd yowl with excitement.

Once the door had been opened, she'd sprint like Carl Lewis and launch herself into the house, getting carried away and ending up all the way in the living room, but none of us ever got upset about that. Miki would get on her hands and knees and play tug-of-war with a towel, rolling around on the floor with Sakura until my mother chided her, "You sure you're a girl?"

When Sakura was sprawled out on her side, I loved to use her as a pillow, which made everyone laugh.

After we'd been playing for a while, my mother would say, with impeccable timing, "Hey! Who's gonna clean up this dog hair all over the place?"

Which meant that Sakura's time was up, and she'd quietly go back to lying by the front door.

Even when we were in bed, we could still hear Sakura groan—"Gmph"—or the sound of her scratching the back of her neck with a hind leg, which would deliver us into the most blissful sleep. Knowing Sakura was there made us feel safe, even in the dark.

Adjusting to our new environment had been a bit of a challenge, but things picked up again after Sakura arrived. My brother and I would race straight home after school to play with Sakura in the yard, and life was like how it was right after Miki was born. It made our mother smile to see us so animated.

"If Sakura were a bird, she'd think you two were her mother."

In addition to the luxury of being able to afford his own

house, my father was so happy to have a dog in the yard, he threw himself into working even harder. My mother was so impressed with Sakura, who kept away from her beloved flower beds without ever having to be told, that she doted on her like a new daughter.

Miki was happy Hajime was playing with her again. And more than anything else, she seemed besotted with Sakura, who would lay beside her, her breath rising and falling as she slept. My sister, who up until now had rarely ever smiled, would beam whenever Sakura was around. Even in her sleep, she called out that beloved name: "Sakura."

A Step Toward Adulthood

Around the same time that Sakura first slept outdoors, my brother announced that he too would sleep alone in his room.

Thanks to Hajime's efforts, and also to the steady influx of new transfer kids, our school had become much livelier. While the town used to only have big houses, a new danchi public housing complex had brought a lot of families in from the suburbs. This meant that not all of them were well-off—there were working-class kids like us, kids whose mothers had jobs to make ends meet, and kids from big families, plenty of whom didn't have the luxury of planting flowers in the yard, to say nothing of having a dog. It was around this time that some new kid had shown up and tried to start a fight with my brother, who had recently had a resurgence in popularity.

"Who made you the boss of this school?"

Even among all the goody-goodies, there was still some bluster and color. In other words, slowly but surely, school got to be more fun again.

Some kids started teasing me about my name in the usual way, which I was happy about. There was also a girl who, when we made even the briefest of eye contact, joked that I must be in love with her, and it made me laugh.

Befitting for a new town, all kinds of things were starting to happen. Strangely, these seemed to coincide with us getting Sakura—somehow, this timid, not-the-prettiest little girl-dog, who'd arrived with a pink petal attached to her tail, had managed to bring joy to our days.

Miki still lapsed into her torpors, but when she played with Sakura, she'd roll around, not caring if anyone could see her underwear—though if any of the boys who tried to flip up her skirt came around, she would be on her feet and ready to swing punches.

The following spring, my brother started junior high school.
Even so, I'd get the standard, "You're Hajime's brother? You don't look much like him," but I also still got the special treatment. I guess my life revolved around my brother too, but I was used to it by then. He was popular wherever he went, and it was perfectly natural, just like how sunflowers grow toward the sun.

At the time of his renewed popularity, my brother was still sleeping in the same room as me in our bunk bed, even though he had his own room now. When Hajime suddenly announced that he wanted to sleep in his own room, my parents accepted it as a natural progression and I too understood, even if it made me sad. I reckon that my brother must have been awakening to his own physical needs.

Hajime was tall for a sixth grader—he had pretty much outgrown his randoseru school bag. It was a small town, so by then even the junior-high-school girls knew who he was. He taught me many things. The first time I ever came across a porn mag was in his room, right before he started junior high.

I figured Hajime must have wanted the space to—how should I put it?—sort out his own body that was developing faster than his friends'. But Miki wasn't having any of it. Aside from playing with Sakura, the times she was able to sleep in the same bed as Hajime meant the most to her.

Once my brother's three-month-long Sakura craze mellowed, he started playing soccer after school, even going to practice on his days off. Miki had often gone to visit his classroom, but Hajime always seemed busy, surrounded by his classmates, and she had hesitated to speak to him there.

Sleeping in bed with Hajime was the only time she had him to herself, so this being taken away was too much to bear, provoking her latest display of willfulness.

"I want to sleep in Hajime's room too!"

Hajime seemed genuinely troubled by her outburst. He loved Miki, just as he loved Sakura, but the changes his body was going through were real. It might have helped had he explained to her what was going on, sort of like how my mother had taught Miki about sex, but of course that was beyond him. He comforted her as she sobbed uncontrollably and, once she had worn herself out and fallen asleep, he did his best to take a step toward adulthood by closing the door to his room.

That first night, I couldn't sleep. Miki's breathing rose and fell as she slept beside me, exhausted, in the lower bunk bed. Above me, where my brother had always been, his bedding was cold and empty.

"Gmph."

Sakura sighed in her kennel, and I brooded over this idea of becoming a grown-up.

Growing up, it seemed to me, wasn't about sleeping by yourself—it was about not sleeping.

Whether it was my mother's mother-cat sounds or my brother's insistence on having his own room despite Miki's sobbing, they were both willing to sacrifice sleep for whatever it was that had captivated them.

I wasn't sure if there was anybody in particular whom Hajime liked, but I knew that what his body desired was someone special, just for him.

That night, had he forsaken us to be on his own, with thoughts of someone else to keep him warm? And was he experiencing a solitude that went beyond sleeping alone?

Tentatively, I thought about Yukawa-san.

In the letter she had given me, she'd written:

—*Hasegawa-kun, I've always liked you.*

There were marks where the letters had been repeatedly erased, and I now associated the sweet scent of her eraser with Yukawa-san. I had inhaled that scent many, many times.

When I recalled Yukawa-san's pink-framed eyeglasses, the color of a baby's skin fresh out of the bath, and the way she seemed so shy about wearing them, I got a thrill in my belly, like someone had pinched me.

I wondered if this was what it felt like to be in love with someone. But that was too embarrassing to even consider, so I thought better of it. I watched Miki turn over in her sleep, nestled on my arm, and then I drifted off myself.

Yajima-san

The first time I had the desire to sleep by myself was when I was in sixth grade, just like my brother. This was around the time when Miki found out the story from my mother about how Hajime had been born, how it was the first time my parents had sex, and by then she knew a lot more about male-female relationships. Miki had been sleeping in the top bunk bed, but she readily accepted my request to sleep alone, taking her pillow and futon bedding under her arm and returning to her walnut-tree–wallpapered room.

My brother seemed glad to hear this and surreptitiously brought me porn mags.

Around this time, Hajime got a girlfriend. She was, according to him, "super mature," and he ended up losing his virginity to her. Once he got a taste of sex, much like a monkey, it was really all he could think about. In order to come to terms with his own body, my brother acquired lots of porn mags.

The day that Hajime first brought his girlfriend home was kind of dramatic.

"My girlfriend's gonna come over this Sunday."

My brother said this with as much nonchalance as he could manage, then cleared his throat in exasperation and went back into his room.

In the living room, my mother and father, for their part, pretended as if this was no big deal—"Oh, okay"—but as soon as Hajime was gone, they became hysterical.

"Hear that?! Hajime's got a girlfriend!" my mother said.

"A girlfriend, huh? Really? Look at him go."

As for me, I knew about Hajime's girlfriend, having heard about her from him, though this would be my first time seeing her in person.

But Miki's reaction was the most extreme.

It had just occurred to me to worry about it when Miki started flinging open and then slamming the refrigerator door closed, and poor Sakura, who just happened to come into the kitchen, got pinched on the bottom. Moments ago, she'd been on the receiving end of gentle and loving belly rubs and then, out of nowhere, this sharp pain.

"Ynph!" Sakura yelped miserably. *What did I do wrong?*

On the day that Hajime's girlfriend was set to visit, Sakura had never been cleaner. I'm the one who gave her a bath, in the hopes that the girlfriend, upon arriving at her boyfriend's home, would see Sakura and say, "How cute!" and, even if she didn't actually like dogs, would reach down to pet Sakura. To make sure her hand didn't stink from touching Sakura, I took care to bathe her even more thoroughly than usual. Sakura hated water, though; with her skinny tail tucked between her legs, she nervously kept trying to lick her own face as if to say, *Isn't this taking l-l-longer than usual?"*

After the third shampoo or so, Sakura finally looked as clean and fluffy as a newborn chick. The vigorous scrubbing may not have washed away the spots on her face, but now any movement she made caused a soft and pleasant scent to waft about, making her seem like quite the girly girl.

My mother and father were trying their best to act like everything was normal, though I had to laugh—they were obviously more dressed up than usual for any given Sunday, and there was a big silver platter heaped with fruit on the table as if to say, "Oh, we *always* keep this here."

Meanwhile, Miki had retreated to her room to sulk in bed.

My first impression of Hajime's girlfriend was that she was even more mature than I'd expected. Her hair was long and curled down her back, and she had on pink lip gloss. She was wearing a faded denim outfit and had a sharp look in her eyes that seemed to say, "Don't mess with me." She was quite the beauty, but not the type of girl that grown-ups necessarily approved of. My father, being a man, welcomed this pretty girl unreservedly but my mother, carrying in a homemade apple pie (the second time she'd ever made one) with the expectation of a warm reception—"Oh, I *love* apple pie!"—looked a bit disappointed to see the girlfriend casually sitting there on the floor, one knee raised up, who responded with a cool "Ah, thanks."

As for me, after having imagined her enamored with Sakura's cuteness, it was kind of a letdown to watch her just go straight upstairs without so much as acknowledging Sakura's existence. Sakura just sat there placidly, emitting her fresh scent as she seemed to ask, *Who dis? Who's the honey?* She was trying to please everyone.

Miki continued to sulk in her room, not leaving her bed.

"Kaoru, what'd you think of her?"

That evening my brother summoned me to his room and bashfully solicited my opinion.

"Whaddya mean?"

"Whaddya mean, 'whaddya mean?' Did you think she's pretty?"

"Sure, she's pretty."

"And . . . ?"

"Uh . . ."

I couldn't say *Scary*, so I fell silent.

Hajime seemed to be crazy about her. Here's what I knew: Her name was Yuko Yajima, her father wasn't in the picture, and she lived with her mother in the danchi complex near the junior high school.

In our town, a fair number of so-called delinquent kids had begun to appear around that time. There was nothing delinquent about Hajime or his character, but he could relate to kids who came here from other towns and who were from families that weren't so well-off. With his cheerful and carefree personality, he could easily make friends with anyone.

Because he was so popular, one time he got called out by a kid in a higher grade—which I guess is par for the course for exceptional people. But my brother wasn't the type to cut and run. Instead, he stood his ground ("So what if I'm popular?"), and his swagger earned him the respect of the older kid.

Yajima-san fell into the category of those so-called delinquents. But she was different from the rest. Unlike the other girls who reeked of cigarette smoke or talked like boys (saying things like "Bite me!"), Yajima-san always wore perfume and smelled nice. And while everyone admired the mature quality she had about her, she seemed indifferent to it and could usually be found sitting off on her own, apart from the others.

When my brother would talk about Yajima-san, he'd speak in this keyed-up yet serious tone, as if he'd just watched a cinematic masterpiece.

"It's like . . . I just dunno what she's thinking about."

"What do you mean?"

"Like, when we're on the way home from school, I'll be all happy and talking about stuff, like what happened that day or about Sakura."

"Right."

"And Yajima-san, she'll be laughing and listening to me, but now and then she'll look sad all of a sudden and I have no idea why. When it happens, it's like she's off in the clouds, and no matter what I say, she'll just smile at me."

"Hmm."

"Y'know, sometimes I worry whether she really likes me or not."

"Of course she likes you."

"She says she likes me. But . . ."

"Huh?"

"But, well . . ."

"What?"

"I don't think it was her first time."

"First time for what?"

"First time for *it*."

"Oh, for *it*."

Why was he worrying about that? I wondered.

But Hajime was my parents' firstborn, after all, and he was strangely concerned with stuff like this. Although I was only a kid at the time, I was still confident that, whenever I got a girlfriend of my own, even if I wasn't her first, that kind of thing wouldn't bother me.

I'd always been the one stuck between Hajime and Miki, the easily forgotten sibling, so why would I care about being second or third? I was convinced that this position actually suited me quite well. Best to approach everything with a sense of resignation—that way, I was never disappointed. I never had to slink away to lick my wounds.

"Who do ya think was her first?"

Hajime was used to being first in everything, and now someone had stolen his thunder; the idea that his first time could've been Yajima-san's second, third, or worse really seemed to have shaken him. I felt sorry for him, but it also seemed ridiculous to me, so I just nodded vaguely.

Someone else in our family had also had their top spot taken away: Miki. Hearing the unfavorable report about Yajima-san from my mother, Miki's mood turned even more sour.

"What does Hajime see in her?"

"I've no idea, but she sure is gorgeous."

"Hmph."

"Such a fine young thing, she even turned your dad's head."

"Hmph!"

When girls got together to talk trash about another girl, it was never pretty. It was common to overhear girls in my class badmouthing any girl who stood out even a little bit, and when they furrowed their brows and pouted their lips while waving their hands around melodramatically, they were just as scary as any creepy yokai creature. But then when the girl they'd been ragging on walked past them, they'd go, "Oh, So-and-so-chan," flapping their hands at her, "see you *la-ter*!" I didn't get it.

Whenever Yajima-san came over, Miki would scrunch her nose up all the way and start marking various cacophonies. She'd play my recorder atonally or screech her nails down the windowpane, behaving like a much younger child than the third grader she was. But she never went anywhere near Hajime's room. Miki must have been afraid of knowing what was going on inside. My brother would even lock the door when they went in—one time my mother had to warn him about it.

At first Sakura seemed to be nervous around Yajima-san and would greet her from afar, giving a gentle tail wag, but after gradually getting used to the girl's presence, she shyly approached her with a more proper greeting:

Hello there. I'm Sakura Hasegawa. Woof.

The Power of Love

The day that Yajima-san first petted Sakura on the head, I was taking Sakura out for a walk. We had just come out the front door and, happy to see the school-uniform-clad couple, Sakura madly wagged her tail as if to say:

Hajime-kun, welcome home! Yajima-san, do you remember me? I'm Sakura Hasegawa. Woof. Right now, Kaoru-kun and I are going for a walk.

With a slightly awkward expression, Yajima-san looked down by her feet at Sakura, who was trying hard to be affectionate, and gently rubbed Sakura's head with her slender and beautiful fingers.

Sakura's eyes closed and, as if being careful not to startle Yajima-san, her body wriggled with the bliss of having her head rubbed. After this first tentative pat, Yajima-san murmured gently "So soft," and then enthusiastically continued rubbing Sakura's head. By then, Sakura was back to her usual stink, with no trace of shampoo scent, but Yajima-san didn't seem to mind and just kept right on petting Sakura's head.

As I stood there watching, somehow the two of them seemed like devoted sisters, and I basked in the warmth of this happy scene. Hajime must have felt the same way, saying "You like that, don'tcha girl?" as he and I joined in scratching Sakura's neck, not wanting to disrupt the head-rubbing.

Now I too was crazy about Yajima-san.

Maybe because of her mature demeanor or her pink lips, people saw her as a delinquent to keep an eye on, but the truth was that she was just an extremely shy girl.

After her parents divorced when she was little, Yajima-san had lived alone with her mother who was—how should I put it?—a woman with many lovers. She brought home a steady stream of men, though their looks were so varied, you'd think she had no type at all. Yajima-san had been well-acquainted with adults and sex from a young age—even more so than Miki—and she knew that when a man showed up it was best to leave the house. And it wasn't only for the same reason as when we had heard the sounds my parents were making; the men who came home with Yajima-san's mother were always problematic.

These men may have varied in the way they looked but, personality-wise, they all resembled Yajima-san's father. What they had in common was an aggressive and toxic masculinity. These men often beat her mother without restraint, apparently even violently kicking her in the back. It fell to Yajima-san to clean up the broken dishes and to care for her bruised and bloodied mother. Witnessing the sobs emanating from her mother's split lip made Yajima-san think, *I guess this is just how things are between men and women.*

Tears and saliva mixed in with the blood, which stank and was shiny in the light and sticky when it dried, and yet these things were completely unpredictable. To prove it, Yajima-san tried it out, giving her slender and supple body away to a guy she couldn't care less about and, as expected, she was just left with streaks of dark-red blood on her thighs and a dull pain between her legs.

Yajima-san's predilection for zoning out had to do with the way that she dealt with the world, her sense that "this is just how things are." She had never experienced what it meant to be in love, and so she paid no attention to the boys who came for her, attracted by her looks—it was almost as if she wasn't there.

This meant that, in a certain way, my brother was a game changer for Yajima-san. Hajime told her, with his whole body, "I'm in love with you." He showered her with love and affection. That was how we Hasegawas did things and my brother, having learned from our mother how spectacular sex was, treated Yajima-san's body like the world's most precious china. And whenever she stared off into space, he always asked her, "What are you thinking about?"

Yajima-san had assumed that she wasn't thinking about anything in particular, but Hajime's question made her realize for the first time that, actually, she *was* always thinking about something, and because the area around her eyes would grow hot whenever he asked, she realized that that something was making her sad.

She was astonished by our relentlessly and ridiculously sunny house that was in stark contrast to her own always-dark home, by our beautiful mother who would whip up handmade treats Yajima-san had never even imagined could exist, and by our father who, more often than not, would be sitting there smiling, quietly reading a book. In Yajima-san's mind, fathers didn't read books; she was more used to creepy smiles from men. To her, a father like mine was "beautiful and dignified," and the way he looked when he smiled left her in awe.

Perhaps she also realized that, just like when she first pet Sakura on the head and discovered how soft her fur was, the rest of the world might be softer than she thought.

Yajima-san started coming to our house more often, though she stopped wearing that pink lip gloss after my mother said to her, "Your lips can't breathe with that stuff on them!" She even started opening her mouth wider when she laughed, trying to imitate the way my mother laughed (which was more like a guffaw).

Only Miki remained secluded in her room, sulking.

By the time I got to junior high school, Hajime and Yajima-san were famous as a couple. My ever-popular brother and the extremely beautiful Yajima-san had kind of been a hot topic ever since they started dating, but in my first year there, what everyone talked about was how devoted they were to each other.

Around that time, Yajima-san chopped off her long hair, wearing it in a short cut that showed off her refreshing, doe-like beauty. Those who knew her with long curls around her face and her lips painted pink were surprised by this change in her appearance, but the boys were startled by how lovely her naturally salmon-pink lips were, and the girls sighed with envy at the nape of her neck, graceful as a young sapling in the sun. But above all, it was clear that Yajima-san's whole body was happy to be in love, and whoever encountered her was struck not just by her beauty but by her soft and carefree glow.

I took pride in the fact that my brother was almost entirely responsible for this change in Yajima-san. As for Hajime, thanks to Yajima-san's wholehearted and full-bodied love, he too was brimming with vitality, seeming to grow sturdier and sturdier.

I recognized the extraordinary power of love.

Yukawa-san

Around this same time, I had been exchanging letters with Yukawa-san.

—*Hi Hasegawa-kun? How are you?*

—*Today Sato-kun spit up his milk again. Remember how you used to always do that?*

—*I'm going to the movies with Yokoyama-san and Mika-chan.*

Chockful with silly and banal details, these letters steadily grew in volume just as Sakura steadily grew in size, but after that first letter from Yukawa-san, she never again mentioned her feelings for me, nor did I ever write anything about liking her too.

Unlike my brother, I had yet to understand the joy of being in love. I sort of got the sense that, when you liked someone, it could make your heart ache or flutter as you were falling asleep, but I didn't know if I was capable of the kind of love that inspired a person to love me back with their entire being, the kind of love that never failed to bring a smile to their lips.

I just knew that when I thought about Yukawa-san, a warm feeling would spread in my chest, like the first sip of hot cocoa on a cold day, and before I knew it, that warmth would travel between my legs, until it felt as if there were another version of myself gently pushing me from behind.

Fantasizing about Yukawa-san was very pleasurable. At some point my hand would turn into Yukawa-san's pale and slender hand, the same hand that had trembled when she gave me that first letter, and the sigh that escaped my lips became one with hers as well.

Afterward, I'd feel disheartened that Yukawa-san wasn't there, and then I'd feel ashamed and pathetic for thinking of her when doing such a thing.

I was utterly bewildered.

I wanted to ask my brother for advice, but at the same time I felt the need to keep my feelings for Yukawa-san to myself. They pained me, even made my chest tight, but the stronger these feelings got, the more I imagined that what I felt for Yukawa-san might actually be love.

My school uniform used to swim on me but as winter arrived, I started to fill it out. Miki said it looked like now I could hold my own head up. In other words, I looked like I fit in more. I could finally go to the water fountain where the older kids hung out without being intimidated. And even better, I grew a lot taller. Come to think of it, ever since starting junior high, I'd gotten lots of invitations to join the volleyball club or the basketball club, which must have had to do with being tall. Maybe it was from all that milk in the hot cocoa my mother made for me, but before I even realized it, I was the tallest of the first-year students.

My brother was tall too, but in his case, he had broad shoulders and a solid chest; he had a strong build and gave the overall impression of being a big guy. I, on the other hand, was "just tall"; I weighed about the same as the other boys and, since I didn't work out, I had not an ounce of muscle. With my lanky frame, I towered over my classmates, but I was sorely lacking in presence.

There are some girls, though, who like a guy just because he's tall. Lucky for me, several girls confessed their feelings. None of them were my type, plus there was the fact that Yukawa-san loomed ever larger in my heart, so I turned them down, but what they said still made my day.

The declaration that made me feel especially good came from a girl in my class who was in the basketball club. She was confident, the kind of girl who stood out among the other students. She always wore her hair in a ponytail, and she played with it as she said to me, "I like you, Hasegawa—you're good at things but you're not a show-off."

It just so happened that was exactly what I had been aiming for.

As a member of the go-home club, I had no know-how of sports, but nevertheless, in gym class and at field day, I managed to show some decent athletic ability, placing third in the marathon event.

Which made everyone go, "Wait, who's that?"

But among all those pointing and wondering, there were a few people who said, "That's Hasegawa-kun's younger brother."

I was the guy who did alright without trying too hard, who never stood out but managed to play well—that had been my intention all along. But I hated to talk about it.

Like I said, my brother was always the hero at school.

In soccer, he played forward, and while this might sound like an exaggeration, when he was on the field, it was like there was a spotlight always following him. Especially when one of his teammates scored, he had this thing he did, and it was quite a sight to see. Instead of running at them like everyone else in a scramble to embrace them, he would look up at the heavens as if he were relishing the joy of the moment, and then his knees would buckle a little in a sort of genuflection. It was like the way an animal flexes its muscles before its next movement. He'd trot slowly toward his teammate, who would then race at my brother as if he were the one who'd made the goal. Yet maybe because of my brother's carefree smile or the goodwill that he radiated, there was nothing awkward about it; they'd always hug him like his happiness was the best part.

There were people like Hajime—born heroes, without pretense or self-consciousness, who charmed everyone they met—and then there were people like me. I was content to fulfill my role, and in my own modest way, to hear a few people say, "Who's that guy?"

I wasn't jealous of my brother, but I remember feeling the need to affirm my identity as the hero's younger brother.

And so I totally flipped out when the girl from basketball club confirmed that I'd done just what I'd set out to. I was on the verge of forgetting all about Yukawa-san, but I quelled my beat-skipping heart and let the basketball girl down gently.

"I'm not interested in dating anyone right now."

I thought this was a cool way of rebuffing her; it made me seem single-minded and direct.

One day I got another letter from Yukawa-san.

It contained the same silly and banal details, but this time something was different. There was a postscript:

This coming Sunday, the band club has a recital at the civic center near your house. I want to see you, if you're free.

It felt like blood was pumping through my veins with tremendous force. Like the Mekong Delta or the Nile River—I don't know, like some enormous river somewhere—had crested inside me. Inconveniently, the blood then stalled between my legs so, with apologies to Yukawa-san, I fulfilled my urge as I read her postscript over and over again.

Rather than *I'd like to see you,* or *Maybe we could see each other,* she had written *I want to see you*, which, to my mind, proved Yukawa-san's love for me. *I want to see you* had such a sweet ring to it! Those words enabled me to fool myself that Yukawa-san had been my long-time girlfriend. I was already thinking about what to wear on Sunday.

It wouldn't do to look like I was trying hard to look cool. Better to seem like I'd just put on whatever was around and yet I still happened to look cool. Flummoxed, I decided to go with my brother's hand-me-down blue down parka with a pair of perfectly faded Levi's. This felt appropriately unpretentious for my character to wear on a first date.

That's right—a date! My first ever!

I spent most Sundays lying around watching TV or playing with Sakura. That day, my brother had gone out with Yajima-san. Miki had been in the living room with me, watching TV with a grumbling, running commentary directed at the screen. She expected me to concur with each complaint, but I was off in my own world so, bored with me, she'd gone out into the yard to play with Sakura in the cold.

I was grateful for this. It was one o'clock; I had plans to meet Yukawa-san in front of the civic center at two-thirty. I was delighted by the fact that Yukawa-san didn't seem concerned about the other girls in band club seeing us together—a sign that our relationship was solid.

Since I hadn't seen her in three years, I imagined what Yukawa-san must look like now. In her letters, she had mentioned clues like "My hair is much longer" or "I stopped wearing glasses," which helped me to form an image.

I sank into the sofa as I dreamily pictured how her presumably longer arms and legs might move and the way she might bat her lush eyelashes at me. It made no difference to me what was on the TV.

The People's Forest had become a popular date spot for couples from my school. A kid in my class, Morioka-kun, had his first kiss there (but he told everyone about it, so then she dumped him), and my brother and Yajima-san had first held hands there. I didn't know whether I'd have the guts to grab Yukawa-san's hand but still, just going to the People's Forest with a girl seemed very grown-up, and I was feeling courageous.

It was still early but I couldn't sit still so I left the house and Sakura, ever aware, came running up to me.

Kaoru-kun, where you going?

Her shoulders heaving as she panted, Sakura dropped her favorite toy, a tawashi scrub brush, at my feet and waited for me to pet her. She was so adorable, I wanted to give her a big cuddle but, wary of my hands getting smelly, I held back. Sakura offered her head, under her chin, her belly for a rub—*Here, here, here*—but once she realized none were coming, she gave up and picked up her tawashi again.

"Sorry, Sakura. We'll have a walk later."

I realized that Miki had come up behind Sakura and was eyeing me. Feeling self-conscious, I turned to go and was surprised to hear Miki say, "Go for it!"

Had I been drinking something, I definitely would have sputtered it all over the place.

"W-whaddya mean?"

"What, don'tcha have a date?"

I was speechless. Though I knew better than to deny it—I

definitely didn't want to get on Miki's bad side—I begged her, "Keep it a secret, okay?"

Miki looked at me like I was a fool.

"A secret? Everyone knows."

Had I been eating something, I definitely would have choked on it and probably died right there.

"W-what do you mean?"

"Kaoru, you've been brushing your teeth since yesterday, you put on brand-new socks—it's a dead giveaway. The only one who doesn't know might be Sakura."

I'd been more of a fool than I thought. Or no, not a fool, but love had made me dumb. *Ah, stupid love!* Realizing that everyone knew about my first date but that no one had said a word gave me newfound respect for the Hasegawa family, and I vowed to make today's date a success (not that I knew what defined "success"). This would be a day that neither Yukawa-san nor I would ever forget.

Inspired and encouraged, I opened the gate.

Sakura, apparently still the only one unaware of my date, waved her tail at me as I walked away.

See you later! Ain't love grand? Woof.

Mint Gum

Hajime came home late that night and went straight to his room without even giving Sakura a pat on the head. The sound of him closing the door followed immediately by the sound of the radio made it obvious to us that he was fighting back tears.

Sakura was a bit glum from being rejected first by me and now by Hajime, and was leaning up against Miki's knees, since Miki could always be trusted to pet her without worrying about washing her hands.

My brother's uncharacteristic mood was certainly unsettling, but I was in not in a position to consider his feelings.

The date had been a disaster.

"Hasegawa-kun?"

At the sound of Yukawa-san's voice, I turned around without hesitation. The river that had sprung inside me since the day I read her letter was now as powerful as the Mekong Delta, or the Amazon, or the Nile—I was sure she could hear its roar. But that torrent abruptly ceased the moment I laid eyes on Yukawa-san. And once it stopped, that flow evaporated like rain returning to the sky.

Standing there before me was—how should I put it?—a totally different girl.

It was the same Yukawa-san who wore glasses during class, the one with the timid gestures and upturned eyes and the comforting presence, but her appearance was completely transformed.

Her face was covered with pimples. A few big ones here and there were clustered together with other ones, as if they were trying to team up and spread further. Her oily complexion made her face shine like it was wet and the blemishes on her forehead distorted the shape of her eyebrows, making Yukawa-san look as if she were either laughing, crying, or angry.

"Don't you recognize me?" Yukawa-san asked nervously.

Other female classmates walked past, stealing glances at the two of us just standing there. In my left hand, I was squishing a piece of gum—if I squeezed it any harder, it might have disintegrated. This hand that I'd thought would be holding Yukawa-san's was now tainted with the artificial mint scent that Sakura would sniff and sniff when I got home.

"How about we take a walk?"

Without responding to Yukawa-san's question, I pointed at the park. The trees swayed, unsteady and forlorn without their leaves, and a beautiful, fluffy white dog, like the kind that Miki had wanted, was walking past them.

Yukawa-san nodded, looking a little sad herself.

The gum had squished out of its wrapper, and I poked it with my finger. It was gross, but I didn't want to take my hand out of my pocket, so I just left it there and started walking.

"The concert."

"Huh?"

"How'd it go?"

Yukawa-san was carrying a large, hard case. There must have been some kind of wind instrument inside, and it seemed heavy—every so often she'd shift it from one hand to the other as we walked. I knew it was my role, as the guy, to offer to carry it for her, but I was too shy to say anything about it, so I pretended not to notice and kept walking.

"It went well, but I was so nervous."

"You've been doing it since elementary school, right?"

"Nope. I started in junior high."

"What do you . . . ?"

"What?"

"What instrument?"

"Oh, trombone."

Yukawa-san hoisted the case onto her shoulder and mimicked playing a trombone.

"Want me to carry it?"

"Huh?"

"That looks heavy."

"Oh, this? It's fine, I'm used to it."

She rapped on the case and cracked a smile.

"What about you, Hasegawa-kun?"

"Yeah?"

"How come you're not in any clubs?"

In our letters, I had reported on every detail: what my classmates were like, what my teachers were like, the way that Sakura licked my face. And Yukawa-san had done the same, telling me about all kinds of things: her father falling down the stairs when he was drunk, fights among her classmates, band camp. Growing out her hair, not wearing glasses anymore, her wisdom teeth hurting. But she hadn't written a word about what had made her unrecognizable.

"No reason."

I was angry at Yukawa-san for not saying anything about her appearance. My feelings were totally misplaced—I knew painfully well that Yukawa-san was still Yukawa-san, regardless of what she looked like. But it made me want to punch whoever had done that to Yukawa-san's skin. With all my strength, I wanted to beat the crap out of whatever was powerful enough to end the love between Yukawa-san and me in the span of an instant. And yet, I was the one afraid that someone might see us walking together. I was so capricious that all it took was a change in her appearance for me to completely abandon the Yukawa-san I had pined for so deeply. I wanted to disappear.

We kept on walking for a while, exchanging recent news about ourselves in dribs and drabs. And that was it.

On the way back, Yukawa-san asked, "Will you write me again?"

That simple, innocuous question should have made me smile, it should have made me happy, like the rain that had fallen so gently on our moving day. But now, it tugged heavily on my heart—like sludgy earth, like muddy but intangible sediment—and refused to let go.

"Sure."

I tried to make my response sound as normal and carefree as possible, but Yukawa-san's expression was the saddest yet. It was as if a doctor had informed her that she'd contracted a serious and incurable disease. With a look of resignation, that of someone who simply accepts everything, she held the front of her duffle coat tightly closed and straightened her spine.

After we parted, she took a few steps and then boldly turned back toward me.

"Thank you, Hasegawa-kun." She smiled as she said this.

The sun was setting later now, and Yukawa-san was lit from behind so I couldn't see her clearly in the glare. My body heat had melted the mint gum, and my hand was sticky from it, which made me want to take a bath. I wanted to soak in the bath and then crawl under the covers in bed. And stay deep under there forever. It wasn't the backlight that prevented me from seeing Yukawa-san's face clearly—it was that I was ashamed.

"Thanks."

My voice was hoarse, like an old man who had lost the ability to do what was expected of him, a far cry from that of a boy in love. Left behind, I just stood there like a total idiot. If you looked closely, the sleeves of my blue down parka were shabby and darkened with grime, and my bangs, which I had trimmed myself, were uneven and kept getting in my eyes. I may have been the tallest kid in my class but as I stood there, hunched over, my shadow looked awfully small. I was such a small person.

After that, there were no more letters from Yukawa-san.

About two months after Yukawa-san's letters stopped, Yajima-san moved to Kita-Kyushu. At some point her mother's new boyfriend had become Yajima-san's stepfather, and he was set to build a bridge in Kita-Kyushu.

Yajima-san was right smack in the middle of studying for entrance exams and she put up considerable resistance to the move, even enlisting the help of her homeroom teacher—who had watched Yajima-san transform from delinquent slacker to diligent student—in her big persuasion effort, but her mother's mind was as unyielding as newly frozen ice.

Yajima-san's love life was all too easily subsumed by her

mother's love life, and Yajima-san's dream of going to the same high school as my brother and being manager of the soccer team was not to be.

That day when my brother had been crying in his room, he had wished with all his heart to grow up as fast as he could; even if they were far apart, he was determined that his feelings for Yajima-san wouldn't change.

Even though they were only fifteen years old, when they said goodbye, they vowed to each other that someday they would get married. Yajima-san's mother may have been thirty-six, but that didn't mean that she had a greater capacity for love. When I think of a mother putting her own need for love above her daughter's happiness, and of the all-consuming power of my fifteen-year-old brother and Yajima-san's love for one another, it takes my breath away.

It was a very cold winter, that year when I was thirteen.

PART 4

Sakiko-san

Just as the wind was getting a lot warmer, the Hasegawa household was swept up in a bit of a storm.

One day I came home from school to find an unfamiliar-looking letter in our mailbox. It was a lazy spring day and, having just started my second year of junior high, I still had too much time on my hands. At first I worried that the letter was from Yukawa-san, but it wasn't from her or from Yajima-san. The letter came from a woman we didn't know and was addressed to my father.

I figured I'd give it to him when he got home. For some reason—I really can't say why—I knew better than to let my mother see this letter. On the back of the pale blue envelope, the name Sakiko Mizoguchi was written in pretty, seemingly female handwriting. For some reason I also had a feeling, derived from the fact that Sakiko was written in katakana rather than in kanji, that they were on relatively close terms. I had no reason to think that my father was fooling around or anything like that but, being a guy, I decided to keep quiet about it to my mother.

Ah, but aside from my mother, there was another fearsome female member of our family. And her powers of perception were as sharp as an owl's at midnight.

Somehow, Miki had managed to get her hands on the letter

from Sakiko that I thought I'd secretly hidden away, and from which, to my horror, she then proceeded to read aloud in front of my mother.

Dear Akio, how are you? It's been so long since I last wrote a letter, so this is super stressful.

"She calls him Akio?! How can she be so chummy with him?!"

My mother was already angry enough to take the simmered hijiki salad—a favorite of my father's—that she'd made as part of his dinner and toss it into the garbage bin. The poor seaweed, still steaming, looked like a mess of someone's tangled hair in the bin.

Thanks to you, Akio, the place is doing well. The only problem, if you could call it that, is everyone is jealous of you. ("Jealous" was also written in katakana, lending it a certain innuendo.)

"Jealous! Jealous of what?!"

Next went the deep-fried pork cutlets (those were our dinner too!)—it was now chaos in the bin.

I'd like to show you my gratitude, Akio. Come by for a meal, my treat of course.

In went the miso soup and the rice too. (A total loss!)

Remember Chottotei, the place we used to go to all the time? I miss their renkon manju.

How is your family?

I've gotten old. I'm embarrassed for you to see how I've aged. (Apparently she was really fond of using katakana.)

That evening, my father would find himself seated before my mother in the formal seiza position, being interrogated about this "Sakiko" person. We had never seen my mother's eyes look so sharp and angry before, and we were surprised to see that my father's eyes had turned red around the edges.

What my father fumbled to say was that Sakiko-san had been a high school classmate of his.

Soon after they graduated, Sakiko-san had fallen into the so-called water trade, saving up money little by little working in various forms of nightlife and entertainment over the next thirty years, and last year she had opened her own place. At that point, my father had lent Sakiko-san "a little" money and had "occasionally" stopped by to say hello, and he wasn't sure but he guessed that the place was popular, so that must be the reason for this thank-you note.

"Why is she so chummy with you?!"

"Chummy? Um, well. I guess, because we went to high school together . . ."

"And how many years has it been since you graduated from high school?!"

"Uh, thirty years? No, thirty-one years . . . ?"

"Like that even matters!"

My brother and I held our breath as we watched all this unfold. No one could stop my mother; even Sakura came over and touched my mother's leg with one of her own adorable front paws. *What happened? What's wrong?*

But my mother didn't even notice.

"Hajime!" my mother yelled.

Startled to be called upon so suddenly, without thinking he automatically muttered, "Sorry." Then he looked at me sheepishly, and all I could do was look back at him with my own wry and inane smile.

"Go into my room and bring me the album from inside the wardrobe!"

"The album?"

"That's right!"

"What album?"

"The one from Dad's graduation, isn't that obvious?"

She may have thought it was obvious, but my brother had never laid eyes on an album from my father's high school graduation or even knew it existed.

Ah, but as I said before, in our family there was a girl with fearsome powers of perception like an owl's at midnight, who ruled like a queenpin.

"I'll get it!"

Maybe it was just me, but Miki seemed thrilled as she raced up the stairs and, about five minutes later, came back carrying my father's dust-covered album. My brother and I were amazed she had been able to locate it so quickly, and seeing the pleasure she derived from doing so sent a little shiver up our spines.

"So then, point me there!"

"P-point you where?"

"Point her out to me!"

Just then, my father looked like the most miserable man in the world. If, thousands of years from now, human faces were completely different and they were creating specimens of what ancient men's faces used to look like, there is no question that my father's face would be on display as "Miserable Man": *Here you see what an ancient human being's face looked like when he was feeling pathetic.*

My father mumbled a kind of excuse, "That's a bit . . ." and he seemed quite reluctant but, cowed by my mother's fury, he finally started to flip through the pages.

The look in my mother's eyes as she watched him was fierce.

"Oh-ho, you weren't in Class One. Not in Class Two either, was it Class Three?!"

Miki offered, "Class Four, right?" And then she egged my mother on, "Maybe she was the teacher?" My brother and I were now even more fearful of Miki.

After quite some time, my father's hand finally landed upon Class Eleven.

"Wow, there were a lot of classes in your school," I blurted out, genuinely surprised.

My father looked at me, somewhat relieved for the digression. "We were the first baby boom."

But my mother wasn't about to let him off the hook. "Which one is she?!"

My father's jitters had reached their peak. Even Sakura had given up on getting our attention and was staring curiously at my father's face, noticing that he'd gone white as a sheet.

But a few minutes later, we would be the ones who were nonplussed. After all that page turning and all that time waiting, the name my father pointed to was:

Sakifumi Mizoguchi.

Sakiko-san was Sakifumi-kun, quite the burly looking guy.

Lie with Love

In high school, my father was on the rugby team. Sakifumi-kun was also on the rugby team, but his brawniness wasn't put to use—he managed the team, along with two other female students. But Sakifumi-kun was unrivaled in the brisk and efficient way that he took care of the players. When he did the laundry, their clothes were as white as a freshly washed daikon, and his sweet-and-sour-pickled honey lemons excelled at dispelling their fatigue. Members of other sports teams knew about his powerful massages, and they'd queue for their turn. Once when a rugby player was injured, Sakifumi-kun had carried him in a sprint to the nurse's office.

Sakifumi-kun thought of himself as a woman. During those three years in high school when his service as team manager was greatly valued, he never spoke about it to anyone. The only person who knew how he really felt was my father, because Sakifumi-kun had confided in him. "I love you, Akio," Sakifumi-kun had confessed.

At first, my father had been taken by surprise. Sure, Sakifumi-kun gave him the lemons that had the most honey, the uniforms Sakifumi-kun washed for him were scented with something besides detergent, Sakifumi-kun seemed to pay a lot of attention to his plays and always gave him sound advice—but my father had never suspected the feelings that were behind Sakifumi-kun's gestures.

"Thank you," he had said, "but I don't know what to say." My father then explained how much he relied on and appreciated everything Sakifumi-kun did for him, and they pledged to maintain their friendly relationship on the team the same way as it always had been. My father's attitude only strengthened Sakifumi-kun's feelings for him, but he gracefully accepted my father's response, and the rest of their high school days passed that way.

Soon after they graduated, Sakifumi-kun started in the night trade, which was also around the time when he began his transition.

Three days later, we stepped foot in a nightclub for the first time.

In a bit of an off-the-wall move, my mother had insisted, "I've gotta see this place."

And Miki had chimed in, even more off the wall, "Me too!" Which would have left my brother and me in the dust.

"A-a-absolutely not!" my father sputtered, shaken up all over again.

But in the end, he caved to the female contingent, and he brought the entire family to visit the bar run by Sakifumi-kun, now Sakiko-san. It was called Lager Woman.

Sakiko-san, having heard from my father that we were all coming, greeted us wearing a gorgeous dress, with sequins all over that made it look like she had the Milky Way draped over her shoulders.

"Irassha-i!" she welcomed us.

A shadow of melancholy seemed to pass over Sakiko-san's

expression when she took in how pretty my mother was, but then her eyes crinkled when she saw how much my brother and Miki resembled my father, who was trying to make himself shrink.

"I've been expecting you!" Sakiko-san said.

She placed her hands on each of our shoulders. Her hands were bigger than anyone's I'd ever seen—even bigger than my father's—and they were warm. We loved Sakiko-san immediately.

"Have a seat!"

She led us to lustrous white leather chairs that were set in a semi-circle. Maybe because they were so shiny or because of the glimmering glass table in the center, it seemed like they belonged on a spaceship. Once Sakiko-san sat down with us there, we really felt like we were on a journey into space. We may not have been drinking saké, but we felt as if we were floating through the air.

"This is like a spaceship." Miki said what we were thinking, and Sakiko-san laughed with pleasure.

"That's right! You aren't on Planet Earth anymore, you've landed on another star."

It was true. Looking around us, the bar was full of women dressed and made up in ways unlike anything we'd ever seen before.

"Now don't go talking about what you see here today at school!" Sakiko-san laughed resonantly when she said this. Her voice sounded like the one you might hear announcing the start of a festival. It was so evocative that even a girl who had just lost something precious would find herself laughing right along with Sakiko-san's loud and gleeful cheer.

What we were most concerned about was how my mother

and Sakiko-san would get along. Normally when my mother laughed, the corners of her eyes turned down and it seemed like those gentle curves reached all the way to the horizon, but that day she seemed a little tense. She'd had a manicure, which Miki was really excited about, but my mother kept fidgeting, picking up her glass or playing with her hair, and, wearing higher-than-usual heels, she crossed and uncrossed her legs.

Observing my mother, Sakiko-san said, "Thank you for coming today," but stopped there, looking a bit troubled. She smiled and seemed to be trying not to let her discomfort show, but then she awkwardly looked down again.

My mother and Sakiko-san were, in a sense, rivals.

Even us kids could tell as much. Sakiko-san was still in love with my father. And, upon seeing his beautiful wife, she was at a loss for words.

So we were very caught up in how my mother would act and how all this would play out. Would she be reassuring, the way she was when Miki had asked about how babies are made? Or would she be like Sakiko-san, staying awkward and quiet and keeping her eyes downcast? Whatever was going to happen, now was the decisive moment.

Oh, but my mother! She knew how Sakiko-san felt, painfully well. Because she too was in love. With that same ridiculously shy fellow, the one who giggled constantly as if someone were tickling him, who always flubbed it when he had something important to say.

My mother regarded Sakiko-san, this other woman enamored with the same man. Her pupils glittered with the reflection from the ornate chandelier in the bar, but that light was no match for the pitch-blackness of those eyes, which could even put unwary ghosts to sleep. They immediately regained their moist, lacquer-like gleam, and her nose, which could instantly detect a person's sadness, twitched gently. Then, her soft lips parted with the words that suited them best, "It's fine, don't worry," she said. "Thank you for having us."

Seemingly surprised, Sakiko-san's eyes opened wide, and she stared back at my mother. Thrown off by my mother having finished her sentence for her, Sakiko-san hurriedly clinked her own glass against the one that my mother was holding.

It made an almost comically slight sound—*chin!*—and the two of them both finished their drinks in one go. We were pretty shocked; none of us had ever seen my mother down saké like that.

"Thank you!" Sakiko-san said.

The two of them laughed hysterically and drank a lot more. After that, they acted like they were long-lost friends, telling secrets and giggling as they looked at my father.

My father looked embarrassed to have them laughing at him, but his eyes squinted in heartening satisfaction to see his buddy and his beloved wife getting along so well, and he drank some more too.

That's right—both my mother and father drank a lot that night!

For the first time, we saw my mother knock over a glass, acting even more like a kid than Miki, and we watched my father belt out songs at the top of his voice. They both caroused, seeming to forget that their kids were there, and it was fun for us to see them that way.

When my mother staggered off to the toilet, Sakiko-san turned to us and asked, "Do you love your mom and dad?"

The question embarrassed us boys but Sakiko-san's eyes,

rimmed with jet-black liner and sparkling like stardust, were so kind that we replied, "Yes, we love them."

Sakiko-san let out a charming burp.

Apparently, my father was known among the regular crowd at the bar—he had been called over to another table, where he was drinking with a group of them. Every so often he would look over at us, grinning and waving cheerfully.

"Someday, you darlings will find someone to love more than your mom and dad."

It was hard to hear Sakiko-san over the laughter of Lily-san, a woman at the next table. Lily-san had slapped a customer pretty hard, shouting "Hey! Take me with you!" and he was forcing a smile. Miki was watching them with keen interest.

"Which means . . ."

I could no longer tell who Sakiko-san was talking to, and she didn't seem to care that her voice was being drowned out by Lily-san.

"Someday, sometime, you will lie to your mom and dad."

My brother and I pressed our hands to our knees, eager to hear what Sakiko-san was saying, like we did when an older kid we trusted had an important lesson to share. Miki had gotten bored with watching Lily-san and was blowing bubbles in the leftover cola in my brother's glass, trying to decarbonate it.

"Even though you really, really don't want to have to lie to them."

Sakiko-san closed her eyes as she spoke each word slowly. Her right hand held mine, and I could tell from the way she squeezed it at times that she wasn't talking about us, but herself.

"But when you absolutely have to, darlings, lie to them with love. Tell a lie that makes it hard for you too. Because your mom and dad love you. That much I know for sure."

Miki had been blowing bubbles so hard, the carbon dioxide in my brother's glass overflowed and the cola spilled onto the table.

"Oops," she said as she tried to suck up the spilled cola with the straw.

Sakiko-san had said that she would accompany us to the station when we left, but her dress had gotten caught on something and many of the sequins had fallen off, so she politely excused herself.

"I hope someday nobody has to lie to anyone."

I may have been the only one who heard Sakiko-san say this.

That night we took the subway home.

My mother and father held hands on the platform. We decided to give them some space, so we got into the car next to theirs. Dangling from my mother's slightly rosy earlobes were a pretty pair of earrings that she didn't wear often, which matched the sparkly blue ring on her finger—she loved my father. My father had on one of the faded-from-overwashing polo shirts he always wore, and whenever the train swayed, he placed his hand on my mother's waist, his arm gently curving around her hip—he loved my mother.

I think that, as the children of two people in love—in other words, us back then—we were a little more mature than other kids. We saw my mother and father as parents, of course, but we also saw them as a loving couple. And while we might have found that image of them encouraging, for some reason it also made us sad.

SAKURA

Miki stared out the subway window intently, even though there was nothing to see. Every so often she murmured, "Sakura."

That winter, Sakiko-san's mother passed away.
We heard about it from my father, who told us that Sakiko-san had been in elementary school when her father had passed away and that her mother had raised Sakiko-san and her older sister on her own. Apparently, she had been in the hospital for a long time.

For the funeral, Sakiko-san went back to being Sakifumi-kun, wearing a double-breasted suit and swept-back hair. There was no semblance of the gentle and kind woman we had met at the bar. In fact, it took us a minute to realize that the man who called out to us "Thank you for coming" was Sakiko-san.

But we knew by the gesture of placing a hand on our shoulder, and by those enormous hands themselves, that this was Sakiko-san, and that she was grieving the loss of someone she loved dearly.

Nevertheless, she performed her duties as chief mourner with poise and aplomb, never shedding a tear throughout the entire funeral ceremony.

"My only regret is that I was not able to give my mother a grandchild."

The photo of Sakiko-san's mother seemed to beam with pride, watching over as her son greeted everyone.

Around that time, Miki had been going through a tremendous growth spurt—remarkable even to Hajime and me, who were around her all the time—and she was looking more like a young woman. It had only been about six months since she'd slurped up spilled cola off the table in Sakiko-san's bar, but ever since we had eaten her celebratory sekihan at the dinner table (even though we hadn't known it was to mark her first period), Miki had grown a lot.

Her soft hair framed her face perfectly, accentuating the beautiful shape of her head, and her hips—higher than anyone else's in our family—were supple like a tree sapling. As always, her almond-shaped eyes conveyed boredom, but if they ever fixed upon you, they inspired a curious sensation, like wanting to run barefoot outside even though it might be raining.

Sakiko-san showered Miki with compliments—how shiny and pretty her black hair was, how becoming her mourning clothes were on her. Miki gave a little smile, quietly taking Sakiko-san's hand. And that was when Sakiko-san, caught utterly by surprise, allowed her shoulders to shake as she sobbed for the first time that day.

Monochrome

Is it just me, or does it seem like whenever the weather gets warm, a lot of people out on the street go a little nuts?

Someone like Ferrari was nuts the whole year round—though in the winter he kept to himself among the junk cars—but once summer came around, we'd often hear Miki say, "Some weird old man showed me his weenie." So it seems like everyone kind of loses their mind when it gets hot.

That summer was another scorcher, and when the heat got to us, we would play in the water in our yard. Sakura hated water, so when we'd turn on the spigot full blast, she'd scurry into her doghouse and stay in there. My brother and I would splash around, naked to the waist, dousing our heads with water. Then we'd sprawl on the grass, having our own kind of crazy fun.

Miki would watch us from Hajime's balcony, declaring that I was too skinny or spitting on us and laughing.

One day my mother came rushing out into the yard, shouting in our direction, "Sakura!"

My brother and I looked at each other and thought to ourselves, *Uh-oh, she's lost it too!*

But Sakura, good girl that she was, went and planted herself at my mother's feet, avoiding the dreaded water. *Yes, yes, what can I do for you?*

"They arrested Sakura's doctor."

It was a strange thing for my mother to say. By "doctor" of course she meant the veterinarian who had examined Sakura at the clinic, the one who looked like a yokai.

The yokai really, really loved animals. The golden retriever with an injured leg, the Persian cat missing its right eye, the abandoned bantam rooster, the python who tried to swallow the bantam. But there was something strange about his love for them. Maybe he loved them too much, or he treated these animals as if they were his lovers.

Maybe the yokai had also gone nuts from the summer heat too. A nurse had discovered him "doing something" with a Maltese named Marie in an un-air-conditioned exam room after the clinic was closed. We were especially curious to know what the thing was he'd been doing, but my mother offered nothing more than "It's awful!"

Sighing, she said, "Sakura, we're so lucky, aren't we? Lucky he didn't do anything to you." She held Sakura tightly against her own chest, which made Sakura grimace.

Before we knew it the clinic had been torn down and a sunakku bar with a vague name like Melody or Music or something popped up in its place, only to be gone itself within six months.

In contrast to this madcap summer mood, the practically daily calls and letters from Yajima-san to Hajime abruptly stopped that summer. It was as if the birds, whose singing every morning we took for granted, had suddenly fallen silent. Without the pretty colors of those envelopes, the mailbox seemed like it alone was now in monochrome.

As for me, not hearing Yajima-san's voice, intent with love, asking "Is Hajime-kun there?" over the phone felt like I'd lost something I needed to believe in.

My brother would come straight home from soccer practice to peer inside the mailbox. But, finding it as empty as a classroom after everyone had left for the day, his shoulders would slump dejectedly. When he tried calling her, the line would be busy, or it would ring twenty times before disconnecting. It sure seemed as though Yajima-san knew he'd be calling, and she was trying to avoid him.

Hajime mostly moped around, his head hung low like a dandelion that had mistakenly bloomed at the water's edge. He started skipping the soccer practice that he'd been so keen about, and when he was home, he would shut himself up in his room. They had vowed to get married, but their love was already facing a major crisis.

My mother and I worried about him—whenever we'd peek into his room, he'd just be sitting there tossing around a soccer ball or randomly looking at a magazine. He'd look up as if he'd just remembered something and say, "Oh, crap." It became his catchphrase, to the point where Miki started using it too. The same Miki who took people's newspapers from their mailboxes.

Back then my daily routine involved studying for my entrance exams in the next room, where I could hear those words echo: "Oh, crap." Occasionally Miki would go into my brother's room, and I could hear them talking about something, except at those times, Miki—who always talked ridiculously fast—would speak slowly, as if mulling over each word. Through the wall, sometimes her voice sounded like my mother's, and it made me think about how much time had passed.

Since I'd started my third year of junior high, people seemed to think that I was pretty smart—even smarter than I myself thought I was. Sure, on year-end and aptitude tests, I'd always come in second without studying much but, in my case, that wasn't exactly the same as being good at school. Whereas Hajime and Miki had an amazing ability to remember things, I on the other hand had an amazing ability to memorize things. I could leaf through a textbook and somehow it would sink in. I'd look at the test question and think, "Right, that was on page forty-two, in bold text in the sidebar."

And so on. Math, science, Japanese, social studies—I memorized all of my textbooks.

I too had a version of Hajime's and Miki's power of instant recall, only for me it wasn't intellectual prowess; instead, it manifested with this ability to memorize things. As soon as the test began, the things I'd memorized would burst into my head like a flash, but the moment the test was over, I'd forget it all as if I never knew it. While I was studying, it was like my brain would hoard everything, comically swelling up, and once the test was done, it would deflate like a spawned salmon.

I gained quite a lot of weight during those six months of active study. It stands to reason, since I'd been absorbing three years' worth of textbooks. I'd been the tallest in my class, the beanpole of the school, even. In the hallways, younger kids would cede the way for me. My mother and Miki said I was better off bigger, that I'd been too thin—but I didn't like the way such a dramatic weight gain seemed to impede the way I moved around. And what I liked least of all was that I was now taller than my brother. Ever since he'd lost contact with Yajima-san, his appetite was noticeably lacking and his cheeks had grown hollow, like an ancient Greek statue.

One day I was handing Sakura's leash to Hajime when I noticed I'd surpassed him in height. My brother was home on suspension because, on a school trip to Nagasaki, he'd run off from where the students were lodging to try to see Yajima-san. While he was AWOL, he'd gotten into a fight on the street downtown and attracted the attention of a policeman, which led to the teacher-chaperone giving him hell. Once back home, Hajime's homeroom teacher and my mother had pressed him, "Why would you do such a thing?" but he wouldn't say a word; he just sat there, folded in upon himself like an ascetic in India. My brother had always been such a big presence, so it pained me to see him looking so small, especially in contrast to his love for Yajima-san.

Once he did emerge from his room, next came a phase of hours-long walks with Sakura (thereafter, whenever he was going through a rough time Sakura was always taken along as his companion).

I'd been just about to go out with Sakura when my brother approached and said, "I'll take her."

Even though I'd been looking forward to a walk, I also knew what a struggle it was for him lately, so I handed him the leash.

"Sure, thanks." As I said this, I had to look slightly down at him. My brother, for his part, was surprised to find himself looking a bit upward at me. There can be something pitiful about a person's expression when they're caught off guard. I didn't want to see my brother like that.

"Thanks, Kaoru," he murmured and then fell silent.

I wanted him to say more but he didn't, he just reached down to put Sakura's leash around her neck.

Sakura, being shorter than everyone in the family, was used

to looking up at us all so she couldn't relate to Hajime's mild shock. She just wagged her tail madly, nipping affectionately at my brother's wrist as he attached the leash.

Where're we going today, Hajime-kun? Woof.

For the rest of his suspension, my brother didn't go for any more walks. And the mailbox remained as empty as ever.

Genkan

Something else happened while I was studying for my entrance exams. I learned about sex.

The girl I learned about it from was the student who always scored highest in my class, Tamaki Susukihara.

Whenever the test results were posted in the hall and I'd see her name—須々木原環—at the top of the list, I'd do a double take, wondering which characters were her last name and which were her first name. Everyone in our school year seemed to feel the same way.

"Genkan's number one again?" They'd roll their eyes.

They seemed to think that the "-hara" part of her name was superfluous and had given her the nickname "Genkan" by combining another reading for the last character of her family name (原) with another reading for the character for her first name (環).

But I thought she had a beautiful name.

Genkan (since that's what everybody else called her, I figured I'd go along with it too) was one of those kids who had returned from living abroad; her family had been in the United States. When she transferred to our junior high in the fall of our first year, the other students pretty much avoided her because of her Americanized mannerisms and labored Japanese, and she had a hard time following our classes in Japanese. Apparently, Genkan had been pretty angry with her parents for not putting her in an American school, but they wanted her to work hard and to fit in with other Japanese.

But it turned out Genkan had real guts.

Every day after school, she studied like hell. She read her elementary-school Japanese textbook to death and listened to recordings of her Japanese lessons over and over. At home she completely switched from speaking English to Japanese, and she studied Japanese history backward and forward.

Then, in a feat that seemed unimaginable to us, by the end of our first year, she had read *The Pillow Book*, *The Tale of Genji*, and, like, all the Japanese classics. She knew so much about Japanese history that even our social studies teacher was intimidated. Her name would appear every so often at the top of the test results around the same time that mine was starting to pop up there too—the two of us were becoming a threat to the nerd cohort.

For our third year at junior high, Genkan and I didn't have any classes together. But occasionally we'd pass each other in the hallway, and the sweet scent of perfume would waft by me, and I'd think, *Yup, she does seem like she lived somewhere else.* That was about it.

Then one day, as I was strolling out of school, listening to the Run-DMC tape I'd borrowed from my brother and casting a backward glance at my classmates studying their asses off in the library, I saw the bridge that was right by my junior high. Just on the other side of it was a park where I always took Sakura for walks. It was warm that day and I was feeling relaxed. I'd taken off the scarf that was always wrapped around my neck and decided to take a little detour through the park on my way home.

In the distance, a dog that resembled Sakura was sniffing the ground on its walk, while all around me leaves swirled from the trees, like they were inviting me to dance.

Thinking I'd buy myself a canned coffee, I was reaching into my pocket to make sure I had change when I heard a girl's dulcet voice: "Oww-ch!"

With a hundred-yen coin in my hand, I turned to look in the direction of the voice. A girl with long hair was crouched down, holding her ankle. Her hair was long enough to reach her waist, glossy and shiny, and right away I recognized Genkan—she thought the school rule "Hair past your shoulders must be tied back" was ridiculous.

Genkan was only about fifteen feet away; I was surprised that I hadn't noticed her walking behind me. It seemed like something was wrong, so I forgot about the canned coffee and headed toward her.

"Are you okay?"

I crouched down beside her and caught that sweet scent.

"It seems like I sprained my ankle," Genkan said in perfect, standard Tokyo dialect, because that was the Japanese she had studied so thoroughly.

In the hallways at school, where everyone spoke in Kansai dialect, Genkan's voice stood out for the beautiful way she spoke Japanese. I don't why, but it made my heart race.

From what I could see, Genkan's ankle wasn't red or turning purple, but she did have a beautifully colored woven anklet wrapped around it, which made her not-all-that-delicate ankle appear more slender. It occurred to me that Genkan might be applying herself to looking cute.

"You're Hasegawa-kun, right?" She looked up at me.

Just then, I gazed back at Genkan, looking her straight in the face for the first time. I'd never seen a girl's face so up close before, and I'd never had anyone stare at me like that before either.

Genkan's eyes were so "Japanese" in that they were what a foreigner would probably imagine as quintessentially Asian: mono-lidded, unassuming, and slanted toward her ears like a fox's. Her eyebrows, rather than left unkempt, were groomed and perfectly arched on her forehead, just like my mother's. Her lips glistened like she had just eaten something fried very quickly.

I was bewildered by these "feminine charms" that had suddenly been thrown my way, and I sputtered a little.

Genkan watched me cough with a kind, maternal gaze, and then she looked me in the eyes and asked, "Would you come home with me?"

It all happened very quickly, really.

Genkan's lips touching mine, our naked bodies entwined, the thing that didn't even compare to doing it alone—it was over in a flash.

Genkan was very grown-up in how boldly she went about it, giggling as she told me that she'd had me in her sights for a while, and today she had finally snared me.

I was really confused.

I'd never had anyone use my arm as a pillow before, and now, Genkan was pressed up tight against my side, her body as soft as Miki's had been the first time I saw her, and the sweet scent Genkan gave off now was different from her perfume.

Having her breasts, though modest in size, pressed up against me like that was enough to exert a certain pressure, and her legs, entangled with mine, seemed to tickle with a will of their own, and I couldn't hold back the excitement that this aroused. The thing that had happened was over in such a flash, and I wanted Genkan over and over, and when we were done again both of us lay there, limp and exhausted.

Genkan declared my body to be "wonderful" and then proceeded to tell me how much the sight of me walking appealed to her, how the kanji for my name (長谷川薫) made her smile, how when she happened to see me in the park she wanted to get naked with me. She had kept talking the whole time we were doing the thing, and hearing her voice that sounded like it came from far away had made Genkan seem like an unfamiliar being from a distant star.

There was a map of the world hanging on her wall and as I stared at it, I was struck with a sudden wanderlust.

My family was pretty liberal, but Genkan's parents were on another level. The next day, Genkan showed up at my classroom and said, "It's from my mom and dad," and handed me a small package. Genkan's unexpected appearance attracted everyone's curiosity, though I made out like it was no big deal and just took my seat. But when I looked inside the package, I couldn't keep a straight face. There were three condoms awkwardly stuffed inside.

The first thing that popped into my head was, "I can do it three more times."

Although I had no interest in dating Genkan, what can I say? I'm a guy.

The reason I may not have had any feelings for Genkan—

admittedly, my interest was not in her as a person but in her body—could have been that, because it had happened so quickly, my heart hadn't caught up with my body.

Nevertheless, before I even knew it, everyone considered Genkan and me an item. Always-number-one Genkan dating always-number-two me became kind of buzzworthy. There were still girls who made their cute confessions to me, and I know it sounds selfish, but each time I'd think, *Aw, man!* I also wondered if Genkan had set me up.

Genkan persisted in coming to my classroom regularly. Sometimes she'd bring me a bento lunch, other times she'd bring a favorite book. Instead of "Hasegawa-kun!" she started calling me "Kaoru!" She even rubbed my belly in front of everyone. "Kaoru, you'd better 'work out' more!"

The nerds were quick to look up this new phrase "work out" in their English dictionaries, but the kids who didn't care about studying saw her acting so casual with me and smirked, "Are those two doing it?"

Truth was, the guys who were still virgins often asked me to school them on sex. But I didn't have any specific advice to offer. Just like my brother, now that I had gotten a taste of sex, I was like a monkey, surrendering myself to pleasure—but when it came to technique, Genkan had been completely in charge. I was embarrassed to admit it, but all she had to do was move her body and that was it, I was done. And when she used her tongue, she got me worked up all over again. Those three condoms were used up in no time.

Genkan's parents seemed to know about her passion and the vigorous pace at which we used up those condoms, but neither Genkan's nor my grades were affected and, perhaps most importantly, they loved the gifts of food like cream puffs or yokan jelly dessert that I always brought with me, so they had no objections to our relationship. As my relationship with his daughter got more and more serious, sometimes Genkan's father would invite me to go fishing.

I got into the high school that I wanted. My homeroom teacher had really pushed me to try for a better school, but I wasn't looking for a hardcore high school experience. I wanted a more low-pressure environment.

The school I'd be going to was closer to the city than where we lived, but the campus had a kind of sleepy countryside vibe. There were uniforms, but everyone just wore the pants or the skirt and then got to wear whatever hoodie or shirt or blouse they liked. Girls had pierced ears and perms, but nobody was loud or rebellious; everybody was just doing their own thing, and the teachers didn't seem to give them a hard time.

My school may have been pretty permissive, but it was nothing compared to the school Genkan was going to. Our matriculation ceremonies were two days apart. For hers, Genkan got a bright red manicure and got her nose pierced too. She put on a dress that was the same vivid color as her nails and sashayed out the door.

"Don'tcha think that's a bit too much?" I had worried.

But when she came back, she said, "No way! I was the plainest one!"

As opposed to when we were in junior high, Genkan now seemed to enjoy surrounding herself with eccentric friends. She was in her element, taking to it like a fish to water, and she became more aggressive when she used her tongue on me. I was surprised when she started speaking to me in English when we were doing it, but I just thought, *Hey, well, nothing wrong with that*, and just kept right on going.

Whirlwind

"Hey, Hasegawa, introduce me to your sister."

This is what I heard most often from guys I knew during the time in between junior high and high school. I heard it so many times that it was like a broken record.

As soon as Miki entered junior high, she became the belle of the ball.

She rarely smiled, and her features had become more refined, taking on an imposing aloofness, like a hydroponic hyacinth or something. Her coolness was not unlike Yajima-san's, but Miki's beauty and destructive power were more overwhelming.

Everyone referred to me as "Hasegawa-kun's little brother," but had Miki and I ever overlapped at the same school, I probably would've been known as "Hasegawa-san's big brother" and there would've been even more requests to "introduce me to your sister."

With all the attention Miki got for her beauty, she would then gorgonize people with her massive attitude. The legendary brutishness that had gone hand in hand with her popularity in kindergarten was now even more deeply ingrained in her personality.

On her second day of junior high, Miki got called out by the older students. Here's a basic summary of what happened:

SAKURA

What first ticked off the older girls was that the scarlet ribbon on Miki's sailor uniform had a shorter bow than everyone else's, and her skirt was also inches shorter. In Miki's defense, she was inept at tying bows and had hiked up her skirt so that it'd be easier to move around in. The thought of trying to attract boys' notice had never entered her mind. If she could have gotten away with it, no doubt Miki would have peed standing up, farted up a storm, and gone to school without brushing her teeth and smelling like Sakura. Not much had changed since kindergarten.

So when the older girls started in on her—

"Hey, aren't you the little brat?"

"Who do you think you are with that skirt?"

—Miki wasn't the least bit threatened. "You have enough time in your busy schedules to call me out?"

Then, just as the older girls were about to retort, Miki spit at them and took off running. Stunned, the girls ran after her, shouting, "Wait up!"

They must have thought that four or five of them could beat her down and make her cry, but Miki's fighting prowess was something else.

Being good at fighting isn't just a matter of physical strength. Against your opponent, you also have to rely on the element of surprise. (Or so Miki told me.)

Demonstrating the top-notch and remarkably experienced technique she'd honed in kindergarten, first she used her innate ability to instantly sniff out which of them was the queen bee, then she picked up some rocks that were on the ground and threw them in a random direction and, while everyone's attention was distracted, she punched that girl in the face as hard as she could. It was enough to send the girl flying! Of course, Miki had used her fist.

While everyone stared with surprise at the splayed-out girl, Miki then kneed a girl who was close to her and left a shoe print on the back of another girl's uniform, before calmly walking away—entirely unscathed.

She left two girls untouched "so they could tell everyone else not to mess with me."

I looked back at Miki in wide-eyed amazement while she relayed all this, looking bored as she ate Happy Turn rice crackers.

When it came to attracting attention, Miki may have been Hajime's equal, but Miki differed from him in that she quickly drew people's ire. Back in kindergarten, her teachers had been the enemy, whereas now, she was pitting herself against the older girls.

Miki's policy (not that I knew whether she actually defined it as such) was never to shrink from a fight. No matter how cheap or how nasty they fought, be it unprompted or premeditated, Miki was always ready for action at the drop of a hat, fierce and powerful. But Miki's belligerence was not for sale; she was a passive aggressor, never one to start anything. In that regard, Miki was a very lazy girl.

You might have thought that Miki's bloody strife would have gone on forever, but it came to a sudden end. This happened on the historic day when, for the first time in her life, Miki was the one who started the fight.

Miki happened to be in the second-floor hallway, looking down at the courtyard. The rest of her class had gone to gym, but Miki was on her own, wandering around (if and when she forgot her gym clothes, she oddly took it as license to brazenly skip class). In the courtyard was the usual gang of delinquents, including the girls who had started that fight with Miki. I guess they should have known that it would come to bite them in the ass (although young people really are something—do they ever learn?). Those girls were skipping class, as usual, looking for a place to smoke cigarettes on this idle, early summer afternoon. But the calm of that moment was about to abruptly shatter. The sky started raining buckets, brooms, chairs, desks, and, finally, a girl. Imagine their surprise—those girls completely lost their shit. These items had come perilously close to landing right on top of them and the last thing to fall—their nemesis—was now sprawled on the ground nearby, where—despite clearly having broken some bones—she was scowling at them. Those girls, seized with panic and fearing for their lives, never started another fight. As for Miki, this inexplicable and, for that reason, terrifying exploit earned her forever-after legendary status.

Laid up at the hospital with her leg in a cast, Miki was lost in her own world, impervious to my mother's tears or my father's yelling or her teacher's lecturing. My brother and I may have loved our irrepressible sister, but this was one time when we simply couldn't fathom what had motivated her.

The one upside of all this was that, from then on, Miki didn't get into any more fights.

During this time, my brother and I often stayed up late talking in his room.

Hajime's room may have been the smallest one in the house, but it was the room I liked best. He had lots of soccer magazines and books, records and CDs, and though he didn't straighten up all that often and it was kind of a mess, everything in his room got plenty of use so there wasn't much chance for dust to accumulate.

It was from my brother that I learned about Earth, Wind &

Fire. I also borrowed Al Green and Run-DMC CDs from him. I was fascinated by the artists he introduced me to, and everything my brother talked about was interesting. For my part, I told Hajime all kinds of things: what happened at school, what I'd watched on TV that day, and of course, I talked about Sakura. Hasegawa family meetings were now few and far between, so I cherished the time I spent talking with my brother in his room.

Most of all, he seemed happy to welcome me into the world of grown-ups, as if it were happening to him all over again. I wasn't able to articulate my feelings for Genkan and Hajime wasn't one to pressure me about whatever things I was too shy to share.

But whenever we'd get to talking about guy stuff, about our urges, it was a given that Miki would come around. She'd fling the door open and ask, "Whatcha talking 'bout?"

Since coming home from the hospital, she never used her crutches, instead getting around by hopping on one foot. We'd hear, thump, thump, like a taiko drum, and Hajime and I would grin wryly at each other. Miki was just a whirlwind of a girl.

If my mother possessed all the warmth of the world, Miki seemed to swirl with all the winds of the world. From the moment she was born, she'd been the center of our attention—she had a peculiar ability, just by entering a room, to make everyone stop what they were doing, and that had only intensified with each passing year.

Sometimes she'd show up with Sakura in tow and we'd all squeeze into Hajime's cramped little room. Sakura would be so thrilled to be allowed into my brother's room, she'd practically pee all over the place. But she would contain herself, swinging her bottom around girlishly and licking our faces in turn.

What is it? What were you talking about? Sakura would say, foul-breathed.

"You stink!" we'd complain, but her fishy reek reminded us of the sea, and there was something comforting about it. That smell would transport us to a faraway beach, relaxed and at ease, until we'd hear my mother's voice shout from downstairs:

"So! Who's gonna vacuum?"

And we'd all look at each other and burst into laughter.

Kaoru-san

Once Miki's leg healed (with astonishing speed), she joined the basketball team. My mother was delighted to see that Miki had stopped getting into fights, and my father was relieved, knowing that she needed an outlet to dedicate herself to. Miki's late-February birthday meant that she was one of the youngest in her school year, and she had always been noticeably smaller than the other kids in her class, but her growth spurt seemed to know no bounds. Just as I was the beanpole in my class, Miki now stood in the back row when they gathered for morning assembly at school.

The basketball team was also the first time Miki considered the meaning of the word "friend." With her height and her uninhibited attitude on the court, unexpected for a beginner, she earned a regular spot on the team, which had never happened for a first-year student. Though Miki may have been the object of the other girls' jealousy and envy (and fear), girls seem able to cozy up to another girl even while experiencing those contradictory feelings. But such female instincts were completely beyond Miki's comprehension.

One of them might say, "Hasegawa-san, wanna get something to eat with us?"

And Miki would respond, "Huh? What for?"

Miki didn't mean any harm. She simply had no idea why they might want to have a meal together. And it followed that she wouldn't have any inkling that her response could offend someone. Which was why Miki had such a hard time making friends.

Certainly, Miki experienced loneliness, but she didn't seem to grasp that it had anything to do with how she diverged from other girls.

"Hasegawa, your sister's weird."

Next to "Introduce me to your sister," this was what I heard most often.

The truth was, I found Miki rather eccentric myself. Before, her response to any attack had been to counter with megaton-level destructive force, but since she had stopped fighting, she seemed indifferent to everything. Though she worked hard at basketball practice, she never got worked up about cute boys or tried to look or act pretty or any of the other sweet-and-sour things girls did to make themselves attractive. At recess she would just sit among the flower beds in the courtyard, staring up at the sky. She looked exactly like that old man my brother and I had met in Ding-Dong Park.

Even when boys started getting crushes on her and confessing their feelings, Miki would gaze back at them with that same daydreamy look in her eyes. Hardly anyone at school had ever seen Miki smile.

The girl with the same name as me arrived along with the thunderheads that appeared on the horizon, which settled in as if they owned the place.

Kaoru-san transferred during the summer of her second year at junior high. Even though she was two years younger than me, I couldn't bring myself to call her "Kaoru-chan." To me, Kaoru-san seemed endowed with a certain dignity, as if from a very young age she'd always been older than anyone else around her.

Also on the basketball team, this girl stood as tall as Miki, and was just as eccentric. Actually, "girl" did not seem like an appropriate descriptor for Kaoru-san. Her slightly stooped posture, her short haircut, her calf muscles that flexed as she walked, her taut, strong-willed, mono-lidded eyes—these all made quite an impression.

I'd seen her out and about several times and, seeing her expression as she sat drinking water under the trees in the park, the way she wiped the drops of water from her mouth with her sleeve, I felt like I was watching a very cool-looking guy.

In fact, there were enough girls who liked Kaoru-san that it frustrated other guys. Girls snuck into afterschool basketball practice just to watch her, and girls gave her chocolate on Valentine's Day. During cleanup, she would carry two desks at a time, and when a girl was lifting something heavy, as a matter of course she would offer to carry it. In the middle of second period, she would devour an enormous bento, and then at lunch, she'd buy a jumbo katsu sandwich and a jumbo yakisoba-pan—suffice it to say that she could wolf down anything that was jumbo-sized and still be hungry. As a result, people found her unapproachable, and she wasn't very sociable anyway so, naturally, she was often alone.

In other words, Kaoru-san and Miki were very much alike.

Kaoru-san was the first to make contact. She wasn't one to suck up to people, nor to brush anyone off; Kaoru-san just liked Miki's sheer immensity, and for Miki, it was refreshing to be treated without pretense by someone of the same sex, and she liked Kaoru-san's guileless personality, so the two of them started hanging out a lot.

These two Amazons walking side by side were kind of imposing—one a head-turning beauty, the other strikingly handsome. You couldn't help but notice them, and more than a few girls wanted to be friends with them.

The day that Kaoru-san came to our house, it caused almost as much of a commotion as the first time Yajima-san came over. She was, after all, Miki's first female friend. Once again Sakura got squeaky clean and, in place of that improbable fruit platter on the table, there was an arrangement of anemones and peonies. My brother put on a proper pair of jeans instead of the ratty Adidas tracksuit he always wore, and I futilely brushed my teeth over and over.

Kaoru-san showed up wearing a gray Champion parka and skinny black jeans that fit her tall and slender body to a tee.

"Hey there," Kaoru-san said offhandedly. For some reason, she had brought a large number of tawashi scrub brushes as a gift.

"My father makes them."

Sakura was the most delighted.

She'd never seen so many of her favorite tawashi all at once—the thought of the texture when she bit down on one, the unpredictable way it bounced when she dropped it on the ground, and how the rough fibers tickled her paw pads when she rolled it with her foreleg made her drool copiously. She practically swooned with happiness.

"What's your name?" Kaoru-san asked as Sakura ardently crammed a tawashi into her mouth, grunting and looking decidedly unfeminine.

"Go on, say hi, Sakura." Miki slapped her on the bottom, which snapped her out of her frenzy.

Ah, oh. How embarrassing, please forgive me. I'm Sakura Hasegawa. Woof.

Sakura wagged her tail affectionately at Kaoru-san.

Kaoru-san rubbed Sakura vigorously and with such a familiar ease that my brother asked, "Do you have a dog?"

Kaoru-san replied, "We only have four dogs."

She added, "We also have twelve cats, two squirrels, and four Java sparrows."

Kaoru-san was pretty wild.

She and Miki shut themselves up in Miki's room and, even when dinnertime came around, Kaoru-san still hadn't left. My mother brought them a fourth serving of apple pie and asked with concern, "Are you sure you shouldn't be home by now?"

"It's fine, but is it any trouble if I stay?" Kaoru-san responded with her own question.

"It's no trouble at all, but won't your parents worry?"

"No, they won't worry. I have so many sisters, they don't even notice who's there and who isn't," Kaoru-san said nonchalantly.

Miki, who was sitting cross-legged beside her, added the supplementary detail, "Kaoru-san's mother is blind."

Incidentally, the "many sisters" in her family numbered eight—a houseful of women.

"I'm the eighth one," Kaoru-san said.

All told, Kaoru-san polished off four of my mother's croquettes, two servings each of rice and miso soup, and another helping of apple pie before heading home around ten that night. Pretty late for a girl in her second year of junior high.

"Her parents really won't worry about her?" My mother fretted as if Kaoru-san were her own daughter.

"Nope," Miki replied flatly, as if talking about her own family.

"If you say so, but a girl walking home alone so late at night..."

"Kaoru-san'll be fine, she does karate."

My father interjected on my mother's behalf. "She may know karate, but she's still a junior high school girl..."

"She's a black belt."

Both my father and mother fell silent.

Kaoru-san was cool in every way.

World Class

"Seems like you're dating that fox-faced girl."

Miki said this during dinner, informing the rest of the family about my love life with Genkan. Kaoru-san sat in her usual seat at the table (at that time Kaoru-san ate with us almost every other day), her mouth full of rice from a third bowl that she'd helped herself to.

"Ah."

Disturbed to realize that this news had spread to Miki and her friend, I responded vaguely and with as much masculine equanimity as I could muster, but my mother's barrage of questions commenced anyway.

"Kaoru! Why didn't you tell us?"

"What's she like?"

"Why don't you have her over here?!"

When I didn't answer any of these questions (or rather, because my mother's barrage didn't allow room for any response), Miki and Kaoru-san started conversing matter-of-factly instead.

"She used to live abroad, right?"

"But she really does have a fox-face."

"She looks like she might start barking."

"Foxes don't really bark, do they?"

"Yeah, I dunno what they call it."

"Isn't it more like a yip?"

"They sound so sad."

"Was she in America?"

"Yeah, America."

"They're more advanced over there; you can get your driver's license at sixteen, right?"

"Yeah, much more advanced."

Miki and Kaoru-san never looked at each other when they talked; they didn't force any smiles either. The rest of us had gotten used to it, but at first this brusqueness had made us worry that the two of them were having a fight or something. Someone who didn't know them might doubt that they were actually close friends.

My father beamed as he listened to what the two of them had to say, delighted to know that his second son had a girlfriend—but he got a little impatient that there wasn't more information about Genkan other than "a fox-faced girl who had come back from America."

"What's her personality like?"

He opted for a very pointed question.

"I saw her saying 'Hi!' to Kaoru and giving him a high-five."

"And I heard her say, 'Shit!'"

Now my father was somewhat concerned by Miki and Kaoru-san's blatantly American characterization of Genkan.

"But, you like her, don't you, Kaoru? She must be a nice girl?" he asked.

To be honest, I still didn't know whether I liked Genkan or not.

My loins got hot whenever I saw her, but it seemed to me that was just my body remembering physical pleasure, more than feeling love for her. It wasn't like those warm and fuzzy thoughts I'd felt for Yukawa-san; this was different—more glaringly lewd, and seemed far removed from what you could call love.

"She's nice," I replied to my father's question, and left it at that.

Meanwhile, Yajima-san was still out of contact with my brother, the Hasegawa who was capable of world-class love. Given how kind she seemed, I found it hard to believe she'd had such a sudden change of heart. But my brother seemed ready to give up on her.

"Maybe she found someone else," he would seethe.

And yet he still regularly checked the mailbox, or if he saw Miki bringing in the newspaper or advertising circulars, he'd ask, "Is that all there is, Miki?"

Miki would respond, somewhat aggravatedly, "What else would there be?" and toss the paper on the table. It was basically the only time when there were any signs of tension between my brother and my sister. Miki seemed annoyed by the fact that Hajime couldn't get over Yajima-san, and Hajime resented that Miki didn't seem to mind if he brought other girls around but got moody at the mere mention of Yajima-san.

Hajime still took Sakura along on his long walks—her flanks became quite sleek, and whereas before she only ate a single can of food, now she gobbled down two.

I didn't join any clubs or teams in high school either. I had lost some weight, and since I now had such broad shoulders, at every recess there were still invitations to play various sports, but I preferred to just loaf around the house listening to music. My physical activity was limited to doing it with Genkan, and once school was over, I wasted time reading books in the library.

I got this trait from my father. My mother had always been well liked, with her beautiful features and cheerful personality, and she was sporty. She enjoyed being outside and active; even now, on the weekends, she'd go out and hit a tennis ball against a wall. She often fought with Hajime over whose turn it was to walk Sakura.

My father, on the other hand, was the handsome philosopher type, much more of an introvert. He was the kind of guy who liked the shadows. He'd rather stay home reading a book than go out, and he preferred the leisure of seeing movies at the theater to bar-hopping.

So, on weekends or holidays, it often happened that everyone else would be out and my father and I would be home, just the two of us. Not that we'd say much to each other, but we enjoyed relaxing together in the comfort of our own home and would smile whenever we'd catch one another's eye.

It was impossible to say whether Miki took after my mother or my father. When she was little, she had certainly been one to run wild through the fields, but that wasn't necessarily the case anymore. She was disciplined about basketball practice, and during games she played as aggressively as ever, but it seemed to me that this was more to fend off boredom than because she really loved it.

The only time she ever really smiled was when she was with Hajime. Even when Kaoru-san came over, the two of them didn't go anywhere; it seemed like they just sat around in her room doing nothing.

At school Miki was the same as ever—the only thing that had changed was now Kaoru-san was always with her. At recess, it was a given that she'd be hanging out in the courtyard, and if the boys tried to make time with her, she'd stare back at them with a dead look in her eyes.

Custard à la Mode

In early October, about three days after we had switched our school uniforms to the winter version, a male classmate asked me something curious:

"Hey, is your sister a lesbo?"

This kid—I've forgotten his name but he and I went to the same junior high. Back then he was totally average, he didn't stand out, but I guess he wanted to debut a new look for high school because suddenly his hair was stiff and shiny with some kind of gel and he acted all smug. He was the kind of guy you couldn't quite trust.

Taken aback by the way he clapped me on the shoulder like we were buddies, I couldn't really process the question, so I just stood there for a second. The spot where I was standing was directly in front of a kissaten called Yorimichi, and as the automatic door whooshed open, the older lady who worked there called from inside, "Come on in!"

I liked Yorimichi's custard à la mode. Other kissas served it with too much fruit and not enough custard, and what's more, they paired it with apple and orange and strawberries, fruits that don't go all that well with custard, which is a shame for custard-enthusiasts like me. But Yorimichi's custard à la mode was gracious: a custard the size of my fist arrived on a huge plate decorated with an obscene amount of fresh cream, as well as overripe bananas and canned peaches, which may not have been the most colorful accompaniments, but what made these fruits ideal to my taste was their utter lack of firmness. I frequented Yorimichi almost every other day.

The lady from the kissaten saw me standing there like an idiot in front of the open entryway and she called out merrily, "All right, one custard, coming up!"

But then, as the automatic door closed shut, having given up on me for not going inside, I heard her say, "Hasegawa-kun?"

Huh, so she knows my name, I thought in the back of my mind as that kid's question, "Is your sister a lesbo?" seeped into my body.

All I could manage to spit out was the word, "Why?" but it ended up sounding as if I were muttering this to myself.

Here's the story:

This kid's younger brother was in the same year as Miki and, like everyone else, had a crush on her. Actually, the brother had been in the same class with Miki for four years, starting back in elementary school but, whereas I couldn't remember the older brother's name, Miki didn't even recognize this kid's face, much less remember his name. Still, he was rather persistent—he'd confessed his feelings to Miki three times, but each time she'd just looked back at him blankly and shook her head, giving him the cold shoulder. And you'd think after three rejections that he'd have gotten the hint and given up, but the fact that Miki remained unattached inspired him to dare a foolish fourth try. The kid seemed to have the makings of a stalker—he steadfastly believed that the reason Miki was unattached was because she was waiting for him and, heedless of the fact that she didn't know his name let alone his face, he'd made the troubling demand, "Enough already—be my girlfriend, Hasegawa!"

Unsurprisingly, even Miki thought there was something odd about what he'd said.

"What do you mean, 'enough already'?" And, for the first time, she really looked this guy in the face.

Locking gaze with her almond-shaped eyes, the kid flipped out.

He must have said something like, "Haven't I told you exactly how I feel," or "You know how much I like you," or some other line. He must have thought he was being romantic. Only now did Miki realize that this was not actually the first time he'd confessed his feelings for her.

And who knows what Miki said—she might have asked, "How many times have you told me you like me?" or possibly even worse, "Just who are you, anyway?"

This kid's pride, tiny as a mouse's to begin with, was in tatters. And he must not have been very bright because the only way he knew how to deal with his emotions was to get angry. He did, however, have enough sense to know that he couldn't win against Miki using violence, so he played dirty: Using the facts that Miki had never had a boyfriend and that she and Kaoru-san were always together, he spread a rumor through the whole school that Miki Hasegawa was a "lesbo." What a creep! As further evidence of what a tool he was, he conveniently failed to include how many times he'd told her about his crush and how many times she'd rejected him, and of course nothing about how she didn't even remember what he looked like.

Though everyone at school was in awe of the inseparable Miki and Kaoru-san, they'd already been a bit skeptical about how neither of them had ever had a boyfriend and the way the two of them seemed like they were more than just friends. Now add to that a lesbian suspicion. For all the guys Miki had unswervingly rejected as well as those girls she had beaten up on her second day of school, this was the perfect spark, and the rumor spread like wildfire.

Some kids were even crude enough to say, "Good thing they can't have kids!"

Nevertheless, this had no effect on Miki's or Kaoru-san's behavior. Instead of disputing the rumor, their attitude was like "So what if we are?" and they spent even more time together—Kaoru-san was at our house as much as ever. This, however, only gave more life to the rumor.

Miki had swiftly gone from being the object of everyone's admiration to being the subject of cruel gossip. Whereas before others had been cowed by her remarkable aura and would cede the way for her in the hallways, now they avoided her with downcast looks. If they happened to meet her gaze, even the girls couldn't help but admire the Venetian-glass-like beauty of her eyes, but they tried to only give her sidelong glances.

But Miki and Kaoru-san carried on as usual. Kaoru-san came over to our house practically every day and they would shut themselves up in Miki's room.

"What could they be doing in there all this time?" my mother would wonder.

Usually I'd simply shrug off whatever my mother said, but now I started to overreact. Even though I knew it didn't matter what was going on between them, and that I should just leave them alone, I'd knock on Miki's door with any excuse to peek inside, like bringing them snacks or borrowing a book. I couldn't talk to my brother about the rumors at school, and obviously I couldn't say anything to my mother and father either.

Occasionally my mother would ask Miki and Kaoru-san, "Are there any cute boys at school?"

Without giving it a moment's thought, they would both answer in unison, "Nope."

My mother looked disappointed but my heart would be pounding, knowing what was going on at school. Sometimes Miki would catch me stealing a glance at her and Kaoru-san and she'd demand, "What is it?"

Fainthearted and unable to broach the real subject, I'd mumble, "Nothing," and scarf down my croquette or hamburger.

I stopped going to Yorimichi. The custard à la mode I'd been so enamored with no longer held any appeal. Because the spot in front of it was where I'd first heard about the rumor, custard à la mode was now inextricably linked in my mind with Miki's love. When I thought about Miki, my mouth would fill with the taste of those gooey peaches, brown bananas, and that pungent eggy custard, and I'd feel nauseous. Even the sight of the dessert's plastic replica out front made me think of Miki, and my heart would ache.

The Letter

"You're feeling down, aren't you, Kaoru?"

This came from Genkan, whom I used to see almost every day but now, maybe because things had been so busy since starting high school, we only saw each other for two or three hours on the weekend. Since there always seemed to be what Genkan referred to as a "party" happening somewhere, I just killed time until she was free. Considering how much crazy sex we'd been having, there was a significant decrease in that too, and as a sixteen-year-old guy, I'd be lying if I didn't say that was a drag—but since I still hadn't explicitly told Genkan that I loved her, I was too chickenshit to say anything about wanting more. So I restrained myself.

Now that Genkan was in high school, she seemed to have taken on an even more mature demeanor, and it wasn't just the earrings that dangled from her ears or the glossy lipstick she wore. She appeared to radiate a womanly air—in the way she'd hold my gaze or her skeptical expression when she heard an unfamiliar phrase in Japanese—which I found unnerving.

What Genkan referred to as "parties" were these supposedly fun and exciting gatherings of "aspiring painters" or "aspiring models" or "aspiring photographers"—always "aspiring" somethings—where, according to Genkan, everyone was "amazingly talented!"

In other words, a bunch of creative types getting together. Which is really not my kind of scene. I mean, I wouldn't have gone even if she invited me, but Genkan never did invite me—not once!—which kind of made me feel like crap.

Anyway, I wasn't quite sure what kind of people Genkan meant by creative types, but I had a feeling they were liberal-minded folks, so I figured it might be worth asking her advice about Miki. Without using her name, of course.

"Hey, Genkan."

"Come on! Didn't I tell you to call me Tammy?"

Since Genkan's actual name was Tamaki, apparently she was going by Tammy now. She painted her eyes with thick black eyeliner to make them appear bigger, but they were still Genkan's same narrow eyes and no matter how they looked, they still belonged to someone named Tamaki Susukihara. Calling her Tammy just didn't feel right.

"So, um . . ."

"What is it?"

"Have you ever had feelings for another girl?"

"Huh?"

My bizarre and out-of-the-blue question caught Genkan, aka Tammy, by surprise. She looked the way she might if some random person came up to her on the street and said, "Yo!"

"What? Where did that come from . . . ?"

Thinking back on it now, her response was totally reasonable; however, I was determined to force my way through with this conversation.

"No, I mean . . . when you were in junior high, Genkan"—here

"Tammy" pinched my arm—"did you ever, uh, like a girl who was a grade or two ahead of you?"

"By 'like,' do you mean 'love'?"

"Yeah, love, or something like that."

"Not just as friends?"

"Right. Liking a girl the way you like a boy."

"I haven't."

My shoulders drooped, thwarted by her flat rebuff.

"Why?" This was also a perfectly natural follow-up question, but at this point I had already lost the momentum to ask Genkan for advice about Miki, so I tried to change the subject.

"No, well, just that I heard Mick Jagger had a gay experience when he was in junior high."

Genkan didn't respond.

"No, I guess that doesn't really have anything to do with it."

She was still silent.

"Sorry."

Genkan stared at my face for a moment and then waved her right hand around in the air in exasperation. It seemed just like something an American girl would do, and the extremely natural way that Genkan did it drove me a little wild.

There was a hint of winter already in the air. The sun seemed to be looking down on us from a great distance and every so often Genkan, who was wearing her hair up, pressed her arm up against me like she was cold.

"Here's what I think," Genkan said suddenly after falling silent, and it was my turn to look as if some random person had come up to me on the street and said, "Yo!"

"Doesn't that kind of love seem really complicated?"

Genkan's hair was so thick and heavy it didn't even flutter in the breeze. But occasionally there would be an unexpected gust and instead of her hair, her skirt or my shirt would rustle gently.

"First of all, there's the public attention. We can wish all we like that we lived in a society without discrimination or prejudice, but there are things that people will always whisper about, the same way you lowered your voice when you asked me that question just now. They say it's a free country, but in America a lot of gay people are victims of violence and even murder. Here in Japan, I can only imagine what it's like. When I came back here, I realized how unpopular it is to stand out. Anyone who's different gets rejected. But not in an overt way—instead it's more subtle, everyone talks under their breath about it, they band together and put a lid on it. They pretend not to see it."

I remembered how when Genkan had transferred to our school, everyone had kept their distance from her. Though that seemed mild compared to what Miki was dealing with now.

The hand that Genkan had whirled in the air before was now wrapped around mine.

"When you're in love with someone, you want to show that love no matter where you are, right? Holding hands like the way we are now, or hugging and kissing. But Japanese people get uncomfortable even when it's a boy and girl, don't they? Imagine how much more courage it would take for two girls to do that. Then there's the matter of sex. I don't really believe in platonic love. Making love is more instinctive, you know? Plus, I like sex with guys."

I had been taken aback by how intense Genkan's expression was as she talked, but now she smiled impishly and glanced at my trousers.

"For now, at least."

I was startled to hear her say "for now." Not only that, but it had also never even occurred to me that she had enjoyed sex with anyone other than myself. Whenever we did it, Genkan's entire body always made me feel adored—she poured her whole heart into it. And now I saw that I had been complacent about her feelings for me. The notion that at some point those feelings might be directed toward someone else caught me completely off guard. It made my heart ache. This pain was different from the complete helplessness I felt when I thought about Miki's situation—this version seemed to well up from within my whole being, a paralyzing fear that threatened to pin me down under the dull weight of it. It was the first time in my life I experienced jealousy.

"Genkan." I had blurted the name without thinking and she stared at me.

I kissed her on the mouth, not giving her the chance to get mad at me for not calling her Tammy.

My hands were clammy with sweat, but I couldn't help myself from putting them on her shoulders. Maybe because she wasn't wearing any lip balm that day, her lips were a little chapped, and their touch reminded me of Yukawa-san.

I had really wanted to touch Yukawa-san.

I had wanted to touch her soft hair that got tousled by the wind or to touch her fingertips, calloused from playing the trombone. I had really loved Yukawa-san. Why hadn't I been able to tell her that?

When that poor girl had asked me anxiously, "Don't you recognize me?" why hadn't I been able to say, "Of course, you're Yukawa-san." Regardless of what her skin looked like, she was still the Yukawa-san I loved.

How small was I?

The girl I was kissing right then and there, whose body I knew so well—I was terrified of losing her. It felt as though Genkan were slipping away from me. Even though I had been unable to love her, in my heart at that moment, I wanted her more than anything.

When our lips finally parted, Genkan asked me, "Do you really love me?"

Her words sparked something that had been smoldering inside me for so long.

Dear Yukawa-san,
How are you?
It's been a long time since we last saw each other.
Are you still in band? The one at my high school seems like it's pretty famous. They performed at a prefectural competition and did really well, and I think they've been on TV too. But their trombone player is a guy, which must mean you're pretty strong if you can play an instrument like that.
I'm still not in any clubs or teams. Back in junior high, I just thought it was too much trouble, but now it's different. Now I'm fat. I've been gaining weight since about the time I last saw you and now I'm over 440 pounds. Also, since getting fat, I get pimples too. When you saw me I only had a few on my forehead but now they're all over my face. It's like one pimple gangs up with another, and then they make more—it's awful. I wipe my face constantly, but it just gets sweaty and oily again and they don't go away. I went to see a famous dermatologist and I keep washing my face, but it's no good.
I forgot to mention that I'm writing this letter from the

hospital. My legs were hurting me. The doctor said that maybe it's because they can't support my weight. They're swollen and purple—they look like some weird animal's legs.

Do you have a boyfriend? You're so smart and pretty; if you don't yet, I'm sure you'll have one soon. I bet they all like you. I'm hopeless. I've never had a girlfriend, the girls don't even talk to me.

I always loved you. Ever since elementary school, back when you only wore glasses during class, I've only ever loved you. That day when we last saw each other, I was too nervous to say anything, I loved you too much. You're so beautiful. Someone like me doesn't deserve you, and so I couldn't tell you how I really felt.

We'll never see each other again. I don't want you to see me this way. If you did, I'm sure you'd be disappointed. You'd look at me like I was a monster, and I wouldn't be able to take it.

I'll always love you, and only you. I hope you have a happy life.

Goodbye,
Kaoru

The envelope that I put in the mail had no address written on it.

Look-Alike

My brother was going to be living in a dorm at university.

On the day that he left home, Miki wouldn't come out of her room.

"Be sure to listen to what the dorm mother says!" My mother slapped him on the back, speaking louder than usual, but her voice was drowned out by a sudden gust of spring wind.

My father and I both wished him good luck or said some other vague thing to him, then moped around.

My brother said, loud enough so that Miki could hear from her room, "The dorm's close by, I'll be back soon!" and then he laughed.

Sakura, unusually restless, paced back and forth between Hajime's legs and mine.

What's going on? What is it? Where you going?

My brother crouched down and put his arms around Sakura's head. Pleased by the embrace, Sakura wagged her tail in sync with the sound of Hajime's heart, then licked his cheeks and ears. My brother laughed like it tickled, but then a sudden and slightly sad look came over his face and he said, "Take care, Sakura."

After dinner one night, about a week before Hajime left home, Miki and I had hung out in Hajime's room for longer than we ever had.

My mother made some hot cocoa for us and, without any of us saying a word, we gathered in my brother's room. When we showed up there, he looked up and smiled, then turned down the volume a little on his stereo. Listening to music in Hajime's room, like Al Green's sad and husky voice or Stevie Wonder's clear and resonant singing, somehow made us feel grown up.

"Remember, when we were watching TV the other day?"

A milk skin would quickly form on our hot cocoa. I never liked it so I always got rid of it, but my brother would say, "It's full of nutrients," and he would gulp it down.

That day, I took my skin and offered it to him, but he just kept right on talking.

"And we saw that Michael Jackson look-alike."

"Did he look just like him?"

"Well, I don't know how much he actually looks like him. Seemed like he'd had plastic surgery, you know?"

"Could he sing and dance like him?"

"Well, sort of, I guess."

"You know, some look-alikes look nothing like the person they're imitating."

"I know, like Stevie Wonder's look-alike—he was wearing sunglasses, but if you look closely, he's Indian."

"Ha ha, what's up with that?"

"Right? And did you know that Stevie really can see?"

"You just made that up!"

"That's the rumor."

"How can that be?"

"At concerts, you know how girls bring him flowers? He always gets them from the prettiest girl."

"That sounds like a complete load of crap!"

"And then, one time, he was staying at a hotel in Japan, and the bellboy was carrying his bags to the room."

"Yeah?"

"And he like pointed and said, you can put those over there."

"Ha ha ha."

"And, he was reading a newspaper."

"Yeah, right!"

"Ha ha."

Miki looked pretty bored as she listened to these stupid stories. She had her mood swings when she acted like she was angry about something or other; and yet, she stayed there with us, without making any move to go to her own room. It seemed important enough to her to be able to spend time with Hajime.

"What's the dorm like?"

Miki had cat tongue—she couldn't tolerate hot food or drink—so she never drank the cocoa when it was hot. Which meant that there was always a major skin on her mug. I had ended up wrapping the one that I had offered to Hajime in a tissue and throwing it in the trash.

"Huh? Oh, for freshmen it's two to a room."

"How big is the room?"

"Like eight tatami mats, I guess? No, maybe not that big, more like six?"

"Tight!"

"And with two guys?"

"Yeah."

"Gonna be filthy."

"For sure."

When I was little, it was unimaginable to me that someone from our family would ever leave our home and go to live someplace else. Whatever happened, I thought we'd be cramming ourselves into my brother's four-and-a-half-mat room or bouncing on my parents' king-size bed. There would always be five potential dog walkers for Sakura, and sometimes we'd scramble for the leash. At night we'd each take our turn in the bath, and my mother would take the last bath and I'd hear her singing loudly as she cleaned the tub. That's what I thought. The idea of my brother not being home anymore made us feel edgy and restless, but at the same time there was also a strange sense of security, like he was still connected to us by an invisible umbilical cord. So long as Hajime was smiling, it felt like we'd all be okay, but once his smile wasn't going to be around for us to see close-up, it seemed as though our own might be reduced by half.

"Hajime, think you'll be as popular in the dorm?"

Miki hadn't even touched her hot cocoa. Sometimes I wondered if maybe she actually hated it, but I'd seen her glug it down once it was completely cold.

My brother, unaware of what was going on at Miki's school and what they were calling her, gave a carefree laugh.

"Do you remember Sakiko-san?"

"Yeah, sure."

"She was interesting, right? There was something mysterious about her."

"Yeah, she was mysterious."

"And that Marilyn Monroe impersonator was outrageous, right?"

"Outrageous!"

"Actually, I saw Sakiko-san one more time after that."

"Huh? You mean at the funeral?"

"Oh, right. In that case, I saw her twice. Once more after the funeral."

"What for?"

"You're gonna laugh. I went to her for advice about Yajima-san."

My brother smiled shyly as he looked over at Miki. She was flipping randomly through the pages of one of his soccer magazines, despite not having the least bit of interest in soccer.

"I told Sakiko-san that the girl I loved had stopped responding to my calls and letters. I went to see her before the bar opened. Sakiko-san had on another incredible dress, you know, like before, and there I was in my school uniform, asking for advice about love. It could have been a comedy sketch."

"Ha ha, totally."

"She said, 'If you really love her that much, go see her. I'll tell your mom and dad.' You know how I ran off while I was on my school trip? I told Sakiko-san about that and she said, 'Go by yourself, with your own money and your own steam. If you go on your own, without anyone else's help, and if she still won't see you, then you have to give up. But then you'll know that it's God's will.'"

"Were you able to see her?"

"I didn't see her 'cause I couldn't leave home. Everything was ready—I had bought a ticket, packed a bag. But I didn't go."

"Why not?"

My brother smiled wryly and pointed at Miki's leg.

"Ah, because Miki was in the hospital?"

"Bingo. Remember how crazy things were at home? Ha ha, with Mom crying and Dad so angry? When I saw what a mess things were, I just lost my motivation. You know how I am, I can be hell-bent on something, right? But when it comes to

Yajima-san, I don't know what it is, but I get scared. Yeah. I was scared. When I'd finally got up the courage, just as I was about to do something about it, there was all that commotion and my defenses just sort of slipped away. It was like, whoosh, I was empty inside, and it was over."

I wondered if what he was describing was similar to how I felt when I wrote that letter to Yukawa-san, that moment when Genkan's words had sparked something inside of me.

Regardless of whether Miki had known that breaking her leg had been the decisive factor in this story, at some point while my brother was talking, she had gotten the pages of the magazine sticky with cocoa.

"Oh, hey!"

But Miki completely ignored his panicked cry. Hajime and I exchanged glances, knowing better than to give her a hard time, and smiled back at each other.

Just then, we heard the sound of Sakura coming out of her doghouse and heading out into the yard. Her paws clicked as they padded along on the ground. Sakura was well trained—every night she would always come out to pee in the yard before going to sleep. Sometimes Miki would torment her upon hearing this signal by dashing out into the yard and staring at Sakura while she bashfully squatted to do her business.

We were silent for a moment; we thought it was adorable the way that Sakura thought she was peeing so stealthily without knowing that we were totally aware. In spring, the night sky can sometimes appear a strange color. That night, the sky was tinged pink. The darkness was hazy, which surely meant it would rain the next day, and I wondered if it would be a fine, gentle mist like on the day we moved.

"Lie to them with love."

It was surprising, when Sakiko-san had said that to us, how much she reminded me of my mother.

Lately, my father hadn't been going to Sakiko-san's bar. Not that he would say so or show even a hint of it, but there was no question that my brother going to a private university and living on his own, even if it was in a dorm, would be quite a strain on him. My father now worked overtime more often, while my mother spent extra time poring over the household account book. Even so, our table was always spread with sumptuous and delicious meals, and the family portrait taken in the yard featured all of us (with the exception of Sakura) smiling as broadly as ever. There I had been, standing behind Miki, who was holding Sakura. As on that day, something big and round still enveloped us.

"Michael."

"Huh?"

"What we were talking about before. The Michael Jackson look-alike."

"What about him?"

"What do you think it's like to be someone's look-alike?"

I had been getting drowsy, but my brother's question brought me back to the present.

"How do you mean?"

"Like, it's clear that he had plastic surgery. In order to look even more like Michael Jackson."

"Yeah."

"So what's he thinking?"

"I still don't know what you mean."

"Okay, how do I put this? That guy wants to be Michael in every way, right? He wants people to love him as Michael, he wants to live his life as Michael, you know?"

There were times when my brother showed a kind of eccentric side. He would make a surprisingly big deal about something nobody else even noticed, and then he would become fixated on finding out the answer to it. It was the same fervor that Miki had shown when learning about the marvel of sex from my mother.

I never knew the right way to respond to my brother's questions of this nature. Most of the time, I just answered with some sort of vague acknowledgment. It was the same with Genkan, who would get angry when she'd ask, "What do you think, does this hairstyle look good on me?" No matter how pissed off she'd get at me, I just didn't have a strong opinion about it. So when Hajime asked me this sort of question, I'd always deflect to Miki.

"Miki, what do you think?"

Although she seemed not to have been paying the slightest bit of attention to our conversation, she finally drank down the rest of her cocoa and looked in our direction.

"That's the way it is for everyone."

"For everyone?"

"Everyone is just being who they are, aren't they?"

"Who they are?"

Miki always used her finger to scoop out the cocoa that collected at the bottom of her mug. The dregs stuck to her finger were a mucky brown but, when she brought them to her mouth, they looked like the most delicious thing you'd ever seen. Miki's lips were glossy and looked ready to burst.

"When he's being the Michael look-alike, isn't he just being himself? And isn't he still being himself when he isn't imitating Michael?"

The way Miki talked was like that old man my brother and

I had seen in Ding-Dong Park. She spoke slowly and as if she were talking to herself. And just like we had done that day, the two of us both cocked our heads and pondered the meaning of what she said. But without even cracking a smile, Miki just went right on talking.

"What's that about? I don't think there's anyone who lives their life thinking, *I'm gonna be one-hundred percent myself, one hundred percent of the time!* Not even Sakiko-san, not even Michael Jackson. They spend their life thinking, *This isn't me, this isn't how I'm supposed to be*, so they imitate someone else, or they hide behind makeup."

There was steam rising from the trash can. The skin that I had wrapped in a tissue and thrown away still retained some of its heat.

"But in the end, that's still who you are."

"What you're saying is pretty complicated, Miki."

My brother looked directly at Miki as he said this, seeming truly impressed. The first-born child of the Hasegawa family couldn't comprehend the concept of "a self that wasn't me" or "not how I'm supposed to be." Hajime always lived to the fullest; he never lied to himself. When something saddened him, he experienced that sadness with his whole being, and when something made him happy, he felt that joy in every cell of his body. He had loved Yajima-san to the fullest, and he was ashamed for wavering about it. Then he had been ready to fight for her with renewed vigor, but when that strength was lost, that may have been what put an end to my brother's love.

"There's steam."

"Huh?"

"There's steam coming out of there." Miki was staring dumbly at the trash can.

"Oh, so there is."

Miki had a way of making everything she said, no matter what in the world it was, seem so trifling. Whether it was Miki's love, or my brother's love, or my love, it was all the same, just like the steam coming off the cocoa skin, there to be taken for granted.

Did Miki feel shame? Could it be that a girl like her was unable to talk to anyone about it? And had she given up on it, believing that it was just another trivial part of what happened in our day to day?

There was a change taking place within Miki. For the first time, I sensed that womanly scent. I detected the wistful scent of a woman who was in love and about to confess it to someone. Right at that moment, when one of us was on the verge of leaving our home for the first time, I was keenly aware of how time had passed. Time would change a violent little girl, and me always trailing behind my brother, into something complicated and unruly. There was still something round and warm that enveloped our home, and yet someone's uncontainable sadness was already beginning to make itself known in a big way.

"But, in the end, is that yourself too?"

My brother left home the next day. It didn't rain.

Alien

My brother's accident happened that summer.

He had been back home for about a week for summer vacation.

The clock in his room had stopped, the hands showing 4:55, so he had gone to the konbini to buy batteries. Normally he would have taken Sakura along for the walk, but it was late at night and it was raining, so he decided to take an umbrella and go on his bicycle.

"Does it really matter if the clock isn't working right now?" asked Miki, who was with him in his room.

"No, but I could use some fresh air," my brother said, and he headed out.

At the time, things weren't going well with his new girlfriend. He had started a new life, but he still sometimes got caught up in the past. Coming home to his old room brought back memories of Yajima-san, so it was possible that he might have needed a mental break.

My mother and father were sound asleep in their king-size bed, and Sakura was snoring happily in her doghouse.

It was pretty hot that night.

With Miki and me left in Hajime's room, the two of us didn't have much to talk about, so we flipped through his soccer magazines and just chilled on the bed to pass the time. Miki kept yawning widely but I knew there was no chance she would go to bed until Hajime got back.

The konbini was only about three minutes away by bicycle, yet my brother was taking a long time to return.

"Doesn't it seem late?" Miki said, bored.

"He could be reading a magazine or something," I said, taking the skin off my hot cocoa again.

"I don't know how you can drink something like that when it's hot out."

Despite being slender, Miki was often bothered by the heat and in summer she slept naked. Obviously by the time she'd started junior high she was no longer lounging around the house without any clothes on, but the tank tops and shorts she always wore consisted of very little material.

"Cocoa tastes better when it's hot."

"Really?"

"Doesn't it taste chalky when it's cold?"

"Oh, yeah, I guess it does."

We could hear Sakura outside, emerging from her doghouse and rustling around. That sound, mixed in with the splattering of the rain, made us drowsy.

"Sakura's peeing," Miki laughed, with a sleepy look on her face. "Psssss."

My face was hot from drinking the cocoa, so I brought it up close to the fan and then I joined in with her: "Psssss."

The fan made my voice choppy; it echoed and sounded like I was speaking a language from another planet.

"Pss, pss, pss, pss, pss."

"Kaoru-san's house."

Miki suddenly uttering Kaoru-san's name startled me, as if someone had suddenly called my own name.

Kaoru-san hadn't been over to our house for about a week. It may have been that she'd quit the team and was studying for entrance exams, but I had the feeling those weren't the only reasons why she wasn't coming around.

"It totally reeks of pee over there."

"Oh, because of all the dogs and cats?"

"Yeah. None of them are trained, so they just go all over the place."

"Just like you."

Annoyed, Miki tried to spit into my hot cocoa. I hastily moved my mug away and it just barely missed, landing with a plop on the floor instead. Miki's spittle, bubbling with foam, was white and viscous and it didn't immediately soak into my brother's floor. She laughed as she used the hem of her tank top to wipe it up.

This image of Miki—laughing as she wiped away her saliva, unconcerned about dirtying her clothes—was just like the one I remembered from when she was little. The stubborn and rambunctious girl who wore rubber boots even on sunny days and who sometimes peppered you with rapid-fire explanations.

But there was no mistaking that, over the past year, Miki had gone through a major change. When she was little, she used to wail at the top of her lungs, sounding like she was laughing—but she never kept any secrets from us, and she never brooded over things.

She still gazed into your face with upturned eyes, the way she always had, but her pupils were as big and black as ever and dark as midnight, like they were reflecting the light of the whole world.

The sound of the rain had gotten more intense.

What had been an innocuous splatter was now a bit aggressive—it sounded like it was knocking hard on the roof of the doghouse, and timid little Sakura kept peering up at the ceiling.

I felt like maybe now was the time to ask Miki.

Sakura was so sweet, she must have been worrying about Hajime not coming home and this terrible rain that might wash away all the little stars. As proof of this, every so often I could hear Sakura's tail whack anxiously against the wall of her doghouse.

"Miki."

"Wh-, wh-, wh-, wh-, wh-, at, at, at, at, at?"

This time Miki had brought her face close to the fan and started speaking the unknown alien language. If mine was the language of a red-hot, rugged, and rocky planet, Miki's sounded like the language of a planet where cool, clear water flowed and the most beautiful flowers and trees, the likes of which you've never seen, grew in lush abundance.

"Do you have feelings for Kaoru-san?"

The only sound was the whirring of the fan. Two summers later, Miki would break one of the blades on this fan and it would go out with the garbage, but at that time it was still working fine and keeping us cool.

"Why do you ask?"

Miki's voice didn't waver at all, though the language of the planet of water and flowers and trees was gone. Instead, now her voice sounded much drier, as if it were being wrung from deep in her throat.

"Why'd you ask me that?"

I wished my brother would hurry up and come home. Miki didn't say any more; she went back to flipping through the magazine pages, while I just stared absently at the characters on the fan—"High" and "medium" and "low." Its gust may have been too strong for the two of us there and then. My hot cocoa had formed another skin.

"It's full of nutrients."

I remembered what my brother had said, and figured I'd try it for myself.

I will never be able to forget the sound of the rain that night or the slimy feel of the milk skin as it slid down my throat. It had left an outsize impression in my throat and unfortunately gotten stuck deep in there. I felt like it was trying to obstruct my breathing and, no matter how many times I tried to clear my throat, it would not make its way to my stomach. The rain beat against the window even more fiercely and Miki, tired of counting the rhythm of the rain, rolled over and sprawled on her back.

The phone rang.

Miki and I looked at each other.

That night Sakura let out the biggest and loudest howl, as if all the wolves of the world had gathered to warn of danger.

When the police called, for some reason the first thing I did was look at the clock, but stupidly of course it still read 4:55. At that moment, the batteries that my brother had bought were lying, scattered and crushed, a two- or three-minute walk from our house.

A taxi driving at breakneck speed on that rainy night robbed my brother of the use of the muscles in the lower half of his body and on the right side of his face.

My brother was unconscious for a week, during which time he said, "I saw our dead Granny" and "a big, flowing river." Upon waking up, he asked, "Wh-what about my legs?"

When my mother saw my brother come to, she burst out sobbing but, other than his name, it wasn't clear what she was saying. I still felt like I had the milk skin lodged deep in my throat, still preventing me from breathing properly.

The right side of my brother's face was so dark it appeared to have been dipped in tar, and the area around his eye strangely looked like the image of a black hole I'd seen in one of those old, illustrated reference books. Almost all you could see of his right eye was his pupil, which gleamed like a piece of candy and looked more like Sakura's eye. His squashed nose seemed to have forgotten how to stay upright on his face, and his lips curled up like when he might have laughed out loud.

The one who first handed him a mirror was Miki.

"You're in for a surprise."

He couldn't move the right side of his face but, when he saw what he looked like, the left side that could still move froze in place.

"Wh-what is this?"

His voice faltered, as if he were speaking for the first time in his life. Outside the window, autumn had arrived.

Bothersome

After my brother started using a wheelchair, he seemed to find just about everything bothersome. When he had to go to the bathroom, he'd hold it until the very last minute, or if a magazine was just beyond his reach, he'd give up on trying to get to it. Often he'd just sit there, holding a soccer ball and staring off into space. But most of all, he completely slacked off on the thing that he had always done best—saying funny things to make us all laugh.

Our house was halfway up a hill, which was difficult for my brother to navigate. His legs had always been like those of a prizewinning thoroughbred, but ever since he'd broken his arm in elementary school, he had neglected to exercise the muscles in his arms. He managed to get around well enough where the ground was flat, but he had a hard time keeping the wheels from sliding backward on a hill. Hajime spent more time than ever in his room. Before the accident, there hadn't been a chance for dust to accumulate in his room because he was always using his stuff, but since he didn't really do anything anymore, the room had started to get dirty.

Seeing my brother's face now, anyone might easily forget what he used to look like, but the one for whom nothing had changed was Sakura. Even though she hadn't seen him for a couple of months, when Hajime came home in a wheelchair, at first she looked at him with a slightly puzzled expression, but then she was back to her usual self.

Welcome home, Hajime-kun! It's been quite a while! What's this shiny silver chair? It's cool!

Sakura was so excited to see my brother, she naughtily leapt up onto his lap, and when he said, "Oh . . . I can't feel . . . her weight," and started crying, Sakura promptly licked his face. Then when he still didn't stop crying, she brought over her treasured green tawashi (more heavy-duty than the regular scrub brushes, this one bounced even more than the others).

It was the first time Hajime had ever cried so much in front of us.

I remember very little from the months after my brother's accident and before he came home from the hospital. Even Miki, with her amazing powers of memory, says that time is hazy for her too.

It seems to me that at night, while we're sleeping, we organize the memories of what we've seen while we're awake. These images ought to be remembered, those images can be deleted, something like that. Our dreams offer proof of this: Extreme insomniacs hallucinate because being awake for so long robs them of their ability to put their memories in order. The reason neither Miki nor I remember much from when Hajime was in the hospital is because our brains unconsciously tried to erase our memories from that time. We may have slept every night, but those nights were dreamless, as our brains were working overtime to clear away the sight of Hajime crying in his bed, of him throwing a vase of flowers at us, of his urine-stained sheets. Instead, what I do remember is this: the bright pinks and yellows of the flowers that my mother decorated my brother's hospital room with; the way that Sakura would wag her tail madly as she ran to greet us when we returned from visiting Hajime in the hospital; and how the wind that blew in from somewhere would teasingly caress our heads.

Oddly, though, there weren't any sounds attached to those memories. When I try to recall that time, it feels as though I'm submerged under water or there's a lid tightly clamped over my ears. As if everything is devoid of sound, and there's only a rattling noise like an old 8mm film, going round and round. Then, when I stop trying to remember, suddenly the sound of the present blares at full volume. The rush of a car racing past, my mother's voice talking to someone on the phone, Sakura knocking over a flowerpot—these sounds seem loud enough to burst my eardrums. This strange phenomenon has repeatedly stopped me in my tracks. There've been times when I have been frightened by the sound of girls' voices calling out to each other in gym class, or the teacher's voice during class, or my classmates laughing.

Miki would playfully ride on my brother's lap while he practiced using the wheelchair, and then he would launch her off it. After Miki was sent flying, she would lie there sprawled on the floor, sticking her tongue out at the nurses who'd come over to help her. It was like she was slowly reverting to being a child. When I told her about being frightened by the blaring sounds and about the flowers in the hospital room, she seemed like she wasn't listening to me at all. Then, as if she suddenly remembered, she started rambling wildly.

"Last night I had a dream. I was dancing in a huge dance

hall, surrounded by mirrors. No, wait. They were windows. Glass windows. They were cracked and broken, and so big. Like stained glass windows. No, wait. They just reflected the light—is it true that dreams aren't in color? They're in black and white, right? If that's true, then I must have made up the part about the stained glass. I was wearing a weird dress—yeah, you know, like the one that Sakiko-san had on—and I was dancing, spinning round and round, and then like the tigers around the tree in that story, I turned into butter, and started to melt. No, that's not true. Ha ha, the part I said before is for real. But the butter part is made up. I was just spinning and spinning. The hall was so huge, and I just spun around in place. Around and around and around."

Miki spun around in front of me and fell over with a thud. Then she cackled like mad.

"Hajime's face looks like a monster's, doesn't it?"

I broke up with Genkan. No big deal—she was in love with someone else.

"An aspiring photographer."

By that point, I was bored to death by Genkan talking about "aspiring" somethings. Their "gifts" and "talents" had yet to bloom into anything and their exaggeratedly painted eyes and lips did not hold the same interest for me. Even Genkan's body, which I used to be so attracted to, no longer held me in the same thrall—it was like watching a doll's movements from a distance.

More importantly, my body stopped responding to her.

"What's wrong?"

Genkan had mobilized all of her tactics in her effort to arouse me, but I realized some of those were probably things she had learned from her new lover. I didn't know that for sure, but my affection for Genkan had scattered like grains of sand, and my useless body was all that remained. Nothing happened, no matter what she did to it, and for some reason the image that flashed in my mind was of Sakura sulking as she lay in her doghouse.

Later that same day, I found out that my brother would never be able to use his legs again. Miki had been in the hospital too that night, lying next to him in the bed and tickling the left side of his body. Normally my brother reserved guy talk for when it was just the two of us, but that day he didn't seem to care that Miki was there with us.

"M-my . . . you know . . . it's no good anymore," he said, crying.

My brother's accident had not only robbed him of any feeling in his lower body and his face of its expression, but it also seemed to have affected his tear ducts.

Miki had been lying next to him, listening to her Walkman the whole time, but the brisk sounds leaking from the headphones were no longer audible, so it seemed likely she was aware of what he was talking about.

Just then, my mother came into the hospital room. "C'mon, Hajime! Let's get you sponged up!"

Still crying, my brother replied, "Why bother?"

But my mother seemed to pay no mind to his tears; she just quietly dipped the towel in the hot water and wrung it out.

I hadn't told Genkan anything about my brother.

"You've been cold to me lately, Kaoru."

Now even when Genkan tried to be coy with me, I found it annoying. On weekends, after she came back from those parties where she would soak up all that vibrant energy and be beaming and practically bursting with happiness, I couldn't seem to look her in the eye.

"If you're struggling, you can talk to me, no matter what," she'd said gently.

But I couldn't even tell whether or not I was struggling with what was going on with Hajime.

A struggle sounded like something much more dramatic than what I was facing. A physically overwhelming shock, like a bolt of lightning that flooded your eyes with so many tears, you couldn't even look up at the sky. More like that kind of thing.

In my case—how should I put it?—it was more of a listlessness than pain, a heaviness in the body like you feel on Monday mornings when you don't want to get out of bed, or a gross taste in your mouth like you haven't brushed your teeth in days, or the uncomfortable feeling that you've forgotten something. That was it. I wore a somber look, like I still had that milk skin stuck in the back of my throat. I guess I too found just about everything bothersome.

The truth was that nobody in my family talked seriously or cried about what had happened to my brother. My mother still made the same absurd amount of toast as always and never got upset, even when my brother refused it and threw the plate on the floor.

"Such a waste! I'll eat it then," she said.

My mother ate whatever my brother didn't finish, and slowly but surely, she started gaining weight. My father, on the other hand, was working harder than ever and looking a little gaunt. When he saw my brother's wheelchair, he thought it looked worn out and became determined to buy him a new one, which seemed like a senseless point of pride. Even my brother was like, "What the hell for?" and threw his plate on the floor again.

This reminded me of when Miki was little and used to throw things with surprising precision. We got used to dodging these items and then cleaning up the mess, but my brother's delayed rebellious phase was exhausting for all of us.

Graduation

One day Kaoru-san brought over another haul of tawashi scrub brushes. It was the first time someone outside of the Hasegawa family had come to the house since my brother's accident—in other words, she was the first visitor to see the state Hajime was in.

"My father makes them."

She made the exact same comment as she had the first time she came to our house. Sakura had decimated the supply of tawashi she'd received from Kaoru-san quite some time ago. Sakura was a very well-behaved girl, but when it came to tawashi she would get carried away.

She would run through various ways to play with one—she rolled it around with her forelegs, she stepped lightly on it, she walked past it pretending not to notice it was there—and, finally, she would gnaw on it with her strong teeth. She'd keep at it with an intent look on her face, even when the bristles drew blood from her gums, and if Miki teased her by taking the tawashi away, Sakura would howl and whimper. Sakura had a way of mangling them beyond recognition, so that anyone who came over to our house would find tawashi in various stages of decomposition strewn about the yard.

Oh-oh-oh, so many tawashi! Sakura rolled her eyes and started drooling.

In Sakura's mind, Kaoru-san was the "tawashi person," and whenever Kaoru-san came over to the house, Sakura would run restless circles around her.

"It's been a while, huh, Sakura-chan," Kaoru-san said, giving Sakura's head a tousle.

Just as Kaoru-san tossed all the tawashi brushes to Sakura, who started chasing after them like a cheetah, Hajime came out into the yard.

At that point my brother had pretty much gotten his act together. For about a month, he had thrown plates and glasses, things that shattered noisily; and then for another month it had been slippers and magazines, things that didn't really hurt even if they hit you—and then he stopped throwing things. His rebellious phase had only lasted two months or so.

My mother had gained maybe fifteen pounds while my father had lost ten, but nothing else had really changed for the rest of us.

When I told my brother that I had dumped Genkan, he sympathized.

"Th-that sucks, I know."

And one time, when he had brandished and thrown a glass that had hit Miki and injured her leg, he apologized.

"S-s-sorry . . . are you . . . o-okay?" He even seemed concerned.

Hajime found everything as bothersome as ever, but he no longer sat around in his room, pissing himself or pretending we weren't there, looking away even when we tried to speak to him.

"Hello," Kaoru-san said, looking at Hajime while she continued to play with Sakura.

"H-hello." He appeared to be a little nervous. It had been a long time since he'd encountered any girls other than Miki. While his rebellious phase was still going on, he had called the girl he'd been dating at the time of his accident and told her that he didn't want to see her anymore, and she had taken him at his word. She didn't even try to persuade him otherwise. Though, by appearances, he was the one who had broken up with her, we certainly suspected he had done so preemptively.

In contrast to Hajime's discomfort, Kaoru-san seemed perfectly relaxed as she kept right on patting Sakura, with Miki watching vacantly as she did so. Soon enough it would be warm again, and in the spring Kaoru-san would enter a private high school where she'd been admitted to play basketball.

"My mom is blind," Kaoru-san said, as if she were speaking to Sakura. "So she never knows who's at home and who isn't."

My brother's arms were limply resting in his lap. They had gotten strong from pushing himself in the wheelchair, so that even at rest, they looked muscular.

"But she's always calm because, as she says, things like the air or how stuff smells don't change. When I was little, whenever I hurt myself, she always knew it as soon as I came home, no matter if I was really hurt or just had a little scrape. She could just tell, she said, and it wasn't by how much or how little I cried."

Miki, being mean again to Sakura, snatched the tawashi away from her. Sakura looked panicked and chased after Miki.

"I-I . . ." Hajime stuttered.

Miki lay face down and hid the tawashi under her belly. She had no qualms about putting that drool-covered thing right up against her skin, and she cackled with laughter. Sakura was desperate. She loved Miki, but she loved her tawashi more, and she wanted it back—she bared her teeth and pawed at the ground. Now that Sakura had moved on, Kaoru-san was left empty-handed.

"There are some things that don't change," she said.

My brother just sat there silently.

One day my brother said, "When it gets a little warmer, I'll take Sakura out for walks."

Miki and I had been wrapping gyoza (not for New Year's).

My father's nose had been buried in a book about chess, but he was exhausted from long days of work and had fallen asleep, while my mother had got it in her head that we should take another beautiful family portrait once summer came around, and so was outside planting some kind of seeds in the garden.

Miki, being Miki, was concentrating on wrapping an umeboshi—pit and all—in a gyoza skin and didn't seem to be listening. So I may have been the only one who actually heard what my brother had said.

"Oh?" I responded, but the garlic got into my eyes and I started tearing up. Without a word, Miki handed me a tissue, but I didn't want her to think I was crying, so I just let my tears flow.

"Isn't the garlic really something?" I whined, and Miki looked at me.

"Kaoru, your snot is really something."

Sakura was pretty excited, looking dazzled as she gazed up at the sky. *Ah, I hope spring arrives soon!*

On the day of Miki and Kaoru-san's graduation ceremony, Kaoru-san did something surprising.

When she crossed the stage in front of all the other students, Kaoru-san stuck the diploma she'd just received under her arm and grabbed the microphone from the principal.

The principal's head was as bald and shiny as could be, but his eyebrows were bushy and appeared bigger than his eyes, and the backs of his hands were so fuzzy with hair that they looked bumpy, like ohagi sweet rice balls. Someone had once said the principal looked like he was crossed with a tanuki raccoon dog, so they referred to him as "Mongrel."

"Mongrel" was surprised by Kaoru-san and hurriedly tried to take the microphone back, but Kaoru-san was a lot taller than he was, so when she pushed him in the stomach as if to say, *Back off*, he fell right over and, on the ground, he looked even more like a tanuki.

Everyone laughed at the sight of "Mongrel" seeming to play right into his role, but they all fell silent when Kaoru-san started speaking, "I . . ."

Kaoru-san took a big breath and continued. "I love Miki Hasegawa."

The crowd roared as if they were in a soccer stadium and someone had scored a goal. Some people made whistles and everyone stamped their feet on the floor—Sakura and I were on a walk in the People's Forest, and the sound was even audible from there.

Miki, with her amazing powers of recollection, was able to recount the rest of what Kaoru-san said word for word. As we listened to Miki's long recitation, my brother and I found it hard to believe that the taciturn Kaoru-san had so much to say.

"I don't think of myself as a girl. My feelings for Miki seem natural, even though we wear the same uniform—I mean, that we both wear a skirt. I find it strange to wear a skirt. But ever since the rumor about Miki and me took off, everyone looks at Miki differently, and I've heard people make a big deal about us being lesbians, which I also find strange. Even though my feelings seem perfectly natural to me, everyone else doesn't feel the same way. Um, I guess maybe I'm weird. But kinda weird in the way that, like, my house is full of animals or that everyone at home is female. Yet when I see how everyone reacts, it's like they think someone like me cannot possibly exist. That feels wrong to me. I love Miki Hasegawa. You all think that's weird, but it's no different from the way that all the cats at my house all have the same mother, they're all mackerel tabbies—except for one, who's pure white. It's the same as that. The fact that my mother is blind is no different from how only one of our dogs has floppy ears, or that one of our hens doesn't lay eggs even though she seems totally healthy otherwise. I told Miki Hasegawa that I love her. I said, I love you more than anyone. And she said, she said that she doesn't love me. She said that it's not because she doesn't like girls. That girl, she never once acted like what I was saying was strange, she never thought I was weird the way that everyone else did. Ah, she's such a fascinating person! I love her. And someday"—here, Miki slowed down, as if she couldn't quite remember—"someday, when other people don't think it's so weird, I'll tell her again how I feel about her. When no one will think I'm strange, I'll tell her I love her. You know, I think there are plenty of people like me in the world. I think there are people who others say are weird for different reasons. But I would never laugh at them. No one should laugh at them. What year is this? 2003? Or no, 2004?

Anyway, in a few years everything will surely change. The day will soon come when no one will call us strange. And when that time comes, I hope to see Miki Hasegawa again."

Nobody at graduation laughed at Kaoru-san that day, and there was no weird, dramatic applause either. Everyone was silent as they watched her descend from the stage. And they were more jealous of Kaoru-san and Miki than they'd ever been of anyone in their lives.

Career Fashions

Although at first my brother needed my father's or my help when he went on walks, eventually he could make his way alone down hills, relying on his now-strong arms in place of his withering legs.

More importantly, Sakura was such a clever girl that she learned to adjust her pace to that of the wheelchair, slowing down or speeding up as needed, and in this way, she was like my brother's wife, a most excellent partner.

Hajime-kun, the path is uneven, Sakura would nudge. *Let's go back.*

And she wasn't even a service dog.

After about six months, my brother was going as far as the People's Forest on his own. I loved the sight of my brother getting ready to go out for a walk. He was cool to watch—to see the way he hoisted himself into his wheelchair using only his hands, and the U-turn maneuver he executed with the wheelchair (kind of like a wheelie); then he'd call to Sakura and put her leash on—it was like he was sitting in the cockpit of a giant robot. And like the smartest police dog in the world, Sakura would sit there, perfectly still, until Hajime started moving. The only disappointment was that, once he started going on walks on his own, he stopped taking me or Miki along with him. If we saw him getting ready and went to put on our shoes, he'd wave his hand vaguely as if to signal "I'm going alone," and then head out. It wasn't that we worried about Hajime being on his own, we just wanted to be with him. Nevertheless, he insisted. It was like we had reverted to when we were little and were once again dependent on him. Back then we used to follow him everywhere he went, and when he wasn't around, we would be edgy and restless. Now, during the hour or so he'd be out on a walk, Miki and I would fidget around in the house, flipping the TV on and off, not really interested in watching it anyway.

Seeing us this way would also make my mother restless. She'd ask loudly, "What *time* is it?" while glancing repeatedly at the clock and singing popular songs despite not knowing any of the words. More so for her than for any of us, moving her mouth was a way to self-soothe. If not singing or laughing loudly, she was increasingly likely to fill that time by eating.

She's gotten pretty pudgy, hasn't she? I thought to myself, surprised by the size of her bottom when I happened to catch sight of my mother putting the vacuum away in the closet. The small floral patterns on her dresses had grown larger until eventually she couldn't wear them any longer, and her belts no longer fit—not that she had to worry about her pants falling down, anyway.

My nineteenth August arrived, and Hajime turned twenty.

We decided to make his birthday a festive celebration. Because my brother had always been in such demand, he was never home on August 3. He would spend it out somewhere with either Yajima-san or his friends or his new girlfriend, and by the time he came back, his birthday would technically be over.

Last year he'd been in the hospital, busy seeing our dead Granny and throwing flower vases, so this was our chance to finally enjoy his birthday together as a family. My mother planned to bake a ridiculously sweet cake (her tastebuds were out of whack), and my father planned to come home early from work, a rare occurrence. I was on summer vacation and had nothing to do, so Miki and I decided to go buy a birthday present for my brother.

Even without spinning around a tree, the day was hot enough to melt us into a pool of butter, and as soon as we went inside the department store, the air was so cool that both Miki and I sneezed as if we'd been plucked. We'd been drenched in sweat that now instantly dried and, not surprisingly, we both managed to catch a cold that day.

"So, the present . . ."

"What should we get him?"

Every year, I gave Hajime a CD. But since I'd usually end up borrowing it from him after he'd had it for a while, that just meant I got him something I wanted to listen to. Miki's presents were always random items she bought from who knows where, like a WWF poster with a close-up of a white gorilla or a boar-bristle toothbrush or an eraser set emblazoned with the Japanese flag, none of which my brother seemed very excited to receive. No doubt Miki wrapped these herself—secured with about a hundred staples, my brother would always prick his fingers as he struggled to open her gifts.

Since neither of us had ever given Hajime a present that he actually liked (Miki always seemed so disappointed when he wasn't thrilled by her offerings), this year both of us felt especially compelled to try to make him leap for joy (which we obviously knew wasn't going to happen) and we were eager to find the perfect gift.

"So, the present . . ."

"What should we get him?"

We kept mumbling this to ourselves as we wandered the floors of the department store. A plush bathrobe, an oversized mug, a shiny new soccer ball? None of those things seemed quite right to us and meanwhile, Miki kept getting politely chided by salespeople for carelessly handling the merchandise with her sticky fingers. We kept wandering around—so much so that the security person there to prevent shoplifting had marked us—until, eventually, Miki started whining and plunked herself down on a bench beside the escalators.

When Miki set herself down somewhere, it wasn't a very good sign. She would plop herself down in the courtyard at school and spend fifth or sixth period just sitting there or, exhausted after swim class, she'd park herself on the diving board and just sit there until it got dark. There was something a little off about Miki's sense of time. She couldn't stand to be in the same room with someone she hated for even a second, but when she plunked herself down like this, two or three hours seemed to pass for her in the blink of an eye.

"So, the present . . ."

"What should we get him?"

We uttered these words for the umpteenth time that day, and then both fell silent.

"Uh-oh, we're on the wrong floor."

"What? Didn't it say just over there it's on the third floor?"

A woman in her mid-twenties and a lady, presumably her mother, were looking at the floor guide map that was posted beside the escalators.

"It's in the east building."

"Where are we?"

"The south building."

"How do we get there?"

"It says there's a connecting passage on the second floor."

"What floor are we on?"

"Uh . . . the third."

"Oh dear, we have to go back down again."

The two linked arms and hurried toward the down escalator on the opposite side. As they passed in front of us, the daughter glanced at me and quickly looked away, but when she saw Miki, she seemed stunned. I was accustomed to this—people looking at and then ignoring me, only to be startled when they saw Miki (or my brother)—it had happened ever since I was little.

"Pretty girl," the daughter whispered to her mother, continuing to glance furtively at Miki as they descended on the escalator.

"Oh, she really is!"

I looked over at Miki, who was blandly sucking on something. I held out my hand, assuming she had some kind of candy on her, "Gimme."

"Huh?" Miki looked back at me quizzically.

"Aren't you sucking on a candy?"

Miki stuck out her tongue to reveal a silver button. Following her gaze, I saw that a button from her jeans had fallen off and her grape-colored underwear was peeking out.

"You lost a button?"

"Yup."

"Huh."

Curious to know where those two women had wanted to go, I got up and went over to look at the map guide. What was listed on the third floor of the east building was "Career Fashions."

"Career Fashions," I said out loud.

"What?"

"Those women just now, they were looking for Career Fashions."

"What two women?"

"You know, that mother and daughter."

"What mother and daughter?"

"Miki, your underwear is showing."

"Huh?"

"Your underwear."

"Oh."

Miki had made herself comfortable and was now lying on the bench—her grape-colored underwear still showing, of course. I gave up wondering about what career fashions were and sat back down next to her. Several more people came and went in front of where we were sitting. A guy with incredibly frizzy hair who looked like a musician, an old-fashioned-looking woman with glasses like the ones a certain dead prime minister used to wear, a boy with bandages wrapped around his head with his big-assed mother holding him tightly by the hand. It really was quite the assortment of people, though none of them were like my brother. These days, I encountered many more people who looked right past me and landed on my brother.

These were not the same looks that people gave Miki or the old Hajime, stunned by their allure. These gazes were—how should I put it?—ones of alarm. Their eyes seemed to say "yikes." The first time I confronted this kind of look was when Miki and I were on a walk with my brother in the People's Forest.

It was still cold out, but we were bathed in the setting sun, our shadows cast onto the ground: me the beanpole and slender Miki, next to stubby Sakura and my brother like a king on a throne. When we first moved here, who would have imagined that we'd ever throw such mellow shadows? My brother had always been the tall one, always bounding around, always in motion. Little Miki would try to keep up with him, leaping about and jumping on my back, while Sakura would run circles around all of us, tail wagging. Our shadows used to be so frenetic, it seemed like even the sun had to work hard to keep up with us.

Late afternoon was peak dog-walking time in the park. We passed by all kinds of dogs: dogs whose faces were smushed up in the middle, dogs whose bellies practically grazed the ground, dogs so shaggy it seemed impossible they could see in front of them. One fellow dog approached Sakura, his hips swaying with great interest, but Sakura turned back toward us self-consciously, as if to say, *Ugh! How crude!*

Everyone looked at us, no matter what kind of dog they accompanied. Perhaps we were an odd sight, the three of us walking such a scruffy mutt as if she were a queen and we were her entourage, because they all stole glances at us as we passed them by. At first, they were stunned by Miki's beauty; then they'd glimpse Sakura's spots and unintentionally chuckle. But my brother was the last thing they all seemed to notice, and their expressions always shifted to alarm. One boy just stared, slack-jawed.

Ever since he was little, my brother was used to being the center of attention. The "Hajime legend" that persisted throughout elementary school meant that when he walked down the street everyone—boys and girls, men and women—couldn't help but turn to look at him, drawn by his warmth, like the scent that seemed to envelop us on that early spring day. Only this time, my brother wasn't used to the kind of attention he received, those alarmed stares. Whereas before, he might have found it annoying to be inundated by such friendly looks, now it was as if people were seeing something they weren't supposed to look at, some unthinkable mistake, and those eyes were like a thousand pricks on his shoulders, his arms, and especially his face. He found it utterly bewildering.

We were rather bewildered ourselves. This was the first time we were witnessing these strange looks from everyone, and we'd never seen Hajime so uncomfortable and downbeat. We might not have thought anything was different, it was just our shadows that looked a bit odd now—but the world around us had clearly shifted, and that was more disorienting and confusing than when this had been a new town, and all these streets and parks had been new and unfamiliar to us.

I was feeling unsteady on my feet when Miki said to me, "Ready?"

I didn't know what she was thinking.

"Go!"

Without even waiting for the signal, Miki was already off and running, pushing the wheelchair with all her might. That time too, Miki had been sucking on a button that had fallen off something, but now she spit it out furiously as she made a mad dash for it. My brother stared straight ahead as the wheelchair made an awful clatter. It looked like he was watching a rocket launch in the distance. I ran with Sakura, using the technique I'd learned from Little Miss Obstacle, a double inhale for every exhale, never losing sight of Miki and Hajime. The people we passed must have been even more alarmed to see us now, but they'd be far behind us by the time we noticed, and anyway, my brother's eyes were tightly squeezed shut.

After much indecision, the present we got for Hajime was a thick new leash for Sakura's walks.

"Wait, isn't this a present for Sakura?"

"But he's the one who takes her for practically all her walks."

The leash Miki picked out had a red and green plaid pattern. It was pretty garish. There was no reason to think Hajime was going to appreciate his birthday present this year either. I looked at the clock. It was six-thirty—my mother would be getting dinner ready: nabé of course. Miki and I walked home listlessly, not speaking a word the whole way.

Balls

My father's shoes were by the front door. At some point, my father had started using the boar-bristle toothbrush Miki had given my brother years ago to polish his shoes. Every night, my father would carefully polish his shoes with it, until even his oldest shoes would gleam like a shiny new bicycle. However, maybe my brother's sense of everything being bothersome had spread to my father, because he suddenly stopped shining his shoes. The ones lying limply by the door were a dingy brown, like a puddle of melting chocolate.

The sounds of the nabé simmering and my mother's voice echoed through the house. Her yammering reached its peak at dinnertime. As opposed to Miki's rapid-fire talking, my mother's loud way of speaking was more like a kind of bombardment. Although whenever I later tried to recall what she'd said, I could never remember.

My brother seemed like he was pretty tired. Instead of the usual one-hour walk with Sakura, my mother said that today he'd been out with her for two and a half hours. I wondered how many times she'd looked at the clock and murmured to herself, "What *time* is it?" and I imagined her loudly singing hip-hop songs she'd heard playing in our rooms without actually understanding the words. Her voice sounded a little hoarse.

My father was superb at interjecting into my mother's conversations.

"You don't say?"

"Really, wow."

Only now, he was staring fixedly at the simmering nabé, as if all along he'd been contemplating how the queen would move, and whether his bishop would be safe in that position. At first, when my mother would see that my father was off in the clouds, she'd admonish him, "Are you *listening*?" but lately she acted as if that made no difference to her, so that at home my mother's habit was now a lot like her talking loudly to herself.

"It's good to eat hot food, especially when it's hot out!"

"Ice cream tastes so good in winter, doesn't it?"

"Eating spicy food makes you sweat bullets, doesn't it?"

About all that I can remember from what my mother was talking about that night and how my father was acting was that it had to do with the first one, that it's good to eat hot food when it's hot out.

I remember that Miki, bored with the dinner, got up to let Sakura back inside, and Sakura, sniffing all the smells, gave up and settled under the table, whimpering. And I remember that my brother suddenly spoke up.

Sakura, caught off guard, started wagging her tail happily, trying to please everyone. She peeked up from under the table with an expectant look:

Oh . . . oh my . . . smells delicious.

Miki selected items from the pot to give to Sakura. Wilted cabbage, excessively white enoki mushrooms, floppy kombu that had imparted all its flavor to the broth. But Sakura was not enthusiastic about any of these morsels chosen by Miki. She sniffed at the piece of tofu that Miki had tossed her way.

Huh, I've never seen food that was so lacking in smell before.
Sakura went back to lying down. Miki tried to pry her jaws open and force the tofu into her mouth, but maybe because it was too hot, or maybe because my brother suddenly spoke up, she soon gave up trying.

"D-do you remember F-ferrari?"

Hajime's eyes were like jet-black pebbles, looking off in no particular direction as he said this. It wasn't clear to whom this question was directed, but it drew a blank stare from both my mother and father, although Miki and I were the ones who would have known who Ferrari was.

Ferrari! What a blast from the past! That character who was always wandering around, eyes downcast, muttering unintelligibly. Ferrari, the guy who had taken one look at Miki that day, then stared up at the sky, and whom we'd never seen again after that. The memory made me so nostalgic, I almost dropped my chopsticks.

"Oh yeah, from back in the day! Sure, I remember him."

"Miki, do you?"

"Who dat?"

"Remember, the weirdo? You know, in Park Number One, that c-crazy old d-dude?"

Despite how perilously close she'd come to harm, Miki truly seemed not to remember Ferrari at all. Then, with the same amount of interest she might have shown upon discovering a white hair on her head, she crawled under the table and started tussling about with Sakura.

My mother, her yammering having been interrupted, was now listening attentively to what my brother was saying, like a starry-eyed princess receiving a gift for the first time ever.

Only what he had to say was nothing like the wondrous and delightful thing she'd been awaiting so hopefully.

"I-it's hard to b-believe that now I'm like Ferrari, I n-never thought little kids would point at me and r-run away."

Retaining only the use of his hands since the accident, Hajime had become perfectly ambidextrous. His chopsticks were the roughly hewn, dark brown ones, and he used these to eat his meals.

"Th-they run away."

Whenever we'd seen Ferrari, it made our hearts race. It had felt as if something terrible was waiting for us, in a world where we weren't supposed to set foot. Ferrari existed unto himself—his world seemed different from the world that my brother and I and all our friends from school lived in.

But now, my brother's world was just like Ferrari's. Ferrari, who couldn't even look up at the sky and who didn't know how to harness his swift-footedness. My brother was totally immersed in a world like Ferrari's, unable to escape.

Those looks of alarm when people saw Hajime, those little boys who ran away when they saw him. That had been my brother and me, when we were little. That had been my brother, up in a tree, pointing and laughing at Ferrari. And now he couldn't even climb a tree; he was closer to the ground than any of us, desperately trying to look up at the sky. Now he took pains not to have to look anyone in the eye, and those black pebbles of his gaze always seemed focused on the day after tomorrow. Hajime was deep in his own world, where everything was bothersome, and no matter how hard we knocked at the door, he refused to come out.

"God."

My brother's voice was usually loud and clear.

"God," he repeated.

Hearing him say this word so suddenly threw us all into a fluster. It was like an unfamiliar word that none of us understood. Sakura, under the table, was the only one who seemed to understand and offered a response:

"Woof."

Even though my brother had said "God" after "Ferrari," what popped into my head wasn't the smiling, skinny white guy with golden curls—Jesus—but Ferrari. Those cloudy eyes that had stared at Miki, those huge nostrils that labored with every inhale and exhale, and that tangle of hair that looked like he'd just emerged from a sandstorm. I would carry all these parts of Ferrari in my mind for a long time to come.

"G-god exists, I think. Not in h-heaven, or in outer space, but in each of our hearts."

Miki was using Sakura as a pillow and had fallen asleep. Her leg, splayed out, kicked my shin. Sakura whimpered again, but then she gave up and relaxed against Miki's weight.

"And s-so, every day, in our h-hearts, he throws us a ball, like a p-pitcher."

"A ball?"

My father had become so reticent lately that now the sound of his voice had been reduced in proportion with the scarcity of his words.

"Breaker, breaker . . . this is number two-four."

"What?"

The truck drivers would often get annoyed with how hard it was to hear their orders over the radio. But that night, my father's response to Hajime was surprisingly loud.

"What ball?"

"Y-yeah. U-up 'til now, I've had all straight pitches. Th-they've all come right over the plate."

My brother, for whom all the girls in kindergarten except for one had declared their affection. My brother, who attracted everyone's attention when he came onto the field, as if spring had arrived there and then. If there really was a God like my brother said, then it was true that until now he'd been lobbing softballs to Hajime. And my brother had taken a full swing at those balls coming straight down the middle, hitting home runs. Some of them he'd even knocked right out of the park.

"But lately, I think, God's had some wild pitches. They've been unhittable."

Outside pitches, inside pitches, high balls, low balls—however you wanted to call them, lately my brother had had a lot of strikes. Before, he'd swing with his eyes closed and crush the ball, but now it was more than he could handle. Once he'd let a good ball go by, one after another unhittable pitch would come flying toward him, and before long, he dreaded even just standing in the batter's box. Then, like Ferrari, he often dived to the bottom of his own deep lake.

From under the table came the whack-whack of Sakura's tail wagging.

Did you say 'ball'? I love the way they bounce!

I wondered what kind of balls were being thrown for Sakura.

"Th-they're unhittable," Hajime repeated.

At that point I'd had more than one girlfriend, but right then I longed more than ever for Genkan, who had said to me with a gentle smile, "If you're struggling, you can talk to me." Her face was blurry in my mind, but I could vividly remember her slightly firm breasts and her supple arms.

"If you're struggling, you can talk to me."

Genkan, now is the time. The way that my brother says his life is "unhittable," that's what I'm struggling with the most.

After always throwing Hajime such nice and easy ones, what was the deal with these wild pitches? My brother had always been our hero. Seeing the outline of his back made me smile and feel secure, hearing the reassuring sound of his snoring from the bunk bed above me was all I needed to sleep soundly myself. I had watched him fall in love with Yajima-san and gradually become more manly, which made me realize that I too wanted someone to love. Though while everyone else was busy trying to spruce themselves up, looking for a partner, I was kicking back, listening to the CDs I'd borrowed from my brother.

But now, he just moped around feeling sorry for himself, not even looking us in the eye. And he cried all the time.

The nabé that my mother had ladled into Hajime's bowl was now mixed with his tears and snot. At some point the pot had stopped simmering, and the only sound was my brother's crying.

"They're unhittable."

The clock read nine o'clock. Under the table, Sakura was still wagging her tail.

Did you say 'ball'? I love the way they bounce!

Mail

On December 23 of that year—the day before the eve of a certain someone's birth—my brother died in the People's Forest. He was twenty years and four months old. He had been out on a walk with Sakura that night.

At the beginning of December, I found out something from Miki.

Miki brought her red randoseru school bag to my room. The shoulder strap on that bag had already ripped when she was in third grade, but my mother had made a valiant effort to sew it back on, and somehow Miki had managed to keep it on her back for another three years. On the left side in magic marker was written in big letters, MIKI HASEGAWA, so that whoever passed her by, even grown-ups struck by her beauty who might not have known she was an elementary school student, knew her name.

"Randoseru."

Miki had deposited the bag on the floor and pointed to it as she said this. I wondered if she was getting weird again.

"Yeah, I can see it's your randoseru. What else would it be?"

"Inside."

"Huh?"

"Look inside."

You ain't foolin' me, I thought to myself. A long time ago, Miki had shown up with a cookie tin and handed it to me, and I had gleefully opened the lid only to find the tin stuffed with a mass of caterpillars. Judging from the size of her school bag, I figured this time it was a snake or some kind of small mammal, so I was wary.

"What is it?"

"Look."

Miki seemed pretty worked up. She was very impatient, like someone rushing to buy a train ticket just before the train was about to depart.

But I was still on guard and made no move toward the bag so Miki, exasperated, opened the randoseru herself. She turned it upside down and began to empty the contents onto the floor in my room.

What tumbled out was an enormous quantity of letters. In familiar pastel colors. All addressed to "Hajime Hasegawa."

Three years' worth of letters from Yajima-san.

Miki flopped onto the floor along with the letters and launched into her old rapid-fire style of explanation that I knew so well.

"Every day, yeah, so, every day, you know how he checked the mailbox? Hajime. Every day, every day. So then I did too, I was imitating him and checking the mailbox too. Every day, every day. Then yeah, Hajime got home late, so I was the first one to look in the mailbox. Then yeah so, you know how Mom puts all the mail on the table? Hajime was always checking that too? But I was the first one to look at that stuff too. I saw it first. Then yeah so, you know how Yajima-san's letters, they were always such pretty colors? Light blue, or pale pink, or golden yellow.

I wondered where she bought them, such pretty envelopes, I wondered where they sold them. Right, I thought I knew where I could get them, in the building where the train station is. One of my classmates, she had these notebooks and postcards in mad pretty colors. Yeah, they have those everywhere. But yeah, then yeah so, Yajima-san's envelopes were prettier. They were super pretty. But I couldn't find them anywhere. They were so pretty, yeah, and every day, every day Hajime was waiting for them. Then yeah, I was always, I got to those envelopes before Hajime did. When I opened the mailbox, they were there, really, so very pretty, those envelopes. I, I . . ."

Miki had been the one who put an end to my brother and Yajima-san's relationship.

Miki had taken those pretty pastel-colored envelopes before my brother saw them and she had carefully cut them open and read every single letter, word for word. And she had memorized them all, down to the punctuation marks. As proof of this, Miki now began reciting to me all the letters that Yajima-san had written to Hajime.

Dear Hajime, how are you? The cherry blossoms are already in bloom here. The temperature seems like it's a bit warmer than Osaka. What's it like there? Have you had any rain?

How is Sakura-chan? On my way home from school, there was a dog that looked like Sakura out on a walk, and it made my heart ache.

You wrote that you didn't get my letters, I wonder why? I write one every day and send it to you. Maybe it's the mailman's fault? I'll see what I can find out.

As her narration carried on, Miki looked like a wind-up or battery-operated doll. I just stared at her, dumbfounded as I listened.

Have you forgotten about me? Please, I just want to hear your voice. You wrote that you're in love with someone else, but I will always love you. Please, just let me hear your voice one more time.

When she got to this letter, Miki's tears spilled onto the pages. When Miki cried, it was always a commotion. She cried with everything she had—it sounded like all the birds in the world greeting the morning in unison. This time, however, it seemed as though her body had reached a saturation point and needed to expel a large amount of moisture, so her tears just kept flowing.

Please, just let me hear your voice one more time.

Miki had sent Yajima-san a short letter, as if it was from Hajime:

I'm in love with someone else. Never call me again.

The reason why it was so short was because she was forging my brother's handwriting and that was all she could manage. She had taken a notebook or letters from his room and, with appalling precision, she had copied Hajime's penmanship, one character at a time. Miki, who never studied at all, had sat at her desk every night with an incomparable dedication to this task.

"So yeah, at first, I used calligraphy paper and traced it. I traced his characters. One by one. Hiragana, it's, you know, round. All the letters are so round, it's like they're cold. Like the white of the notebook is cold and they're curled up into themselves. I wanted to warm them up, but if I did that, it wouldn't look like Hajime's writing, right? So, I just traced them all. All of them. I didn't need to use any katakana. Nobody uses katakana when they send letters, do they? Nah? It's like the olden days, writing letters. In Hajime's notebook, yeah, it's all about soccer—who plays forward, who plays midfielder—he's making up his own team. Yeah, so he had French players and Brazilian players. Cool, yeah? The kanji! Right, the kanji were hard, you know, they're so many characters. With hiragana and katakana, there's a limited number, you know? But with kanji it's unlimited. There're too many, and I don't know them. So I picked three and practiced writing those. '好き' for 'love' and '人' for 'someone' and '電話' for 'phone'—that's all. Which one do you think was the hardest? It was '人'! That was the toughest one to get right. Then yeah, you write it like this."

The "人" that Miki wrote in magic marker is still there on the floor of my room. My brother's writing resembles my father's—his letters incline slightly toward the right, and they have a way of making the pen leap with the last stroke. Miki wrote that character, which looked just like my brother's handwriting, on my floor without looking up at me. She had given up hours of sleep, practicing until she was sick and tired, in order to perfectly master his style. This was probably the only time Miki had ever devoted herself so intently, so self-effacingly, to anything in her life. Just so she could learn to write exactly the same way as my brother. And, at some point, the rest of Miki's handwriting started to look like his too. It was like she gave up on having her own writing style.

Without looking up at all, Miki just kept on staring at the "人" that was like Hajime's. It had been almost three hours since she'd started reciting Yajima-san's letters. Pretty soon it would be time for my mother to call everyone for dinner, but her voice seemed never to materialize.

I'd never longed to hear my mother's voice more urgently than I did at that moment. To me her voice was like sunshine piercing through rifts in the clouds, in that miraculous way it does on an overcast day at the beach. That persistent, meddlesome, and slightly nasal voice.

And oh, it was almost bittersweet the way Miki's voice resembled my mother's. In that gentle voice that sounded like my mother's, Miki recited in closing:

We're moving to another town. Even though you love someone else now, I always loved you.

These last words seemed to strain her voice, and despite how much moisture her body had already excreted, her tears were still flowing. Miki's tears fell on the pastel-colored envelopes, darkening the hues as they seeped into the paper. The enormous pile of letters reminded me of the junk cars where Ferrari used to hide in Park No. 1. My heart raced and I felt that anxiety again. Ferrari's world, previously unknown to us, was now here before us. We used to laugh at him, thinking we had nothing to do with him, and now that world we'd paid no attention to was about to engulf us.

I could hear Sakura walking in the yard. The rustling sound

of her padding around on the ground echoed softly in our ears. Somehow, Sakura would always reassure us. I'd been reminded of how that milk skin felt when it was stuck in my throat on the night of my brother's accident and how I had felt so nauseated I almost keeled over. But, hearing the sound of Sakura's paws, like a draft through a barely cracked-open window, I could feel something gently pass down my throat.

Hajime, Yajima-san always loved you too.

But it was too late. I was confused, I couldn't keep things straight—what was too late? why did it matter?—and my mind raced with images of my brother's destroyed face, his paralyzed limbs, and the pastel-colored envelopes that Miki had stolen out of the mailbox and from the table. Unfortunately, these swirled around at the same rhythm as the sound of Sakura's paws—crunch, crunch, crunch—and something about this synchronization made it seem like a tender, precious moment.

Crunch, crunch, crunch, crunch.

I hit Miki. I don't remember whether I punched her or slapped her. But my hand struck her with such force that she reeled to the left. Miki's hair fell loosely from her shoulders in slow motion, and blood spurted, either from her mouth or from her nose, further tainting the pastel-colored heap. There was something lovely and yet indisputable about those scattered drops of red that made me feel even more tender and forlorn.

My impulse was not appeased. I wanted to smash her face in. I wanted to tear her hair out from the roots. I wanted to send her softly curved shoulders flying off somewhere.

The next thing I knew, I was pummeling Miki, to the point

where I had worked up a sweat. And each blow sent the letters flying—light blue like rain, golden yellow like sunshine, chartreuse like spring, and then, yes, the softest, gentlest, palest pink. Like the flower petal that had been stuck to Sakura's tail the day we brought her home.

Crunch, crunch, crunch, crunch.

What I'd thought was sweat turned out to be tears. The second son and the only daughter of the Hasegawa family could have filled a six-mat room with their tears that night.

Just then, Miki let out a howl. Like a flower that still tries to enchant even after its petals have fallen, like solemn thunder at the end of summer, her howl conveyed an urgent, almost mad need for something.

"Help me!" this howl said.

"Help me!" It was the voice of a woman desperately in love with someone.

My brother took that garish leash Miki had picked out for his present and hung it from a tree, and then he wrapped the other end around his neck. Sakura, who had gotten used to it for her walks, just stood and stared at Hajime, stunned, the leash like a poisonous snake coiled about his neck. My brother took a deep breath and, as if he'd suddenly remembered something, got out of his wheelchair. He just rose up out of the chair, lifting his torso, and fell a short distance. That was all it took for him to die. My brother's body didn't sway in the air at all, it just slumped onto the ground, where it grew colder and colder, like the silver button Miki had been sucking on.

In his pocket, there was a scrap of paper.

Another New Year in this body is too much. I give up.

SAKURA

It was not written in my brother's masculine hand that Miki had imitated. The writing did not have the right-leaning, somewhat overzealous appearance as when he had written the kanji for love.

This writing looked lifeless and pitiful, like a forgotten receipt that went through the laundry and would disintegrate into shreds if you touched it.

Sakura had always been a vocal dog, but after that night, she stopped talking.

Studying

The photo of my brother was of him smiling, the way he used to look.

When he smiled like that, it was as radiant as the sea on a clear day—it prompted not just girls but us guys too, young and old, to smile with him. Everyone who saw him smile would think, *Do that again*, and wish the moment would last forever.

But that moment had been abruptly cut short, all too soon.

So many people came to the funeral, including some old familiar faces. There was Little Miss Obstacle, with a kid who was her spitting image in tow, and Mochizuki-kun, whose record in the game of "I Dare You" Miki had broken and who had grown into quite the handsome fellow. Everyone bowed with deep sorrow when they saw us; however, I couldn't help but grin at our childhood pals in attendance from my spot in the front row, unable to contain my happiness at the sight of them. I had the urge to wave at them with both hands, but my mother was gripping my right hand too tightly. That hand bore numerous marks from her fingernails digging into my skin, as if I'd been attacked by mosquitoes. My mother's profile looked like an overripe mango. Like a dangling fruit that, if you touched it, would leak juice, and the slightest sway would send it tumbling to the ground. Her almond-shaped eyes that everyone used to sigh in admiration over were now overwhelmed by her flesh and seemed superfluously stuck in her face. Come to think of it, my mother hadn't worn any makeup since my brother's accident. Her lips that once shined a pretty red were now as rough as an elephant's hide, and her eyelids that used to be painted with bright blue were now as darkly shadowed as a dense forest. When she closed her eyes, the dark circles were so alarmingly intense they made my heart pound.

My father, sitting beside her, was diminishingly small. He used to easily lift my mother up in his arms and hug her so tightly she could barely breathe, but now he was so thin that his body seemed to vanish into the shadow of my mother. He just stared straight ahead, and during the funeral he was so completely immobile that he reminded me of the grandfather clock I'd seen a long time ago at Granny's house. The only time the clock moved at all was when Sakiko-san came forward to offer incense, but then time resumed standing still.

Sakiko-san faced us and bowed slowly. She lowered her head so slowly that I even worried she might topple over. Drops of water then fell onto Sakiko-san's shadow, and I realized she was crying as she bowed to us. Normally, my always-considerate mother would have offered her a pretty floral handkerchief, but instead she just stood there, staring vacantly at Sakiko-san. To make matters worse, next to me Miki started audibly peeing her pants.

I thought Miki had used up all the moisture in her body that night, but what dribbled onto the floor wasn't just coming from Sakiko-san's eyes. Earlier, Miki had gotten up and munched on the incense, then decided of her own accord to close my brother's coffin—she'd done whatever she pleased. When I could no longer just sit back and watch, I whispered to her to stop.

She rolled her eyes exaggeratedly and said, "Yeah, are my eyes white?"

She was impossible.

Then, just when I thought she'd finally settled down and was sitting quietly, here she was peeing herself, like a little girl. Sakiko-san took her by the hand and led her out of the funeral hall. As she left, she turned back to look at the photo of my brother, but she cocked her head as if he were a stranger, and resumed her wobbly gait. Everyone seemed surprised to see Miki acting this way—their faces showed the same look of alarm as when they'd seen Hajime, and then they lowered their gaze.

"Pretty girl." I heard a voice murmur from somewhere in the hall.

For the first time in my life, I was filled with so much hate that I wanted to murder someone.

Miki didn't go to high school. If before she had occasionally done something that resembled studying for entrance exams, even that now ceased completely. Instead, after my brother died, Miki gave up on everyday things. She didn't go to school, and for a while she didn't even brush her teeth after getting up in the morning. She couldn't be bothered to eat meals, and she let her nails grow long and sharp like a wild monkey's.

Miki spent her days in her room in a daze, occasionally coming out to let Sakura into the house, then hugging her tightly and petting her for what seemed like forever. It was almost as if she were trying to make a model of Sakura out of clay—she rubbed her hard and gave the flesh on Sakura's back a good squeeze. Sakura always looked like she was in pain, like this was all rather uncomfortable, but she never said anything; she would just be still and let Miki do whatever she was doing.

I, on the other hand, decided to study my ass off for my entrance exams. I still had my amazing power to memorize things, so I could have just looked at the textbook the day before the test and gotten a decent score, but I decided to try properly studying for the first time in my life.

Rather than simply memorizing the entire textbook, I tried to read and understand all the words that were written in it. I figured this way I would learn and remember things for the future. Before, I'd blimp out when I would memorize books for exams, but now, as I went through the process of comprehending every single thing, my weight dropped just as dramatically.

For example, in biology, I'd look at a photo of a dissected frog. The only things that were likely to be on the test were the names of each organ and their functions, but now, in order to fully understand what a frog was, I wanted to know why the organs were shaped the way they were and how those functions were determined. When we studied the refractive index of light, I wondered, just what is light anyway? And when imaginary numbers came up in calculus, I spent three hours contemplating what "imaginary" meant. When we were learning about the French revolutionaries, it occurred to me to ask, why did they all have those curls on their heads—was that the fashion back then? And wait a minute, what about the chonmage hairstyle here in Japan—did that make it easier to wear a helmet? Then why did they wear a topknot? This went on and on; there was no end to it.

I spent an entire month studying like this in the library and I lost thirteen pounds, only to realize that I hated studying. Hilariously, I failed all my exams.

After that I gave up studying—and for that matter, I gave up thinking. From then on, my girlfriend or my friends would often say to me, "I don't know what you're thinking," but the truth is, I wasn't thinking about anything at all.

My girlfriend at the time was very serious. She was taken with the fact that I was often in the library, reading books. But it wasn't like I was trying to learn something new from those books or to discover how to live my life—what I liked was that, when I was reading a book, I didn't have to think about anything. Still, she was always asking me about the books I'd read. The fact that I couldn't remember a single thing about what was in any of them made her doubt whether I'd actually read them.

"I don't remember."

"What don't you remember?"

"What the book was about."

"Why not?"

"What do you mean?"

"Didn't you read it?"

"Yeah, I read the words on the page."

That's how these conversations would go. More and more often, she'd claim not to understand me, just like my next girlfriend, who was a year older, and the one who was two years younger, and the one who was half-Chinese/half-Japanese, and the one I have now, with the perm—they all said the same thing:

"I don't get you, Kaoru-kun."

I don't get me either.

When spring came around, I gave up on studying and decided I would just remember things. The way Hajime and Miki remembered stuff, like ordinary minor events, I'd imprint everything about them in my mind. Like the way that my mother drank the last drop of wine in her glass at night when she was sitting in the kitchen, or, when my father burned his chess board in the yard, what the fire looked like when it rose into the sky, or the way Sakura tore the last tawashi from Kaoru-san to pieces. I arranged each of these in my head, like individual pictures.

I wasn't going to test prep or any school at the time, but had I been, I would have been taken for a scrawny freshman. I was six feet one and weighed 125 pounds, my hip bones stood out like the tendons on the back of my dead great-grandpa's hands, and my neck was as gaunt as the legs on the spiders that Miki liked to catch.

Sakura still didn't bark. But when I'd show her the leash for a walk, she'd fawn all over me and grunt in the same voice that had reverberated through the animal clinic way back when. She kept the prized remnants of her tawashi scrub brushes inside her doghouse and, when we encountered other dogs on the street, she would lay bare her fighting spirit. I was surprised by her aggression—Sakura had always had such a refined temperament—but, more than anything, it was just odd to see her behaving like a dog.

Back then, at any given moment, my mother was always snacking. It could be a doughnut that looked like someone had accidentally spilled honey all over it, or a piece of cake smothered in so much whipped cream it looked as if the person piping it must have sneezed while they were doing it. She'd always make the same excuse:

"Sugar is the only thing that nourishes my brain!"

But all that nourishment that she made sure to give her brain must have been counteracted by the vast quantity of alcohol that she consumed in the kitchen late at night. My mother repeated herself an absurd number of times, and she dropped and broke all kinds of things at the most unexpected moments.

Despite how passionately my father had loved my mother, it now seemed he had forgotten all about it. Their king-size bed would sag on the side where my mother was sleeping, like a ship that was about to capsize. My father's sunken cheeks were dull and dark, like a bottomless swamp that, once you looked at it, threatened to pull you under. It was true; seeing him in this state made me so anxious that I couldn't concentrate on anything else.

Every so often he'd mutter, "Kaoru, where's Miki?" or "Gonna rain again tomorrow." These phrases were like ominous incantations that darkened our spirits, and my father's periodic sighs seemed to drive away whatever brightness was in the room. Like the Grim Reaper in my mother's tarot deck, the happiest man in the universe had now become the receptacle for all our sadness and pain. This change shocked us—we'd always thought that my brother and my mother had been mainly responsible for the warmth and happiness of our home, but only now did we realize it was Akio Hasegawa who had played that role. Our happiness had been overwhelmingly reliant not on the blazing summer sunshine of my mother's sonorous singing or my brother's strong legs kicking the soccer ball, but instead on the more muted and reserved autumnal sounds of my father moving the pieces around on his chess board or wiping his glasses clean when he looked up from his book. We didn't know that it was my father who had protected us, that he was the one who had prepared a warm refuge for the eventual winter. By the time winter did arrive at the Hasegawa home—an honest-to-goodness winter if ever there was one—my father had expended all the warmth in his body, and he was just so very tired. My father was utterly exhausted.

My brother had never been as fond of sweets as my mother,

but whenever we visited Hajime's grave, my mother always brought something sweet for him. After the half hour or so ride to the cemetery, only about half of the sweet would be left, but she still insisted on offering whatever was left at his graveside.

"Hajime is the one who taught me that sugar is nourishment for the brain!" she would say, and then press her palms together for a long time.

This reminded me of my brother drinking the milk skin on his cocoa.

"There are a lot of nutrients in there."

The Sound of Rain

When we were little and it would rain, we'd go nuts because we couldn't go outside to play, and we'd stare at the raindrops that slid down the outside of the window as they fell, or we'd go out anyway and get all muddy—either way, we'd be restless and fidgety. When I'd wake up in the morning and hear the sound of rain, that melancholy would make me feel a little more grown-up, and when it started raining in the middle of the night, it would make me feel safe—warm and nestled in my futon like a baby—and I'd curl up and go back to sleep.

Of all the people I knew, Miki could sense when it was going to rain better than anyone.

It could be a perfectly clear, perfectly dry day, without even the merest scent of it in the air, and she'd say, "Gonna rain."

Then, as if Miki had given the signal, dark clouds would roll in and—drip drop—the rain would start to fall, almost self-consciously. Miki would seem worried about it hitting the ground; wide-eyed, she'd look up at the sky and just stare. She wouldn't say a word, but her face seemed to be loudly welcoming the rain back home.

That was Miki, who always used to wear rubber boots, even on sunny days. So that when it would start to rain, she'd go and play in it ardently, like an old man who'd found his calling.

She'd lick the raindrops that slid onto her shoulders, gaze lovingly at the drops that bounced back up from the ground, even put her ear to the ground to better hear its sound. And most of the time, after the rain would stop, she'd catch a cold. Miki would seem miserable, sneezing from her stuffed-up nose, but then she'd eagerly await the next rainstorm.

Miki was like a hydroponic flower, the rain her constant companion.

Even after Hajime died, she and the rain were always together. The rain that had fallen on the night of his accident had messed with her a little bit, but she still never used an umbrella when she went out in it, nor did she ever wipe or dry off when she got soaked. That night, the raindrops that fell from her bangs onto her cheeks glistened, as if consoling her with a caress of iridescent light.

There was another night when it had rained. It had started late, which was Miki's favorite.

According to her, rain that's already falling when it turns to night is completely different from rain that starts during the night.

"When the rain starts late at night, it seems like it's raining all over the world. Like there's nowhere that's sunny, you know? Like it's the middle of the night all over the world and, just like us, everyone is under the covers in bed, intently listening to the sound of the rain. Silently, silently."

When Miki was little and it would start raining late at night, she would call out softly for my brother. But he'd always be fast asleep, as soundly and bravely as a king whose job it was to sleep. Knowing that he wouldn't wake up, Miki just kept calling for him, as if that put her even more at ease. I would lie there, in between dreaming and waking, listening to the rain against the window and Miki's soft voice, not minding if morning never came, and eventually I'd drift back to sleep.

When we were little. Those precious moments of happiness.

The rain would gently drum against the roof of our house. Sometimes the rain would be violent, announcing its arrival with authority so that even Sakura's ears would twitch in her sleep.

I had just drifted off to sleep when that sweet and overpowering scent, along with the sounds of it on the roof, awakened me with quite a start. Normally I would have been comforted by the sound of rain and gone back to sleep, but that night I couldn't sleep.

This was different from the sense of foreboding I'd had when my brother had his accident. This was also different from the discomfort I'd felt on the morning of the day we moved. There was something I couldn't hear, deep within me.

Saa, saa, saa.

Botsu, botsu, botsu.

The sound of the rain had distracted me from hearing the voice in my chest. Like a child from a southern island seeing a whale for the first time, all of my senses were heightened, and the sound of my heart seemed so loud, as if I had left it beside the pillow. Like the kind of roar from the earth that you only hear in the desert, filled with the premonition that something was about to happen.

Doku, doku, doku, doku.

Doku, doku, doku, doku.

I heard a voice calling out for my brother.

Doku, doku, doku, doku.
Saa, saa, saa.
The voice was coming from my brother's room.

Just then, brightly colored flower petals flashed before my eyes. Pale chartreuse, yellow, orange, light blue. And pink. They whirled softly, clouding my vision, but when I strained my eyes and looked into the distance, Miki was standing there. She was buried in a mountain of those pastel-colored envelopes, the prettiest envelopes in the world, and she was looking right at me.

The voice I heard calling for my brother again from his room was gentle and lush, and so very sad. The tenderest voice in the world, too tender, and too sad.

The voice sighed. The way that my father had made my mother sound, like a mother cat—that's what Miki's voice sounded like.

And with that, I understood everything.

When it started raining late at night, Miki would go to that room, the sound of the rain in her ears. Miki never paid any attention to her appearance but, on those nights, she brought with her the only comb she had, a blue one, and she would take care to untangle her bedhead of hair. She didn't own any lip gloss, but her lips would be moistened with her own sweet saliva, her mouth always slightly distorted by grief and affection. Her teeth, like ivory peeking from her lips, trembled a little with the desire to bite down on someone, her beloved. Her eyes, having seen too much and overflowing with tears, were shut tightly, twin pools that contained their own stillness. From my pillow I thought I could smell an old, familiar, yet slightly intoxicating scent, like sunlit linen, and for a moment I was frozen in place.

I heard the voice calling for my brother.

That day when Miki stood up for the first time, outside the window she had seen a boy leaping lightly, with a furoshiki cloth wrapped around his shoulders and a baseball cap turned backward, holding it so that it wouldn't fall off as he laughed and made a noise like he was crash-landing in a tree in the forest.

Miki's hand now touched her slender body, which had been unattainable to anyone else.

I heard a sigh.

That had been the very first time Miki had wanted to touch that boy, who glimmered like fresh, untrodden mountain snow. And so little baby Miki had stood up.

She had reached out her hands and that boy had exclaimed, with the innocence of a soap bubble that floats away and evaporates in the distance, "That's my little sister!"

And Miki had been in love with my brother ever since, all this time.

When we were little, when there was something she wanted to say, instead of speaking, Miki would just make a lot of noise. She'd drag something around with a clatter or scratch something that made a screech. We would listen to these sounds that reached our ears, knowing this meant Miki had something to say, and we realized how happy we were to hear them.

Miki's love was gentle—overwhelmingly and, if I'm being honest, frighteningly so. If everything in the world were to disappear and by some miracle only one thing was left, it would be her love.

But ever since she realized that her love was wrong, Miki had stopped making those noises.

Saa, saa, saa.

Saa, saa, saa.

At some point the sound of my heartbeat had faded into the distance. Outside the window, the raindrops were dutifully soaking the ground, and ever so quietly, as it was nighttime all over the world.

The Female Line

On one of those days when the sky was full of cirrocumulus clouds, so many clouds that it looked like a huge school of fish in a great hurry to get somewhere, my father disappeared from our home.

It happened quite suddenly, but the only thing that any of us—my mother, Miki, or myself—had to say about it was Miki's pithy, "Oh, shit."

The flowering quince was dropping all its leaves, as if caving under its own weight. Sakura, who had long since given up stuffing her mouth full of tawashi brushes, stood staring at the way the leaves fell to the ground.

At dawn, before the cirrocumulus clouds had formed, my father looked up at the sky just barely tinged pink and, after lightly patting Sakura—who had just emerged from her doghouse—on the nose to make sure it was appropriately wet, he had swung open the gate. It had clanked loudly but there was no point in worrying about it. My father knew that my mother would notice but, well, he was so very tired. The days at work when he had demonstrated his superior navigation skills, just like when he moved chess pieces around on the board, were long gone. Lately, my father was so totally worn out that at the office he often just sat there in a stupor. For example, he'd call out, "Number one-seven-six, come in," but then he'd fall silent, or he'd give the names of the roads to Hiroshima for the truck that was headed to Okayama—that kind of thing. In any case, it was a problem.

My father was utterly exhausted.

The swift pace at which the amount of alcohol in the kitchen was depleted. The wheelchair that didn't fit into storage and sat there gradually rusting. The last words left behind by his son: "I give up." All these things had sapped my father's heart just as they'd hollowed out his cheeks. Other memories—his wails on the day Miki was born, the smiles when he'd look up at me from reading his book, the hand placed on my mother's waist with his arm gently curving around her hip—had been forgotten by then.

My father was utterly exhausted.

One day, about a week after my father had left, Miki came to my room again.

At that point, we were already accustomed to the absence in the family, like we were to the sound of one of my mother's empty bottles on the floor or to the quince losing its leaves. There had been no contact from my father, but one night, maybe three days after he left, the phone rang.

"It's Mizoguchi."

The voice was familiar. Nevertheless, for a moment I didn't know who it was. I guess my vague reply, "Yes," had been unconvincing, so the person said, somewhat shyly, "It's Sakiko."

It was only after I realized it was Sakiko-san that I became aware of just how much I had wanted to hear her voice.

"Your father's fine," Sakiko-san said softly, and then hung up. I stood there, motionless, holding the receiver. Just what, exactly, did she mean by "fine"? My father was fine, he was alive. My father was fine, he'd come home soon. My father was fine, he's gaining back some weight. None of these options sat well with me. So, I opted to tell my mother and my sister that my father was with Sakiko-san, and that when the call ended, I had heard the sound that a payphone makes.

"Mm-hmm."

The female contingent of my family replied blankly, both of them with similar disinterest. My mother opened the toaster, took out the slices of bread, and spread them thickly with honey, while Miki was absorbed in a pedicure, which she'd started regularly giving to herself around that time (though almost all her toes were smudged).

The night when Miki came to my room that second time, her toenails were painted yellow. The upbeat yellow of the Brazilian soccer uniform—although, sure enough, they were totally smudged, which made it seem like her mind really had been somewhere else when she was painting them.

"My randoseru is gone."

Miki stared at me, sounding unconvinced as she said this. The way she looked at me, I wasn't convinced either, but then a particular image popped into my head.

A man with the morning paper tucked under his arm, an overnight bag in his right hand and, slung over his left shoulder, a tiny little red randoseru school bag. That old, faded randoseru, the shoulder strap mended with awfully thick stitches. Miki's randoseru, stuffed full of her suffering and longing, sadness and jealousy, affection and, above all, love for someone. Miki had handled the red leather so roughly, taking it out so many times and holding it close, wetting it with her tears, that she had long ago forgotten how pretty it had been when it was shiny and new. He must not have known what to do with it—too big to fit inside his overnight bag, but at the same time, too small to carry on his shoulder. He must have sighed deeply, and then, a bit self-consciously, slung it over shoulder. And he must have been rather surprised by how much its load had weighed upon his back.

That night, when my mother hadn't called us for dinner, my father must have been on the other side of the door, quietly listening to what Miki and I said to each other. He must have heard Miki as she recited Yajima-san's letters and then the rustling of those envelopes as they made that appallingly lovely trajectory.

And then, that rainy night, he too must have found out about Miki's love.

"My randoseru is gone."

Miki repeated herself, like a fool. But she had to have known that my father had taken it, and that she would probably never get it back. The look on her face was anxious, a little agitated, and yet cowardly, like a little girl who hands over to her mother the stuffed animal she'd always slept with, or like a little boy who finds a secret hiding place outside and doesn't tell anyone about it.

It occurred to me then that my father might never come back home.

And that, eventually, there wouldn't be any men left in the Hasegawa home.

I turned twenty and entered a university in Tokyo.

At that time, I had never given any thought to what lay ahead for me. The only thing I used my brain for was to retrace my memories—I didn't put any effort at all into thinking about things such as what I wanted to be or getting a new girlfriend. In my head, there were fragments of memories, just like a Picasso painting, that either glimmered with light or sank into darkness, the way that a solemn stained-glass window does in a church. My mind either reflected or absorbed things, but there was nothing about the future in it.

I had saved up my own money. It wasn't as if it had been my intention to go to college, nor was I trying to help with the household bills. There were deposits from my father transferred regularly into the family bank account, so we were able to maintain our life as usual. Most of the family's necessities were what was devoured by my mother. Neither Miki nor I needed to buy new shoes or new clothes or new hats—as far as Miki was concerned, she was content to wear the same clothing every single day.

I just thought I'd save up money. The same way that memories accumulated in my mind, or that Miki put those letters in her randoseru school bag, I just saved up money.

Since I basically didn't go outside except to walk Sakura, the one job I managed to get was as a decoy for an online dating site.

I'm a twenty-two-year-old single woman. I like tennis and karaoke. I'm looking for someone who will sing karaoke with me.

I'm a twenty-seven-year-old married woman. My afternoons are free, so send me a message.

I posed as a frightening number of women—sometimes I didn't even recognize myself anymore. Who was this person in front of the computer, tapping away on the keyboard, sending messages? This skinny, unshaven guy reflected in the dark screen of my computer when I shut it down? Losing myself like this, I was able to sit there brazenly, completely at ease. I must have become a hundred different women. Long-haired women, large-eyed women, left-handed women, buxom women. Women of various ages, with various hobbies, of all different physical attributes. And I knew every detail about every one of them; I never made mistakes in my responses. I was a man with no self. When I wrote those messages, I became those women, unfailingly.

Until one day, I realized something.

A hundred women. Pretty ones, plump ones, skinny ones, tough ones. Women who cried easily, women from Osaka, only children, returnees.

And they were all bored.

They all suffered from the same hopeless boredom of wanting to go off somewhere else, yet in spite of this they were afraid of making a move, so they did nothing. And at some point, I realized that this applied to me as well.

I felt a terrifying emptiness.

So I decided to go to Tokyo. I don't know why I chose Tokyo. I just wanted to go to a place where there were more people than here. I wanted to know what loneliness would feel like amid so much humanity. I wasn't thinking of my future or anything like that, except for a sudden, urgent desire:

I wanted to live on my own.

And with that, I ceded the Hasegawa house to the female line.

My mother, whose beauty had once captured everyone's attention. Her body had been like a beautiful river but, at some point, the waters had swelled and overflowed, and the river became unstoppable. She quaffed down anything with alcohol. Her guzzling was audible, and once she'd finished a bottle, her eyes would widen in apparent surprise at her own thirst, but then she'd reach for another bottle. The river continued to breach its banks, eventually reaching us. We didn't know how to swim in her river, and we were overtaken by the deluge.

And Miki, who always made friends with the rain. She was better suited than anyone to being inundated, and with her legs like carefully cultivated white asparagus and her body that had yet to be possessed by anyone. The one she loved—to the point that it blinded her and drove her mad—was her own brother.

After Hajime's disfiguring accident, she said that it made her happy. "It will keep away the other girls."

Hers was a thoroughly warped kind of love. So warped, and so sad that it could make you think it was the real thing. Miki was not one to cry often, but at times her body would forsake her and seemed to overflow with tears.

And then there was Sakura! Daring and clever, our best girl. So talkative and lively, yet at times reserved—that was Sakura. We learned from her chatter how much the world overflowed with love, and that there was nothing useless in it. For us, it was perfectly natural that we could hear her voice and understand what she was saying, just as she took in everything we said to her with those adorable little ears, mottled with grape-like spots.

The moving truck gradually pulled away from my mother, from Miki, and from Sakura. Their reflections in the rearview mirror might have looked foolish or annoying, but to me they were pure light. Dazzling, iridescent light, the kind of light you can't look at directly. As I felt that light shine in my eyes, I wished that, in my next life, I could be reborn as a woman.

The truck picked up speed and turned the corner. As it turned, I caught a glimpse of my mother waving goodbye, and then I was crying so hard, I slumped down in the passenger seat.

PART 6
The End

Mating Cats

When I return from Sakura's walk, Miki is sitting idly in the yard. When she notices Sakura and me, she makes kind of a strange face and then walks over to give Sakura a hug.

I have the sense that I'm dreaming.

Miki's short hair sways lightly, reminding me of when she was a newborn. Her hair then had been like freshly made ice cream, with a sweet and mild scent. Inhaling that scent, I had been rapt with the joy of having a sister.

"Sakuraaa," Miki says, drawing out the last syllable and giving Sakura's body a good rub. It's been quite a while since she's had a bath, so she vibrates with pleasure from the massage. Who knows what kind of bugs or germs Sakura has on her, but this doesn't bother Miki at all—she plays with her, biting Sakura's tail and burying her face in Sakura's belly.

"Phone."

With her face still in Sakura's belly, Miki voice is muffled.

"Huh?"

"Phone was ringing."

Miki looks up. There are a bunch of hairs from Sakura's belly stuck to her cheeks. Miki doesn't make any effort to brush them away, so I feel compelled to pluck them off, one by one.

"My phone?"

Just then, I hear a familiar ringtone coming from the living room.

Within seconds, the ringing stops. I take out my cell phone and open it to see my girlfriend's name. I close the phone and am about to go back out into the yard when it starts ringing again. I don't feel like answering, but not answering will cause more trouble than it's worth so, reluctantly, I press "accept."

"Hello?"

"Oh, Kaoru-kun, what happened? I was shocked!"

My girlfriend's voice is high-pitched. There are oh-so-many things that she finds shocking. She's constantly grabbing my arm and saying, "I was shocked!"

"By what?"

"The girl who answered just now, who's that?"

"Huh?"

"When I called just now, a girl answered! I was shocked, I thought I had the wrong number! Who is she?"

The only person who would have done something like that was Miki.

"My younger sister."

"What? Your sister? Kaoru-kun, you have a sister?"

"Yeah."

"Whaaa . . . I didn't know that! I was pretty nasty to her! Well, I guess I . . ."

"What?"

"Well, she sounded really pissed off herself."

"Why?"

"She answered the phone with a 'Yes,' and at first I didn't say anything, but then when I asked who it was, she didn't respond. Then she, she . . . do you know what she said to me?"

"What'd she say?"

"She said I have a weird voice! Can you believe it?"

I almost burst into laughter. A weird voice, hm. That sounds exactly like something Miki would say.

"Do I? Do I have a weird voice?"

Kinda, I want to say, but there's something cloying about the way she asks me. It's the same as when she asks, "Do you hate me?" And she'll get me to reply, "No, I love you."

I know she wants me to say, *Not at all, you have a cute voice!* Her expectation comes through loud and clear over the receiver, but I pretend we have a bad connection.

"Uh, sorry. I couldn't hear you very well."

". . . oh, never mind."

Then she asks me when I'm coming home, what I've been doing here, whether I've seen my old school friends (in particular any girls), she grills me on all the details (she even says, "Talk in Kansai dialect!") and then, after she's told me all about what's going on with her, she finally hangs up. By the time I get off the phone, I'm totally bushed.

Next thing I know, I look up to see Miki bringing Sakura into the living room, acting as if nothing's wrong.

"Miki, you answered my phone?"

"Uh-huh."

"That's my cell phone."

"Your ringtone, that's 'Top of the World,' right?"

"It is."

"Top of the world."

"Miki."

"Uh-huh."

"That was my girlfriend."

"Uh-huh."

"Did she have a weird voice?"

"Yeah."

"Weird, how?"

"It sounded like cats mating."

Again, I have to keep myself from laughing. My girlfriend's voice actually does sound just like the noises that alley cats make in early spring

"'Cats mating'?! What are you talking about?!"

My mother bursts into the room, her cheeks bright red. Behind her stands my father, looking completely back at home, if still a little tired.

Miki is about to repeat "cats mating" but before she can get the words out, my mother beats her to it, shouting:

"We're going to the cemetery!"

After my father had left home, my mother had swapped our big van for a kei car with a yellow, restricted license plate. The car is too small for my mother to fit comfortably inside, and with Miki in the passenger seat and my father and me riding in the back seat, even a policeman with poor vision might stop us for exceeding the passenger limit.

My father sits, motionless, tucked in the back with his eyes closed. He's wearing a brown coat that contrasts with the yellow checked seat cover like a sunflower. His face is partially obscured by the armful of flowers that my mother made him carry. With his eyes closed and his face surrounded by the white, yellow, and purple flowers, he reminds me of my dead brother, and I look away.

Whenever I think of Hajime in his coffin, it will always be as my handsome brother.

He had been lying there among so many beautiful flowers,

freshly watered and cool, but his face was purple and swollen, his mouth open in an unnatural way, so that he looked like some kind of bruised fruit. Still, the image in my head is of my handsome brother—his closed lids creating a faint shadow under his eyes, his nose arranged perfectly like a Himalayan peak, and his mouth, were he to smile, revealing pearly white teeth.

At the funeral, I hadn't shed a single tear.

"Miki, did you bring the incense?"

"Yes, I've got it."

"What about you, Kaoru?"

"Huh?"

"What did you bring?"

"I didn't bring anything."

"Oh, really?!"

My mother shouts, and then jams her foot on the accelerator. Surprised by the car's sudden jolt, my father opens his eyes. Now his face looks even more like Hajime's, and I try to avoid looking in his direction.

Even if we don't get stopped for being over the limit, we're clearly speeding as we pass the park that had been demolished to make way for new houses and the civic center where I had met Yukawa-san. This all goes by at an alarming speed.

My mother isn't holding the steering wheel so much as clinging to it, and Miki, in the passenger seat, isn't wearing a seatbelt. She's eating the jellybeans that didn't make it into the gyoza. As she munches on each small bite, she looks like a squirrel.

Crows

My mother keeps my brother's grave very tidy.

The polished gray stone sparkles in the winter light. Set against the whitish sky, it reminds me of when the three of us siblings had wandered around outside of the funeral hall at Granny's funeral.

As we watched the smoke from Granny climb up into the sky, we had meandered among the tombstones. I held Miki's hand—she kept trying to take the manju buns or bananas that had been left as offerings—and kept an eye on Hajime as he walked ahead of us. I was trying hard to follow his quick pace and sudden turns through the cemetery's narrow and labyrinthine paths while leading Miki along at her toddling gait. My brother was sulking a little and taking a haphazard route—it seemed like he was trying to get lost in the maze—as he made his way deeper into the cemetery.

Just when I was about to give up on keeping up with him, Hajime stopped in his tracks.

"Aha."

We hurried to catch up to him, to see what he had found. He was standing there, staring blankly at a perfectly ordinary gravestone. It was decorated with what appeared to be recent offerings: yellow chrysanthemums that gleamed in the sun, and incense that had just burned down and whose scent still wafted in the air. I followed Hajime's gaze and saw written on the stone:

HASEGAWA FAMILY TOMB

I was too young to be able to recognize all the kanji, but I knew that was our name. My brother didn't bother to speak; he just stared at the tombstone. I have no memory whatsoever of what happened next—whether we talked about anything there or just brought Miki back to the funeral hall—but I do recall the sense of foreboding evoked by the stone, glinting in the white light.

HASEGAWA FAMILY TOMB

My mother promptly fills a bucket with water and, despite the cold, vigorously wrings out a cleaning rag. Miki no longer just does whatever she pleases, but she seems to find the graveside visit boring and, glancing at my mother busily wiping down the gravestone, she then looks off in a completely different direction. My father stands a slight distance away from us smoking a cigarette, perhaps in an effort to relax. The purple smoke that swirls around him seems particularly strong, but when I look closely, I see that it's the menthol cigarette I had given him a little while ago. My eyes are playing tricks on me.

"Alright! Let's all put our hands together!"

My mother sits down heavily and presses her palms together, which look like tiny gloves.

"Hajime, we all came to see you today."

Ever since my mother started overeating, she now overdoes everything, down to the most minor everyday things. She's lit about fifty sticks of incense at once, so that their purported "subtle fragrance" permeates the entire area around us.

"Hajime, we all came, to see you today," she repeats, and then sniffles.

In the past, whenever my mother cried, it would make us panicky, like chicks who had forgotten where the nest was. She had a perpetual smile, and her laughter was contagious to everyone around her, so seeing her cheeks wet with tears would throw us into high gear to figure out how to dry them. Like athletes training muscles we didn't normally use, we'd stay close to her side, bringing over her favorite book or telling her about something interesting we'd learned in school, just to hear her laugh once more. And once a smile softened her face again, we'd ask what it was we had done so we'd know how to stop her crying next time, and she'd always say the same thing:

"Just seeing the three of you together, that's all I need."

Unexpectedly and at an early age, the eldest Hasegawa son had joined the family tomb. My mother's sniffles are naturally followed by her crying. No sobbing or weeping, nothing audible. Just a steady flow of teardrops from her eyes, very much like that night I had seen Miki cry. When the Hasegawa women are truly sad, their bodies seem to reach a saturation point. In no time at all, my mother's lap is soaked with tears.

Caw, goes the insipid call of a crow. Its slick body is blacker than Sakura's spots, and every so often it makes a sound in its throat like a cat purring.

SAKURA

HASEGAWA FAMILY TOMB

My brother doesn't say anything. My brother, who had laughingly told us that he could have sex every day until he was spent and it wouldn't be enough, now lies still and breathless under that cold stone.

Miki starts throwing rocks at the crows. She carefully chooses from among the shiny pebbles covering people's graves and then looks up at the sky, dazzled by the light. The stones she throws carve odd arcs in the air before landing on someone else's grave.

Katsun! Katsun!

After I count seven distinct sounds of pebbles clattering against headstones, I go over and squat next to my mother. The tops of her thighs have expansive wet patches that resemble mysterious continents from prehistoric times. She is crying so much, I try to console her by putting my arm around her shoulder, but her shoulders are so broad that I'm not able to reach all the way around, so instead I press my palms together. Come to think of it, maybe my father feels the same way. My mother's body seems to be bursting at the seams with so much sadness, and yet my father is unable to take it all on himself. Her once slender hips and supple shoulders have slipped through his fingers and expanded well beyond his reach, to some distant world.

I close my eyes, and I catch the scent of another kind of smoke. My father is crouching beside me. I hear a muffled sound, and I think he might be stifling a laugh, but from his direction I feel the ever-so-slightest trembling, so I keep my eyes closed.

"Hajime."

Swayed by the trembling, I can't tell whose voice has uttered his name.

Now that I think about it, despite Miki's pinpoint control, not one of those stones even grazed the crows.

Katsun!

Wild Pitches

"Sakura's..."

When Miki bursts into my room, it's less than four hours until the new year. This is around the time when my mother would start cooking the gyoza, even if it is rather on the early side. When we returned home from the cemetery, she exclaimed, "Ah, I'm so tired!" and then spent the next two hours or so ingesting a large amount of sweets.

As Miki bursts into my room, the delicious aroma of gyoza frying is permeating the house, further dispersing the "subtle fragrance" that had infused our clothes.

"Sakura's..."

Her face is as pale as a kid who's just gotten out of the pool early in the season, her lips purple like hydrangeas at nighttime. After muttering about Sakura, she slumps down by the door.

Sakura is lying halfway out of her doghouse with her eyes shut tight. I can tell right away from this unnatural position that something is wrong but, running my hands over her body, I can't find any strange lumps or caked blood or anything unusual, so I figure whatever it is must be internal.

Her breathing is very shallow. As insubstantial as a mosquito in early autumn that you could catch with your hands and that would be obliterated by even a sneeze.

No matter how vigorously Miki pets her, Sakura doesn't wag her tail. Normally it waves like a bargain-sale flag, but seeing her now, you'd think she'd never wagged her tail in her life, and this seems to indicate that it isn't just a matter of her tail but something more serious that's amiss.

"Sakura, Sakura."

Seeing her so listless, I can't help but flash back to those crows, which now seem like a sinister omen. Why hadn't Miki managed to hit them with the stones? I have the feeling that if she'd gotten any of them, Sakura wouldn't be lying here, collapsed on the threshold of her doghouse, her breathing so faint it is practically nonexistent.

Miki has been petting Sakura this entire time. Her eyes are dry, but Miki's body gives off the scent of copious tears and once those thin shoulders start trembling, I know what that means.

"Sakura, Sakura."

My mother jostles Miki out of the way and scoops Sakura into her husky embrace. As Sakura is lifted up, she makes a strange gurgle and, hearing this, Miki draws in a big, panicked breath.

There is a beautiful moon in the sky, which seems appropriate for New Year's Eve, and the glittering stars clustering around it let us know this is the end of the year. Their light seems to reach us so directly, I lose track of when the present is.

"Let's go to the clinic," my father says.

"What clinic?" my mother responds in a low voice. We've never heard her voice sound like that, full of malice and anger. She had spoken without turning around and now, for the first time, the anger and sadness she felt toward my father radiates clearly from her back.

"That place where we took her before."

"That doctor was a pervert, and the place got shut down, don'tcha know?"

Her weight has flattened her voice but when she speaks this time, she enunciates clearly from the back of her throat, the way she used to when she was petite. My mother is so angry, she's shaking. I've never seen her like this before.

"I didn't know."

"How can you not know? How can you not know!"

My mother hugs Sakura. And then, despite how much she'd cried earlier at my brother's grave, her tears well up all over again.

"Why, why?"

My mother's face, smeared with snot and tears, looks awful. Her face looks so ugly, it has a mysterious kind of sanctity. My mother's sorrow begins to give the sky and the air a strange color.

"That happened before you ran away from home, didn't it?!"

Just then, my mother's love for my father becomes frighteningly clear to me. As she shouts at him, each hatred-infused word is the fruit of her pained love for my father. It wasn't misdirected sorrow or anger that had made my mother's body grow so big—rather, she had just continued to expand with her feelings for the man she loved.

"You ran away . . . from home . . . how do you . . . think I . . ."

It's no longer Sakura my mother is looking at. What she sees is all the time that's been lost, from when my brother had his accident, to his death, and up until today.

There should have been another happy time for us. Another

world, in which my brother hadn't had his accident or taken his own life. In that world, my brother would be off at some university, playing soccer and being popular. He'd come back home sometimes, he'd make us all laugh, he'd reassure us, and we'd all sleep peacefully. My mother's hips would still be delicate and slender, and sometimes my father would stroke her hair the way he had when they were sweethearts. Sakura would call out loudly for Miki, and the two of them would chatter away like schoolgirls. Then, when summer came around, we'd take another family portrait.

Our precious, lost time.

That other world, where we were always laughing, always ridiculously happy, always carefree. But we are here, in this world, gathered and weeping around Sakura, who is motionless. Our mother is on the verge of giving up herself. Her large body trembling, she utters words that she's never said before.

"Why did such a terrible . . . ?"

Ah, here's God, throwing us another wild pitch.

The moon shines a pale salmon pink. Just around its edges is an orangish aura, the color like a sunset's afterglow, which makes me wonder again if it might rain tomorrow. I look over at Miki, the girl who can always predict when it will rain, but she is sitting beside Sakura, rubbing her body incessantly. There could be a major global crisis, people all over the world could be fleeing from disaster, and I bet Miki would still be in the same spot, continuing to pet Sakura. For Miki, who has lost the one she loved, and for my mother as well, Sakura is a symbol of their happiness. She represents our good fortune, when the Hasegawa family used to shine bright and had always been laughing. For our family, down by one and now struggling, Sakura is a source of stability and reassurance. All I have to do is touch her warm body to be reminded, with heart-wrenching joy, of that summer day when Miki and I brought her home with us.

Sakura has been bearing the weight of the entire family's memories. Day after day, she wags her tail madly, yawns deeply, and peers at us through the window with concern. She pees bashfully, then grunts with satisfaction and wanders around, her black spots swaying. All these gestures symbolize our happiness. So long as Sakura is there, we can look away from our sadness, ignore our dreadful loneliness, and, even though it might still require a bit of effort, we can manage to greet the morning.

Now our happiness—Sakura—is breathing as if the air is leaking out of her somewhere, and her tail lies there, stiff like a dead mouse. I'm not sure that she's going to make it.

The moon has begun to drift slowly, its orange aura now turning a grayish blue. The cold wind whips up nasty little whirls that seem to rip at our fingers.

Ah, here's God, throwing us another wild pitch.

"Let's go to the clinic," my father repeats himself, speaking clearly this time.

My mother looks up at him, astonished.

"Weren't you listening to what I said? That place shut down," she objects.

I listen apprehensively to this exchange between my parents, like I had when I was little and would peek through a cracked-open door. Whenever they fought, my father always gave in. He would just stare at her, watching as she gesticulated to fully express herself, and then he'd take her hands in his and say, "I'm sorry."

And with the power of those two words, my mother would realize that she may have gone a bit too far herself. Then her indescribable feelings for my father would well up and she would pretend to pout shyly.

But tonight, my father refuses to give in. With the stern look of a grown-up, the likes of which we've never seen on his face before, he says, "We'll find another clinic."

As my mother is about to protest again, he says calmly, "Let's find somewhere else." His voice is low, like the sound of a distant steam whistle, and authoritative. My mother falls silent, her cheeks still wet with tears. My father lifts my mother's arms up high, like when he used to swoop up us kids all together in his embrace. Caught off guard, my mother stumbles, and she stares at my father with surprise, but my father has already gone back into the house to get the car keys.

Catcher

My father is flummoxed by driving the kei car for the first time. It fits him better than it does my mother, who is now squeezed into the back seat, but he takes a long time fiddling with the key in the ignition and adjusting the rearview mirror.

The used van that was the previous family car would occasionally throw a tantrum and die on us. Its engine was known to crap out just while sitting at a light, and it might take four or five tries to get it going again. Nevertheless, my father had doted on that van, cajoling it like it was his darling little girl, and he managed to make it go wherever he wanted.

Now, my father expresses surprise when the new car starts right up, and also by how light the accelerator is.

"Whoa!"

When my father puts his foot on the gas pedal, the car zooms out of the garage with such speed that we nearly crash into the wall around the Onishis' house.

My mother screams my father's name and Miki, holding Sakura in her arms, scolds her for being so loud. "Keep your voice down!"

I sit in the passenger seat without saying a word, my heart racing. My father, at pains to accustom himself to this car's extra-light steering wheel, misses the opening to apologize to these two Furies. He may have missed colliding with the Onishis' wall, but the car is weaving erratically as it speeds up, so that the police won't be the only ones who want to pull us over.

I happen to look in the side mirror and notice that the moon is following us. What had been an orange aura is now a perfectly deep indigo, producing a solemn New Year's Eve mood. Warm light radiates from house after house, where families sit together in a circle, and though we can't hear it, it's easy to imagine that some of them are watching the *Kohaku Uta Gassen* music special on TV.

There isn't a single other car on the road. When we pass the konbini where my brother had gone to buy batteries, we see a high-school-age kid trying to balance plastic bags while on his bicycle. Sakura is curled up very small, her head buried in Miki's lap and illuminated by the blue light of the neon sign. She has the habit of blinking a lot when she rides in a car, but she doesn't even do this now. Every so often, one of her legs will just twitch resignedly.

The yokai veterinarian's clinic had since been reborn as multiple different businesses and has currently taken the form of a dubiously stylish beauty salon. The image of an attractive and extremely blond model with a peculiar hairstyle is smiling at us. Had there been a face on the moon in tonight's sky, it might have looked like this—a sort of detached and derisive smirk as if to say, "Sucks for you!"

It pisses me off, to be smirked at like that.

"Gh-ff-guh."

Sakura starts making a strange burping sound, which sends Miki into a panic.

"Sakura . . ." she says, curling into a ball and burying her own face atop Sakura. Despite how cramped we are inside the little car, the terrifying sense of inevitability feels all-pervasive. It reminds me of what Miki said about Hajime's hiragana that one night:

"Like the white of the notebook is cold and the letters are curled up into themselves."

After which she had proceeded to recite, at length, what Yajima-san had written to Hajime. I wondered whether she still remembered those letters. I bet she could still recite them, word for word, punctuation marks included, as if she had written them herself.

"Sakura, Sakura."

Miki keeps calling out Sakura's name, sounding like she had that night, her voice trailing off. As if, were she to stop, Sakura's body would completely shut down.

"Sakura."

I'm annoyed by the moon relentlessly following us, and I glare at the sky. I roll down the window and cold air streams in, chilling our cheeks.

"And just where do you think we're going?" my mother asks, with her left eye closed against the gust of cold air. "There aren't any clinics around here, are there?"

"There's one—if we go straight on the Two, then turn right at the underpass for the Seven, it's about twelve miles from there."

My father keeps looking straight ahead as he speaks. The traffic light is just about to change from amber to red, but he steps on the gas anyway.

"Huh?"

"It's there." My father says this with such decisiveness there's no room for any of us to question him.

Cars are few and far between on the Two as well, it being New Year's Eve. Our car veers over the lines on the road and ignores traffic lights, doing as we please, just like Miki at the funeral. At the underpass for the Seven, we make a right turn and, after going a little way, we actually do see a sign for "Veterinary Hospital."

My palms are sweating in anticipation and anxiety. I can't imagine how my father knows about this clinic, but we marvel at the sight of that sign, and my father seems a little overexcited in the driver's seat.

He's clinging to the steering wheel as he revs the gas, and before I even register that all the lights are out at the hospital, he has banged a U-turn. The sudden movement causes us all to pitch forward and then topple over and Miki, who had been protectively holding Sakura, hits her head against the window. With these jolts, Sakura lets out another ominous-sounding burp: "gh-puh."

My mother screams at my father again. But my father pays her no mind.

"There's another one, if we take the road in front of Ace Prep School toward the central hospital, then at the five-way junction, we head past the lake."

The moon is a bit blindsided, having to hurry to keep up with us.

My father is firing on all cylinders. Every cell in his body, his blood, his strength—they're feeding his brain even without any sugar.

Everything stored in his head about all the roads in Japan starts pouring forth, and he tells us, in rapid succession, about the roads that lead to various veterinary hospitals located near our house, and then those a little farther away, and then those really far away. As if to reassure us, he keeps talking, describing those old, round, seemingly forgotten mailboxes by the side of the road, or even older election posters that still hang in places, incredible facts about these roads that never see the light of day. My father knows every detail about every road—you never would have thought he's just been sitting in the control room, directing trucks where to go all this time.

"There are plenty of clinics," my father says, and hands me a road atlas. It had been stuffed in his pocket, so it's crumpled and dirty and it seems pretty old. My hands are shaking as I turn the pages, which are all blackened. Every single road has been blotted out with a pencil, rendering it useless as a map.

"The whole thing is black," I mutter.

"I marked every road after taking it," my father says self-consciously.

The man who had directed others to navigate all over Japan's roads has now taken all of them himself. He has spent nights under various skies, in the cold and in the heat, while local programs come through over the radio. He might find a spot he likes and work there for a little while, but then he'll move on again. He can't resist the urge to grip the steering wheel. He has to be on the road. With that beat-up overnight bag on the passenger seat and, in the back seat, that red randoseru school bag.

My father's atlas is pitch-black. And the lead is darker, the closer the roads are to our home. My father has circled our house, over and over again. I look over at him.

"There are plenty of clinics," my father repeats to himself triumphantly. But there is no way for me to determine the location of these clinics.

My mother doesn't say anything. She just sits there silently, watching my father as he turns the extra-light steering wheel. Her expression is not the blank one from late nights in the kitchen, when she reaches for a magnum of something—instead, I think it's probably the one she had in Chinatown, the look when she'd fallen in love and knew she wanted to eat gyoza to her heart's content with this man.

So there we are again, the whole family bringing Sakura to the vet.

This, along with so many nearly forgotten things—"nobody's flowers," Ferrari mesmerized by Miki, making my pee go farther with Hajime, my mother's voice like a mother cat, Yukawa-san's pink glasses, Genkan's modest breasts—have whooshed out the open window, to be left behind.

My father has been talking so much that Miki finally stops petting Sakura and just stares at him. She has the same look in her eyes as when she'd been listening avidly to my mother telling her about the marvels of sex.

"And?" she urges him to continue.

My father is in his element, like a fish taking to water, like Sakura with a tawashi brush, as he soaks up all our attention. He responds to our encouragement, with answers to all our questions and boundless information.

It turns out we've inherited our amazing powers of memory from him. What formidable DNA.

"They're unhittable."

I can hear my brother's voice. *They're unhittable.*

Like a tape that had been on fast-forward and then slowly comes back to regular speed, I began to understand something inside my heart.

SAKURA

My father, like a madman, keeps steering us along the roads, from one clinic to the next. His crazy driving (trash bins overturned, walls grazed) prompts residents to notify the police and rouse the drowsy officers off their duffs. We hear the sound of a siren in the distance.

"Oh, but it's New Year's Eve!" my mother exclaims.

Remembering our family tradition, I make a suggestion.

"Let's bring Sakura back home and eat gyoza."

Upon hearing the word "gyoza," Sakura gives a feeble response, but then she just burps again.

"Miki, you made some 'winner' dumplings, right?" I know the answer, but I ask anyway, and Miki pinches my shoulder tightly.

"Yup."

"You're sure?"

"Yup."

She hasn't let go of my shoulder.

"Miki," my father says. That's right, this is when he says this.

"I got rid of your randoseru."

My mother starts crying. She wails like a little kid, *waahh, waahh*. Sweet Sakura tries to lick her face, but the car is going so fast that the centrifugal force keeps her glued to Miki's lap.

"I got rid of it."

I know without having to turn around that Miki is crying. She's incredibly quiet, but tears are again flowing from her eyes in that certain way of hers. And there beside her, my mother who had given birth to Miki, is bawling as if the roles are reversed and she is Miki's little baby girl. What a raucous scene it is, there inside our car—such authentic tears.

"I . . ."

Miki starts to speak but my mother's sobbing doesn't stop. Is she starting a crying diet? Does she want to suffocate us with her weeping?

"I, uh . . ."

Miki's voice trembles, matching the rocking of the car.

"I-if I fell in love with someone . . ."

The words spill out of Miki the same way that her tears do. Just like when she was little and would make so much noise in order to communicate what she was feeling—sadness, yearning, hatred, isolation, jealousy—now she does so in the form of words.

"I'd tell them, I love you. Without any hesitation. I'd tell them how much I loved them. Yeah, because you never know how long that person's gonna be around, right? You don't know if they'll always be there, yeah. If I love them, I'll tell them. And then, then, if that person loves me too, I'll say thank you, and then, we'll have sex. Sex. Like Mom said, right? The person you love, there's nothing dirty about their pee-pee, yeah? I'll have lots of sex. Mom, the way your voice sounded that time was so beautiful. It was more beautiful than anything I'd ever heard. More beautiful than the sound of rain in the middle of the night, than the sound of the waves, so much more beautiful. Right, Kaoru? We heard Mom's voice while we were sleeping. We listened to the voice of sex and then we were sleeping. I can make a baby, yeah. I can make a baby. I don't care whether it's a boy or a girl. And whichever it is, here's what I'll tell them: Thank you for being born. Right, Mom, isn't that what you said? You had sex, you made that beautiful voice, and then the next day, that's what you said to me: Thank you for being born. I'll say that too: Thank you for being born. Right? When that kid gets a little bigger, we'll play together. I'll teach them hiragana letters, and you know how little kids ask things like, why is the sky blue? Well then, we'll think about it together. We'll look up at the sky together for a long time and wonder why it's blue, and we'll be stumped, we might even cry a little. We'll wonder why it's so big, and we'll be stumped. At some point, that kid will figure it out themselves, why the sky is blue. And then they'll fall in love, right? And when they do, I'll say, you have to tell them you love them. That person might go away somewhere, so hurry, hurry, tell them you love them. Even if my kid throws things like Hajime did, like a fan or plates, it'll be okay, I'll be able to dodge it. With Hajime, is it really true that you only did it once? Yeah? It only took one time for Hajime. He was always, he smiled so much, and then, he died. He died. Hajime. My brother. I loved him. Hajime. My brother. Ah, so much, I, my kid will grow up, yeah, I don't know if I'll have grandkids, I don't know what kind of grown-ups they'll be, or what will happen, but I have to, I have to die before them. I absolutely have to die first. And then, when I die, I'll tell them. I'll be sure to say, Thank you for being born. Mom, Dad. Yeah? Hajime is dead so, yeah, isn't that how you feel? You're glad he was born. Right? Aren't you?"

How's that, Miki? My memory's pretty good too, isn't it? I only heard Miki say all this that one time, but to this day, I can still recall it perfectly.

"Thank you for being born."

My mother's wails now reach the heavens. And then, of all things, as if she's spurred him on, my father starts crying too. His wails are just like on that day in the hospital when Miki was born and he saw her for the first time, and then he thought of us waiting for him back home, all of which made him weep. And Miki's name had come to him: the epitome of beauty, the most precious thing.

So, there we are again, the whole family bringing Sakura to the vet!

In the driver's seat, a man whose wails sound like wolves howling off in the distance, the same man who was once the happiest man in the universe. In the back seat is a girl babbling like a fool, maybe the second or third most beautiful girl in the world. Next to her is a woman who, in the span of a few years, gained more weight than would have been thought possible, but she's so dazzling you can even tell how beautiful she is (even when she's bawling her eyes out). And then there's our girl, who from the day she arrived at our home brought with her a light, sweet, warmth, like the pink flower petal stuck to her tail. Sakura. Sakura!

Ha ha, look Hajime, it's New Year's Eve and we've got the cops chasing us!

They're unhittable.

I can hear a voice. Perfectly clear, I can hear my brother's voice. But no, you're wrong. Hajime, you were wrong.

They're unhittable.

You're wrong, Hajime. God never threw you an unhittable pitch.

We're the ones who kept throwing 'em.

Day after day, we laughed, we cried, we got angry, we fell in love, we lost at love and cried again, and every time, we kept them coming, aimed at the one we called God, asking, *What the*

SAKURA

hell—what's this all about? Why would you do this to me, something so terrible?!

But every time, God just caught our pitches.

No matter how fast, how wild—I hate to admit it, but God caught every one of them perfectly.

What God said was, "Hey there, look, every pitch, they're all alike!"

For us, it was the same old routine.

"Every ball is just like the one before it."

At that moment, Sakura, who has been burping on Miki's lap, says, *Did you say 'ball'? I love the way they bounce!*

And that's when Sakura started talking again.

Sakura

Sakura is sleeping under the bicycles, her breath rising and falling.

The sun looks a bit tired, kind of like a school athlete who has splashed water on his face and comes back out with renewed determination to win—but it shines brightly, if a little too big, as it casts our fresh shadows on the ground.

Bored with looking at Sakura's paw pads, I go into the house. I grab one of the hardened gyoza lying on the table. I bite down on something crunchy and the sweet taste of peach fills my mouth. *Shit.* I got one with jellybeans.

On the TV, the female announcer is all dressed up and talking about the current habits for New Year's across the country. As each correspondent introduces themselves, they wave their hands and shout their name. They're really hitting the ground running, even on the first day of the year.

Miki has crashed out like Sakura. One leg is thrust out from the sofa. Maybe she's wisely given up on the messy pedicures, but her unpainted toenails are a pretty pink color.

I grab another dumpling. This one is filled with M&M's. Fuming, I kick Miki, who groans and starts snoring loudly. I go to turn off the TV and, just as I do so, as if to stop me, the announcer chirps, "Happy New Year!"

We were totally out of our minds last night.

We went to every last veterinary clinic, knocking on the shuttered doors, begging them to open up for us—we might as well have been in a manga or something—but we had no luck anywhere. We even went to an emergency room for people (causing the nurse at reception to snort with laughter at us).

We ventured far afield. It was a very odd experience, driving through totally unfamiliar towns in the middle of the night, on New Year's Eve, no less. As we sped along the straight and open roads, it felt like we were about to soar up into the sky and that we might remain up there for days, without anyone knowing. There was something about those deserted roads, late at night, where a family could disappear into the night sky and it would be unremarkable.

Besides myself, the other three had finally stopped crying and then, whether out of self-consciousness or as a distraction from Sakura's discomfort, they started talking kind of rudely (like the way my mother addressed my father in a more familiar but still not sweet tone, or Miki saying that, had I been the one who was sick, we wouldn't be going all out like this).

That was when, at last, we heard the police siren approaching.

"Not again!" my mother said but, thinking back now on that boisterous New Year's Eve drive, this time the siren was clearly coming toward us.

"Stop your vehicle," a dull voice projected over a speaker.

My father acted oblivious about his erratic driving. "Now what—not with Sakura like this!" he exclaimed with exasperation.

Miki resumed her long-abandoned battle readiness and my father, who had also forgotten to bring his driver's license, was preparing to pounce on the cops. Meanwhile, my mother was working up a good show of crocodile tears.

Without compunction, the cop shined his flashlight inside the car. We were dizzy from the glare and our own impatience. Sakura still lay there limply, not moving a muscle even when the flashlight shined in her eyes.

"What is this? We have an invalid here!" my father shouted.

"Gh-ff-gobb." Sakura let out her most exaggerated burp yet.

"An invalid?"

The young officer was momentarily stunned by Miki's beauty, who was staring him down. Miki started to roll down her window, ready to give him a wallop, just as my father pre-emptively stepped on the gas.

That same instant, there was a loud farting noise.

Judging by its stridence, we were all ready to blame my mother, but she immediately screamed:

"Whoa, it stinks!"

As a stench filled the entire car, I noticed the distinct scent of grass mixed in with the funk, and I turned around.

Miki was covered in Sakura's green poop. Sakura was bashfully wagging her tail.

Ugh, I'm so glad that's finally out!

Miki hadn't been so besmirched since her days of playing "I Dare You."

My father had his license suspended for speeding and driving without his license, as well as for violating traffic laws and disturbing the peace.

And, for the second time in my life, I got to ride in a patrol car. That first time hadn't been very exciting for me. The policeman driving it had seemed big and intimidating, and even though the landscape passing by outside the patrol car window was familiar, I had been worried that we were being taken somewhere unknown. But back then, I had Hajime. He'd held my hand tightly, and even though he was the second youngest one in the car, I knew he would still protect me from whatever happened—that was my trustworthy older brother. Hajime. Who was gone now. His eyes that had peered into mine, his feet that had kicked the soccer ball—those had returned to dust and were far off now. I felt betrayed and despondent; I gave up on everything. I loved my brother, I hated him, there were times when I pitied him. But that all ended today. No, make that yesterday—better to have a clean slate. New Year's Day. Beside me then was Miki. Next to her was my mother. My father was in front of me. And on his lap, Sakura.

"Ah."

Miki looked dazzled. My mother bent her body to look out the window. My father must have had his eyes closed. Not because he was sleeping, but because he was contemplating something that had welled up inside him.

"Kaoru, look."

I know, Miki. Ha ha, I already know, okay? We were lit by a ray of light. No, it'd be stingy to call it just one ray—once it appeared, it showered over us like never-ending rain.

"Look, here comes the sun."

That poor policeman, who'd ended up marking the first sunrise of the new year with this nutty family, slowed down a little.

"The new year has begun."

None of us looked at each other. Instead, all of us Hasegawas were smiling at Sakura's wagging tail.

We all looked a lot alike.

My mother is in the yard, mixing fertilizer into the soil. Next to her big shadow, as if attached to it, is a smaller one. My father's zipper is half-open, something that he never would have let happen in the past. I figure I should let him know, but then I'm stunned by the song that my mother starts singing:

Ii-zaa-raa,
za-aafa-u-ebaa,
shin-yu-bii-ora-u,
yoo-raa-pummi,
aa-zaa-toppo-rawaa

It's the song of the camel. The one the lady in purple with the cat in the satellite-dish collar had sung.

"Mom!"

I rush into the yard in a frenzy, not even caring that I'm barefoot. My fluster even wakes up Sakura. She looks over at me unenthusiastically from under the bicycles.

"Hm?"

"What's that song?"

"Huh?"

"That song you were just singing."

"Ah, *yoo-raa-pummi, aa-zaa-toppo-rawaa*?"

"Yes, yes! That one!"

"Why are you so worked up about it?"

"That song, Mom, you used to sing it, I . . ."

"Huh?"

"The lady in purple, surely she . . ."

As I continue to speak, I start to feel self-conscious. That had to have been a dream. My mother must have been the one singing that, and I must have just heard it, in my dream state.

"What are you talking about, Kaoru?"

My father is looking at me, mystified. He has a smudge of earth on the tip of his nose and, standing there right next to my mother, even though they are totally different, somehow they look like twins.

"You and Hajime used to sing that song all the time, didn'tcha?"

"Huh?"

"You know, when your dad and I would play our Carpenters record, you two would pretend you were singing along in English."

I'm dumbfounded.

"*Is the love that I've found ever since you've been around. Your love's put me at the top of the world.* That's it, right?"

"*Ii-zaa-raa, za-aafa-u-ebaa, shin-yu-bii-ora-u, yoo-raa-pummi, aa-zaa-toppo-rawaa.*"

My father speaks the lyrics in excellent English while my mother accompanies him in song.

And then the two of them once again focus their attention on mixing the soil.

I feel like an old man who's just awoken from being under a magic spell for a long time. Ha ha, so my brother and I had sung that song.

"*Yoo-raa-pummi, aa-zaa-toppo-rawaa.*"

I have absolutely no recollection of that.

Her sleep having been interrupted, Sakura comes over to where I stand.

First you wake me up, and then you ignore me?

Sakura has turned into a sort of imperious old lady. I give her a big hug. She still reeks of that green poop, but I have to reassure myself of the warmth of her body, and I press my ear up against it to listen to her heartbeat. I know that, someday, that sound will stop. Her yielding body will become stiff, like a tree in winter, and then Sakura will go off somewhere. And I'll be left here, crying my eyes out.

"Sakura." As I say her name now, tears are already welling up.

What a wild life we're making our way through. That first sunrise, it seemed so big. Ha ha, here come the tears. I can't help crying, and then, I can't help but laugh.

"Kaoru!" Miki opens the window and looks at me curiously. "It's ringing again."

My cell phone's frivolous ringtone echoes in the winter yard.

"Oh, dear," my mother says, stopping what she was doing.

My father starts singing, again with his surprisingly fluent English. *"Your love's put me at the top of the world."*

And just like that, it's the new year, so dreaded by Hajime.

Miki falling in love with someone is a long way off. A short time from now, she'll get a phone call from Kaoru-san, and she'll learn that Kaoru-san has transitioned to a man.

My father will get a phone call from Sakiko-san, who will report that she's opened a new bar in a new place. My mother will laugh. "You never learn, huh?" They probably don't still make love on that big soft bed, but every so often, the two of them will stop what they're doing and steal a glance at one another.

In addition to calls from my girlfriend, I will also receive a New Year's card from Yukawa-san. Happy New Year. But I don't know any of this yet—I just go on hugging Sakura.

Sakura gets a bit bored with me hugging her. She wags her tail two or three times, but then, back in her dream state, she looks up at the sky. *I hope spring arrives soon.* And Ferrari, he's off on a journey somewhere, to find that certain "something" he still recalled.

In the sky above the Hasegawa home, a brisk wind blows, brave and undaunted by the cold. Somewhere among the clouds, in the treetops, in the flow of the river, beside the old mailbox, on the redbrick wall, in a corner of the playing field, along the Two, on the second floor of the Bamboo Villas, and all over the world, there is someone eagerly awaiting our pitches. That something is big and warm, and true, and no matter how wild those pitches are, it will catch every one of them.

Your love brings me to the top of the world.

Tired of fiddling with my cell phone, Miki comes out into the yard. She's wearing flip-flops that are too big for her, and she looks cold, but she cries out happily:

"Sakura!"

And our new year begins.

Afterword

Sakura is my debut novel. It was published in Japan in 2005, more than twenty years before this English translation came to be.

I was still in my twenties at the time and had no idea what it meant to be a writer, much less what a novel should be. Saying that, though, might make it sound as if *Sakura* was written without thinking; that maybe it reveals just how inexperienced and naïve I was. And yet, not thinking (too much) and being naïve gave me a certain freedom; it emboldened me. After recently rereading *Sakura*, as it was about to be translated into English, I was chagrined. There were passages that made my cheeks go bright red (imagine, if you will, rereading the diary you kept twenty years ago). But at the same time, I was also incredibly proud and delighted. That had been me—I *was* free, I was bold.

I had wanted to write about a loving family. I'd had the impression (at least, back in the early aughts when I wrote this novel) that we Japanese were not in fact comfortable with love as an emotion. Don't get me wrong—of course, Japanese people know what love is. We encounter this notion countless times in movies, manga, and certainly in novels. And yet, the reality is that in our day-to-day lives, we rarely ever say the words "I love you." Especially not to anyone in our family. We hardly ever hug each other either—in my life, I've only ever hugged my mom. I've never hugged my dad or my brother.

I wonder if the reason might be that love, as an emotion, is just too magnificent, too beautiful an experience for us. The more magnificent and beautiful it is, the more we shy away from it. I wonder if perhaps we are daunted by the scale of it.

And so, I wanted to depict a love that fits my own size and my own shape. I wanted to make it clear that we are worthy of love too. And what helped me do that was Sakura. The Hasegawas are a fragile and vulnerable family, but they are unquestionably bound together by their beloved dog, Sakura. Sometimes they communicate with one another by way of Sakura; other times they express their love for each other through Sakura.

The inspiration for Sakura was a mutt named Sunny who lived with my family and me a long time ago. Like Sakura, Sunny was scrawny and scrappy, definitely not the kind of fancy dog I would show off to my friends. But Sunny personified the love we had as a family. There was nothing magnificent or beautiful about our family's love—it was not the kind you would proudly show off to anyone else. Indeed, it was scrawny and scrappy, and yet, what we felt was undeniably love.

I have no doubt that you too have love that is tailor-fit to your size and shape. If this book plays any part in helping you discover what that love is, it will give me no greater happiness as an author.

—SEPTEMBER 2025, TOKYO, JAPAN

A Note from the Translator

I met Kanako Nishi in 2015, shortly after her epic I-novel *Saraba!* had won the Naoki Prize, one of the most prestigious literary awards in Japan. This was just over ten years into her career, and it was an appropriate recognition of her status and stature as a writer. By that time, she had already published many books—novels, short story collections, essays, and children's books—and, of course, even more would follow.

I don't know if you're reading this note before or after reading *Sakura*, or if this may or may not be your first encounter with Kanako Nishi. One of the things that's unusual about literature in translation is that these books often make their way to us in English in a completely different context than how they first appeared.

An author's reputation in their own country may or may not be relevant to readers who encounter their work in translation. Before you crack the spine on one of their books (or download it onto your device), you can choose to know as much or as little about them as you like—but I will tell you anyway: Kanako Nishi is a hugely popular and much beloved writer in Japan. After she burst onto the scene with *Sakura* decades ago, she has since solidified her place at the apex of the literary landscape with dozens of books that demonstrate her versatility and mastery, culminating in the publication of her award-winning and

A NOTE FROM THE TRANSLATOR

bestselling literary memoir about being diagnosed with breast cancer while living in Canada during the pandemic.

It is a privilege to be Kanako's translator and to have been involved in the effort to make her work available to English-language readers—that is to say, you. I sincerely hope to bring many more of her books into translation in the near future.

—OCTOBER 2025, NEW YORK, NY

Here ends Kanako Nishi's
Sakura.

The first edition of this book was printed
and bound at LSC Communications
in Harrisonburg, Virginia, February 2026.

A NOTE ON THE TYPE

The text of this novel was set in ITC Cheltenham, a typeface designed by Tony Stan. It was originally designed by the architect Bertram Goodhue in 1896, before Morris Fuller Benton at American Type Founders expanded it in 1904. ITC commissioned Stan to revamp the typeface in 1975, giving it a larger x-height and refining its italic details. Clean, no-nonsense, and surprisingly versatile, ITC Cheltenham adds a professional touch to designs and documents, making it a popular choice for various kinds of printed matter.

HARPERVIA

An imprint dedicated to publishing international voices,
offering readers a chance to encounter other lives and other
points of view via the language of the imagination.